Trouvelot Étienne Léopold

The Trouvelot Astronomical Drawings Manual

Trouvelot Étienne Léopold

The Trouvelot Astronomical Drawings Manual

ISBN/EAN: 9783337399481

Printed in Europe, USA, Canada, Australia, Japan

Cover: Foto ©Andreas Hilbeck / pixelio.de

More available books at **www.hansebooks.com**

THE

TROUVELOT

Astronomical Drawings

MANUAL

BY

E. L. TROUVELOT,

FORMERLY CONNECTED WITH THE OBSERVATORY OF HARVARD COLLEGE ; FELLOW OF THE
AMERICAN ACADEMY OF ARTS AND SCIENCES, AND MEMBER OF THE SELENO-
GRAPHICAL SOCIETY OF GREAT BRITAIN ; IN CHARGE OF A
GOVERNMENT EXPEDITION TO OBSERVE THE
TOTAL SOLAR ECLIPSE OF 1878.

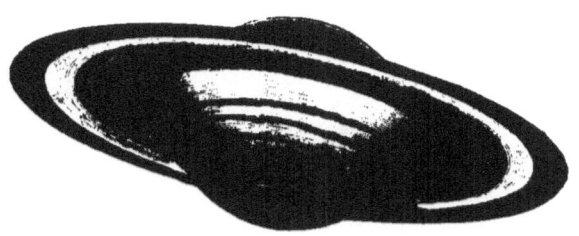

NEW YORK
CHARLES SCRIBNER'S SONS
1882

INTRODUCTION.

DURING a study of the heavens, which has now been continued for more than fifteen years, I have made a large number of observations pertaining to physical astronomy, together with many original drawings representing the most interesting celestial objects and phenomena.

With a view to making these observations more generally useful, I was led, some years ago, to prepare, from this collection of drawings, a series of astronomical pictures, which were intended to represent the celestial phenomena as they appear to a trained eye and to an experienced draughtsman through the great modern telescopes, provided with the most delicate instrumental appliances. Over two years were spent in the preparation of this series, which consisted of a number of large drawings executed in pastel. In 1876, these drawings were displayed at the United States Centennial Exhibition at Philadelphia, forming a part of the Massachusetts exhibit, in the Department of Education and Science.

The drawings forming the present series comprise only a part of those exhibited at Philadelphia; but, although fewer in number, they are quite sufficient to illustrate the principal classes of celestial objects and phenomena.

While my aim in this work has been to combine scrupulous fidelity and accuracy in the details, I have also endeavored to preserve the natural elegance and the delicate outlines peculiar to the objects depicted; but in this, only a little more than a suggestion is possible, since no human skill can reproduce upon paper the majestic beauty and radiance of the celestial objects.

The plates were prepared under my supervision, from the original pastel drawings, and great care has been taken to make the reproduction exact.

The instruments employed in the observations, and in the delineation of the heavenly bodies represented in the series, have varied in aperture from 6 to 26 inches, according to circumstances, and to the nature of the object to be studied. The great Washington refractor, kindly placed at my disposal by the late Admiral C. H. Davis, has contributed to this work, as has also the 26 inch telescope of the University of Virginia, while in the hands of its celebrated constructors, Alvan Clark & Sons. The spectroscope used was made by Alvan Clark & Sons. Attached to it is an excellent diffraction grating, by Mr. L. M. Rutherfurd, to whose kindness I am indebted for it.

Those unacquainted with the use of optical instruments generally suppose that all astronomical drawings are obtained by the photographic process, and are, therefore, comparatively easy to procure; but this is not true. Although photography renders valuable assistance to the astronomer in the case of the Sun and Moon, as proved by the fine photographs of these objects taken by M. Janssen and Mr. Rutherfurd; yet, for other subjects, its products are in general so blurred and indistinct that no details of any great value can be secured. A well-trained eye alone is capable of seizing the delicate details of structure and of configuration of the heavenly bodies, which are liable to be affected, and even rendered invisible, by the slightest changes in our atmosphere.

The method employed to secure correctness in the proportions of the original drawings is simple, but well adapted to the purpose in view. It consists in placing a fine reticule, cut on glass, at the common focus of the objective and the eye-piece, so that in viewing an object, its telescopic image, appearing projected on the reticule, can be drawn very accurately on a sheet of paper ruled with corresponding squares. For a series of such reticules I am indebted to the kindness of Professor William A. Rogers, of the Harvard College Observatory.

The drawings representing telescopic views are inverted, as they appear in a refracting telescope—the South being upward, the North downward, the East on the right, and the West on the left. The Comet, the Milky-Way, the Eclipse of the Moon, the Aurora Borealis, the Zodiacal Light and the Meteors are represented as seen directly in the sky with the naked eye. The Comet was, however, drawn with the aid of the telescope, without which the delicate structure shown in the drawing would not have been visible.

The plate representing the November Meteors, or so-called "Leonids," may be called an ideal view, since the shooting stars delineated, were not observed at the same moment of time, but during the same night. Over three thousand Meteors were observed between midnight and five o'clock in the morning of the day on which this shower occurred ; a dozen being sometimes in sight at the same instant. The paths of the Meteors, whether curved, wavy, or crooked, and also their delicate colors, are in all cases depicted as they were actually observed.

In the Manual, I have endeavored to present a general outline of what is known, or supposed, on the different subjects and phenomena illustrated in the series. The statements made are derived either from the best authorities on physical astronomy, or from my original observations, which are, for the most part, yet unpublished.

The figures in the Manual relating to distance, size, volume, mass, etc., are not intended to be strictly exact, being only round numbers, which can, therefore, be more easily remembered.

It gives me pleasure to acknowledge that the experience acquired in making the astronomical drawings published in Volume VIII. of the Annals of the Harvard College Observatory, while I was connected with that institution, has been of considerable assistance to me in preparing this work; although no drawings made while I was so connected have been used for this series.

E. L. TROUVELOT.

Cambridge, March, 1882.

CONTENTS.

COMETS AND METEORS.

THE STELLAR SYSTEMS.

LIST OF PLATES.

* For Key to the Plates, see Appendix.

⁎ *Reproduced from the Original Drawings, by Armstrong & Company, Riverside Press, Cambridge, Mass.*

GENERAL REMARKS ON THE SUN.

THE Sun, the centre of the system which bears its name, is a self-luminous sphere, constantly radiating heat and light.

Its apparent diameter, as seen at its mean from the Earth, subtends an angle of 32′, or a little over half a degree. A dime, placed about six feet from the eye, would appear of the same proportions, and cover the Sun's disk, if projected upon it.

That the diameter of the Sun does not appear larger, is due to the great distance which separates us from that body. Its distance from the Earth is no less than 92,000,000 miles. To bridge this immense gap, would require 11,623 globes like the Earth, placed side by side, like beads on a string.

The Sun is an enormous sphere whose diameter is over 108 times the diameter of our globe, or very nearly 860,000 miles. Its radius is nearly double the distance from the Earth to the Moon. If we suppose, for a moment, the Sun to be hollow, and our globe to be placed at the centre of this immense spherical shell, not only could our satellite revolve around us at its mean distance of 238,800 miles, as now, but another satellite, placed 190,000 miles farther than the Moon, could freely revolve likewise, without ever coming in contact with the solar envelope.

The circumference of this immense sphere measures 2,800,000 miles. While a steamer, going at the rate of 300 miles a day, would circumnavigate the Earth in 83 days, it would take, at the same rate, nearly 25 years to travel around the Sun.

The surface of the Sun is nearly 12,000 times the surface of the Earth, and its volume is equal to 1,300,000 globes like our own. If all the known planets and satellites were united in a single mass, 600 such compound masses would be needed to equal the volume of our luminary.

Although the density of the Sun is only one-quarter that of the Earth, yet the bulk of this body is so enormous that, to counterpoise it, no less than 314,760 globes like our Earth would be required.

The Sun uniformly revolves around its axis in about 25½ days. Its equator is inclined 7° 15' to the plane of the ecliptic, the axis of rotation forming, therefore, an angle of 82° 45' with the same plane. As the Earth revolves about the Sun in the same direction as that of the Sun's rotation, the apparent time of this rotation, as seen by a terrestrial spectator, is prolonged from 25½ days to about 27 days and 7 hours.

The rotation of the Sun on its axis, like that of the Earth and the other planets, is direct, or accomplished from West to East. To an observer on the Earth, looking directly at the Sun, the rotation of this body is from left to right, or from East to West.

The general appearance of the Sun is that of an intensely luminous disk, whose limb, or border, is sharply defined on the heavens. When its telescopic image is projected on a screen, or fixed on paper by photography, it is noticed that its disk is not uniformly bright throughout, but is notably more luminous in its central parts. This phenomenon is not accidental, but permanent, and is due in reality to a very rare but extensive atmosphere which surrounds the Sun, and absorbs the light which that body radiates, proportionally to its thickness, which, of course, increases towards the limb, to an observer on the Earth.

THE ENVELOPING LAYERS OF THE SUN.

The luminous surface of the Sun, or that part visible at all times, and which forms its disk, is called the *Photosphere*, from the property it is supposed to possess of generating light. The photosphere does not extend to a great depth below the luminous surface, but forms a comparatively thin shell, 3,000 or 4,000 miles thick, which is distinct from the interior parts, above which it seems to be kept in suspense by internal forces. From the observations of some astronomers it would appear that the diameter of the photosphere is subject to slight variations, and, therefore, that the solar diameter is not a constant quantity. From the nature of this envelope, such a result does not seem at all impossible, but rather probable.

Immediately above the photosphere lies a comparatively thin stratum, less than a thousand miles in thickness, called the *Reversing Layer*. This stratum is composed of metallic vapors, which, by absorbing the light of particular refrangibilities emanating from the photosphere below, produces the dark Fraunhofer lines of the solar spectrum.

Above the reversing layer, and resting immediately upon it, is a shallow, semi-transparent gaseous layer, which has been called the *Chromosphere*, from the fine tints which it exhibits during total eclipses of the Sun, in contrast with the colorless white light radiated by the photosphere below. Although visible to a certain extent on the disk, the chromosphere is totally invisible on the limb, except with the spectroscope, and during eclipses, on account of the nature of its light, which is mainly monochromatic, and too feeble, compared with that emitted by the photosphere, to be seen.

The chromospheric layer, which has a thickness of from 3,000 to 4,000 miles, is uneven, and is usually upheaved in certain regions, its matter being transported to considerable elevations above its general surface, apparently by some internal forces. The portions of the chromosphere thus lifted up, form curious and complicated figures, which are known under the names of *Solar Protuberances, or Solar Flames*.

Above the chromosphere, and rising to an immense but unknown height, is the solar atmosphere proper, which is only visible during total eclipses of the Sun, and which then surrounds the dark body of the Moon with the beautiful rays and glorious nimbus, called the *Corona*.

These four envelopes : the photosphere, the reversing layer, the chromosphere, and the corona, constitute the outer portions of our luminary.

Below the photosphere little can be seen, although it is known, as will appear below, that at certain depths cloud-like forms exist, and freely float in an interior atmosphere of invisible gases. Beyond this all is mystery, and belongs to the domain of hypothesis.

STRUCTURE OF THE PHOTOSPHERE AND CHROMOSPHERE.

The apparent uniformity of the solar surface disappears when it is examined with a telescope of sufficient aperture and magnifying powers. Seen under good atmospheric conditions, the greater part of the solar surface appears mottled with an infinite number of small, bright granules, irregularly distributed, and separated from each other by a gray-tinted background.

These objects are known under different names. The terms granules and granulations answer very well for the purpose, as they do not imply anything positive as to their form and true nature. They have also been called *Luculæ, Rice Grains, Willow Leaves*, etc., by different observers.

Although having different shapes, the granulations partake more or less of the circular or slightly elongated form.   Their diameter, which varies considerably, has been estimated at from $0''.5$ to $3''$, or from 224 to 1,344 miles.   The granulations which attain the largest size appear, under good atmospheric conditions, to be composed of several granules, closely united and forming an irregular mass, from which short appendages protrude in various directions.

The number of granulations on the surface of the Sun varies considerably under the action of unknown causes.   Sometimes they are small and very numerous, while at other times they are larger, less numerous, and more widely separated.   Other things being equal, the granulations are better seen in the central regions of the Sun than they are near the limb.

Usually the granulations are very unstable ; their relative position, form, and size undergoing continual changes.   Sometimes they are seen to congregate or to disperse in an instant, as if acting under the influence of attractive and repulsive forces ; assembling in groups or files, and oftentimes forming capricious figures which are very remarkable, but usually of short duration.   In an area of great solar disturbances, the granulations are often stretched to great distances, and form into parallel lines, either straight, wavy, or curved, and they have then some resemblance to the flowing of viscous liquids.

The granulations are usually terminated either by rounded or sharply pointed summits, but they do not all rise to the same height, as can be ascertained with the spectroscope when they are seen sidewise on the limb.   In the regions where they are most abundant, they usually attain greater elevations, and when observed on the limb with the spectroscope, they appear as slender acute flames.

The granulations terminated by sharply-pointed crests, although observed in all latitudes, seem to be characteristic of certain regions. A daily study of the chromosphere, extending over a period of ten years, has shown me that the polar regions are rarely ever free from these objects, which are less frequent in other parts of the Sun.   In the polar regions they are sometimes so abundant that they completely form the solar limb.   These forms of granulation are comparatively rare in the equatorial zones, and when seen there, they never have the permanency which they exhibit in the polar regions. When observed in the equatorial regions, they usually appear in small groups, in the vicinity of sun spots, or they are at least enclosed in areas of disturbances where such spots are in process of formation.   In these regions they often attain greater elevations than those seen in high latitudes.

As we are certain that in the equatorial zones these slender flames (*i. e.*, granulations) are a sure sign of local disturbance, it may be reasonably supposed that the same kind of energy producing them nearly always prevails in the polar regions, although it is there much weaker, and never reaches beyond certain narrow limits.

Studied with the spectroscope, the granulations are found to be composed in the main of incandescent hydrogen gas, and of an unknown substance provisionally called "helium." Among the most brilliant of them are found traces of incandescent metallic vapors, belonging to various substances found on our globe.

The chromosphere is not fixed, but varies considerably in thickness in its different parts, from day to day. Its thickness is usually greater in the polar regions, where it sometimes exceeds 6,700 miles. In the equatorial regions the chromosphere very rarely attains this height, and when it does, the rising is local and occupies only a small area. In these regions it is sometimes so shallow that its depth is only a few seconds, and is then quite difficult to measure. These numbers give, of course, the extreme limits of the variations of the chromosphere ; but, nearly always, it is more shallow in the equatorial regions ; and, as far as my observations go, the difference in thickness between the polar and equatorial zones is greater in years of calm than it is in years of great solar activity. But ten years of observation are not sufficient to warrant any definite conclusions on this subject.

There is undoubtedly some relation between the greater thickness of the chromosphere in the polar regions, and the abundance and permanence of the sharply-pointed granulations observed in the same regions. This becomes more evident when we know that the appearance of similarly-pointed flames in the equatorial zones is always accompanied with a local thickening of the chromosphere. The thickening in the polar regions may be only apparent, and not due to a greater accumulation of chromospheric gases there ; but may be caused by some kind of repulsive action or polarity, which lifts up and extends the summit of the granulations in a manner similar to the well-known mode of electric repulsion and polarity.

As it seems very probable that the heat and light emanating from the Sun are mainly generated at the base of the granulations, in the filamentary elements composing the chromosphere and photosphere, it would follow that, as the size and number of these objects constantly vary, the amount of heat and light emitted by the Sun should also vary in the same proportion.

The granulations of the solar surface are represented on Plate

I., and form the general background to the group of Sun-spots forming the picture.

THE FACULÆ.

Although the solar surface is mainly covered with the luminous
granulations and the grayish background above described, it is very
rare that its appearance is so simple and uniform as already represented. For the most part, on the contrary, it is diversified by
larger, brighter, and more complicated forms, which are especially
visible towards the border of the Sun. Owing to their extraordinary
brilliancy, these objects have been called *Faculæ*, (torches.)

Although the faculæ are very seldom seen well beyond 50 heliocentric degrees from the limb, yet they exist, and are as numerous
in the central parts of the disk as they are towards the border ;
since they form a part of the solar surface, and participate in its
movement of rotation. Their appearance near the limb has been attributed to the effect of absorption produced by the solar atmosphere
on the light from the photosphere ; but this explanation seems inad-
equate, and does not solve the problem. The well-known fact that
the solar protuberances—which are in a great measure identical with
the faculæ—are much brighter at the base than they are at the
summit, perhaps gives a clue to the explanation of the phenomenon; especially since we know that, in general, the summit of
the protuberances is considerably broader than their base. When
these objects are observed in the vicinity of the limb, they present
their brightest parts to the observer, since, in this position, they are
seen more or less sidewise ; and, therefore, they appear bright and
distinct. But as the faculæ recede from the limb, their sides, being
seen under a constantly decreasing angle, appear more and more
foreshortened ; and, therefore, these objects grow less bright and
less distinct, until they finally become invisible, when their bases
are covered over by the broad, dusky summit generally terminating
the protuberances.

The faculæ appear as bright and luminous masses or streaks on
the granular surface of the Sun, but they differ considerably in form
and size. Two types at least are distinguishable. In their simplest
form they appear either as isolated white spots, or as groups of such
spots covering large surfaces, and somewhat resembling large flakes
of snow. In their most characteristic types they appear as intensely
luminous, heavy masses, from which, in most cases, issue intricate
ramifications, sometimes extending to great distances. Generally,
the ramifications issuing from the masses of faculæ have their largest

branches directed in the main towards the eastern limb of the Sun. Some of these branches have gigantic proportions. Occasionally they extend over 60° and even 80° of the solar surface, and, there-fore, attain a length of from 450,000 to 600,000 miles.

Although the faculæ may be said to be seen everywhere on the surface of the Sun, there is a vast difference in different regions, with regard to their size, number, and brilliancy. They are largest, most abundant, and brightest on two intermediate zones parallel to the solar equator, and extending 35° or 40° to the north and to the south of this line. The breadth of these zones varies considerably with the activity of the solar forces. When they are most active, the faculæ spread on either side, but especially towards the equator, where they sometimes nearly meet those of the other zone. In years of little solar activity the belts formed by the faculæ are very narrow—the elements composing them being very few and small, although they never entirely disappear.

The faculæ are very unstable, and are constantly changing : those of the small types sometimes form and vanish in a few min-utes. When an area of disturbance of the solar surface is observed for some time, all seems in confusion ; the movements of the granu-lations become unusually violent ; they congregate in all sorts of ways, and thus frequently form temporary faculæ. Action of this kind is, for the most part, peculiar to the polar regions of the Sun.

The larger faculæ have undoubtedly another origin, as they seem to be mainly formed by the ejection of incandescent gases and metallic vapors from the interior of the photosphere. In their pro-cess of development some of the heavy masses of faculæ are swollen up to great heights, being torn in all sorts of ways, showing large rents and fissures through which the sight can penetrate.

Very few faculæ are represented in Plate I. ; several streaks are shown at the upper left-hand corner, some appearing as whitish ramifications among the granulations representing the general solar surface.

SUN-SPOTS AND VEILED SPOTS.

PLATE I.

BESIDES the brilliant faculæ already described, much more conspicuous markings, though of a totally different character, are very frequently observed on the Sun. On account of their darkish appearance, which is in strong contrast with the white envelope of our luminary, these markings were called *Maculæ*, or Sun-spots, by their earlier observers.

The Sun-spots are not equally distributed on the solar surface ; but like the faculæ, to which they are closely related, they occupy two zones—one on each side of the equator. These zones are comprised between 10° and 35° of north latitude, and 10° and 35° of south latitude. Between these two zones is a belt 20° in width, where the Sun-spots are rarely seen.

Above the latitudes 35° north and south, the Sun-spots are rare, and it is only occasionally, and during years of great solar activity, that they appear in these regions ; in only a few cases have spots of considerable size been seen there. A few observers, however, have seen spots as far as 40° and 50° from the equator; and La Hire even observed one in 70° of north latitude ; but these cases are exceedingly rare. It is not uncommon, however, to see very small spots, or groups of such spots, within 8° or 10° from the poles.

The activity of the Sun is subject to considerable fluctuation, and accordingly the Sun-spots vary in size and number in different years. During some years they are large, complicated, and very numerous ; while in others they are 'small and scarce, and are sometimes totally absent for weeks and months together. The fluctuations in the frequency of Sun-spots are supposed to be periodical in their character, although their periods do not always appear to recur at exactly regular intervals. Sometimes the period is found to be only nine years, while at other times it extends to twelve years. The period generally adopted now is $11\frac{1}{10}$ years, nearly ; but further investigations are needed to understand the true nature of the phenomenon.

The number of Sun-spots does not symmetrically augment and diminish, but the increase is more rapid than the diminution.

The period of increase is only about four years, while that of decrease is over seven years ; each period of Sun-spot maximum being nearer the preceding period of Sun-spot minimum than it is to that next following.

The cause of these fluctuations in the solar energy is at present wholly unknown. Some astronomers, however, have attributed it to the influence of the planets Venus and Jupiter, the period of revolution of the latter planet being not much longer than the Sun-spot period; but this supposition lacks confirmation from direct observations, which, so far, do not seem to be in favor of the hypothesis. At the present time the solar activity is on the increase, and the Sun-spots will probably reach their maximum in 1883. The last minimum occurred in 1879, when only sixteen small groups of spots were observed during the whole year.

Sun-spots vary in size and appearance ; but, unless they are very small, in which case they appear as simple black dots, they generally consist of two distinct and well-characterized parts, nearly always present. There is first, a central part, much darker than the other, and sharply divided from it, called the " *Umbra ;*" second, a broad, irregular radiated fringe of lighter shade, completely surrounding the first, and called the "*Penumbra.*"

Reduced to its simplest expression, a Sun-spot is a funnel-shaped opening through the chromosphere and the photosphere. The inner end of the funnel, or opening, gives the form to the umbra, while its sloping sides form the penumbra.

The umbra of Sun-spots, whose outlines approximately follow the irregularities of the penumbral fringe, has a diameter which generally exceeds the width of the penumbral ring. Sometimes it appears uniformly black throughout ; but it is only so by contrast, as is proved when either Mercury or Venus passes near a spot during a transit over the Sun's disk. The umbra then appears grayish, when compared with the jet-black disk of the planet.

The umbra of spots is rarely so simple as just described ; but it is frequently occupied, either partly or wholly, by grayish and rosy forms, somewhat resembling loosely-entangled muscular fibres. These forms have been called the *Gray and Rosy Veils.* Frequently these veils appear as if perforated by roundish black holes, improperly called *Nuclei*, which permit the sight to penetrate deeper into the interior. To all appearance the gray and rosy veils are of the same nature as the chromosphere and the faculæ, and are therefore mainly composed of hydrogen gas.

Whatever can be known about the interior of the Sun, must be learned from the observations of these openings, which are comparatively small. But whatever this interior may be, we certainly know that it is not homogeneous. Apparently, the Sun is a gigantic bubble, limited by a very thin shell. Below this shell exists a large open space filled with invisible gases, in which, through the openings constituting the Sun-spots, the gray and rosy veils described above are occasionally seen floating.

The fringe forming the penumbra of spots is much more complicated than the umbra. In its simpler form, it is composed of a multitude of bright, independent filaments of different forms and sizes, partly projecting one above the other, on the sloping wall of the penumbra, from which they seem to proceed. Seen from the Earth, these filaments have somewhat the appearance of thatched straw, converging towards the centre of the umbra. It is very rare, however, that the convergence of the penumbral filaments is regular, and great confusion sometimes arises from the entanglement of these filaments. Some of these elements appear straight, others are curved or loop-shaped ; while still others, much larger and brighter than the rest, give a final touch to this' chaos of filaments, from which results the general thatched and radiating appearance of the penumbra.

The extremities of the penumbral filaments, especially of those forming the border of the umbra, are usually club-shaped and appear very brilliant, as if these elements had been superheated by some forces escaping through the opening of the spots.

Besides these characteristics, the Sun-spots have others, which, although not always present, properly belong to them. Comparatively few spots are so simple as the form just described. Very frequently a spot is accompanied by brilliant faculæ, covering part of its umbra and penumbra, and appearing to form a part of the spot itself.

When seen projected over Sun-spots, the faculæ appear intensely bright, and from these peculiarities they have been called *Luminous Bridges*. They are, in fact, bridges, but in most cases they are at considerable heights above the spots, kept there by invisible forces. When such spots with luminous bridges approach the Sun's limb, it is easy to see, by the rapid apparent displacement which they undergo, that they are above the general level.

When the spots are closing up, the inverse effect is sometimes observed. On several occasions, I have seen huge masses of faculæ advance slowly over the penumbra of a spot and fall into the depths of the umbra, resembling gigantic cataracts. I have seen narrow branches of faculæ, which, after having fallen to great depths in the umbra, floated across it and disappeared under the photosphere on the opposite side. I have also seen luminous bridges, resembling cables, tightly stretched across the spots, slackening slowly, as if loosened at one end, and gently curving into the umbra, where they formed immense loops, large enough to receive our globe.

It is to be remarked that, in descending under· the photospheric shell, the bright faculæ and the luminous bridges gradually lose their brilliancy. At first they appear grayish, but in descending farther they assume more and more the pink color peculiar to the rosy veils. The pinkish color acquired by the faculæ when they reach a certain depth under the photosphere, is precisely the color of the chromosphere and of the solar protuberances, as seen during total eclipses of the Sun—a fact which furnishes another proof that the faculæ are of the same nature as the protuberances.

I record here an observation which, at first sight, may appear paradoxical ; but which seems, however, to be of considerable importance, as it shows unmistakably that the solar light is mainly, if not entirely, generated on its surface, or at least very near to it. On May 26, 1878, I observed a large group of Sun-spots at a little distance from the east limb of the Sun. The spot nearest to the limb was partly covered over on its eastern and western sides by bright and massive faculæ which concealed about two-thirds of the whole spot, only a narrow opening, running from north to south, being left across the middle of the spot. Owing to the rotundity of the Sun, the penumbra of this spot, although partly covered by the faculæ, could, however, be seen on its eastern side, since the sight of the observer could there penetrate sidewise under the faculæ. Upon that part of the penumbra appeared a strong shadow, representing perfectly the outline of the facular mass situated above it. The phenomenon was so apparent that no error of observation was possible, and a good drawing of it was secured. If this facula had been as bright beneath as it was above, it is evident that no shadow could have been produced ; hence the light of these faculæ must have been mainly generated on or very near their exterior surfaces. This, with the well-proved fact that the bright faculæ lose their light in falling into the interior of the Sun, seems to suggest the idea that the bright light emitted by the faculæ, and very probably all the solar light, can be generated only on its surface ; the presence of the coronal atmosphere being perhaps necessary to produce it. Several times before this observation, I had suspected that

some faculæ were casting a shadow, but as this seemed so improba-
ble, my attention was not awakened until the phenomenon became
so prominent that it could not escape notice.

With due attention, some glimpses of the phenomenon can frequently be observed through the openings of some of the faculæ
projecting over the penumbra of Sun-spots. It is very seldom that
the structure of the penumbra is seen through such openings, which
usually appear as dark as the umbra of the large spots, although
they do not penetrate through the photosphere like the latter. It is
only when the rents in the faculæ are numerous and quite large, that
the penumbral structure is recognized through them. Since these
superficial rents in the faculæ do not extend through the photosphere, and appear black, it seems evident that the penumbra seen
through them cannot be as bright as it is when no faculæ are projected upon it, and therefore that the faculæ intercept light from the
exterior surface, which would otherwise reach the penumbra.

While the matter forming the faculæ sometimes falls into the
interior of the Sun, the same kind of matter is frequently ejected in
enormous quantities, and with great force, from the interior, through
the visible and invisible openings of the photosphere, and form the
protuberances described in the following section of this manual (p.
20.) It is not only the incandescent hydrogen gas or the metallic
vapors which are thus ejected, but also cooler hydrogen gas, which
sometimes appears as dark clouds on the solar surface. On December 12, 1875, I observed such a cloud of hydrogen issuing from
the corner of a small Sun-spot. It traveled several thousand miles
on the solar surface, in a north-easterly direction, before it became
invisible.

Solar spots are formed in various ways ; but, for the most part,
the apparition of a spot is announced beforehand, by a great commotion of the solar surface at the place of its appearance, and by
the formation of large and bright masses of faculæ, which are usually swollen into enormous bubbles by the pressure of the internal
gases. These bubbles become visible in the spectroscope while they
are traversing the solar limb, as they are then presented to us sidewise. Under the action of the increasing pressure, the base of the
faculæ is considerably stretched, and, its weakest side finally giving way, the facular mass is torn in many places from the solar surface, and is perforated by holes of different sizes and forms. The
holes thus made along the border of the faculæ appear as small
black spots, separated more or less by the remaining portion of the
lacerated faculæ, and they enlarge more and more at the expense of

the intervening portions, which thus become very narrow. This perforated side of the faculæ, offering less resistance, is gradually lifted up, as would be the cover of a box, for example, while its opposite side remains attached to the surface. The facular matter separating the small black holes is greatly stretched during this action, and forms long columns and filaments. These appear as luminous bridges upon the large and perfectly-formed spot, which is then seen under the lifted facular masses. The spots thus made visible are soon freed from the facular masses, which are gradually shifted towards the opposite side.

In such cases the spots are undoubtedly formed under the faculæ before they can be seen. This becomes evident when such spots, not yet cleared from the faculæ covering them, are observed near the east limb ; since in this position the observer can see through the side-openings of the faculæ, and sometimes recognize the spots under their cover.

It frequently occurs that the spots thus formed under the faculæ continue to be partly covered by the facular clouds, the forces at work in them being apparently too feeble to shift them aside. In such cases these spots are visible when they are in the vicinity of the limb, where they are seen sidewise ; but when observed in the east, in being carried forward by the solar rotation towards the centre of the disk, they gradually diminish in size, and finally become invisible. The disappearance of these spots, however, is only apparent, being due to the fact that, as they advance towards the centre of the disk, our lateral view of them is gradually lost, and they are finally hidden from sight by the overhanging faculæ which then serve as a screen between the observer and the spot. This class of spots may be called *Lateral Spots*, from the fact that they can only be seen laterally, and near the Sun's limb.

Solar spots are also formed in various other ways. Some, like those represented in Plate I., appearing without being announced by any apparent disturbance of the surface, or by the formation of any faculæ, form and develop in a very short time. Others, appearing at first as very small spots having an umbra and a penumbra, slowly and gradually develop into very large spots. This mode of formation, which would seem to be the most natural, is, however, quite rare. Spots of this class have a duration and permanence not observed in those of any other type. These spots of slow and regular development are never accompanied by faculæ or luminous bridges, nor have they any gray or rosy veils in their interior ; a fact which may, perhaps, account for their permanent character.

Another class of spots, which is also rare, appear as long and narrow crevasses showing the penumbral structure of the ordinary spots ; but these rarely have any umbra.   These long, and sometimes exceedingly narrow fissures of the solar envelopes, with their radiated penumbral structure, strongly suggest the idea that the photosphere is composed of a multitude of filamentary elements having the granulations for summits.   Such a crevasse is represented on Plate I., and unites the two spots which form the group.

The duration of Sun-spots varies greatly.   Some last only for a few hours ; while others continue for weeks and even months at a time, but not without undergoing changes.

The modes of disappearance of Sun-spots are as various as those of their apparition.   The spots rarely close up by a gradual diminution or contraction of their umbra and penumbra.   This mode of disappearance belongs exclusively to the spots deprived of faculæ and veils.   One of the most common modes of the disappearance of a spot is its invasion by large facular masses, which slowly advance upon its penumbra and umbra and finally cover it entirely.   It is a process precisely the reverse of that in which spots are formed by the shifting aside of the faculæ, as above described.   In other types, the spots close up by the gradual enlargement of the luminous bridges traversing them, which are slowly transformed into branches of the photosphere, all of the characteristics of which they have acquired.   In many cases, the spots covered over by the faculæ continue to exist for some time, hidden under these masses, as is often proved, either by the appearance of small spots on the facular mass left at the place they occupied, or even by the reappearance of the same spot.

Apart from the general movement of rotation of the solar surface, some of the spots seem to be endowed with a proper motion of their own, which becomes greater the nearer the spots are to the solar equator.   According to the observations of Mr. Carrington, the period of rotation of the Sun, as deduced from the observations of the solar spots during a period of seven years, is 25 days at the equator ; while at 50° of heliocentric latitude it is 27 days.   But the period of rotation, as derived from the observations of spots occupying the same latitude, is far from being constant, as it varies at different times, with the frequency of the spots and with the solar activity, so that at present the law of these variations is not well known.   From the character of the solar envelope, it seems very natural that the rotation should differ in the different zones and at different times, since this envelope is not rigid, but very movable, and governed by forces which are themselves very variable.

Although it is a general law that the spots near the equator have a more rapid motion than those situated in higher latitudes, yet, in many cases, the proper motion of the spots is more apparent than real. For the most part, the changes of form and the rapid displacements observed in some spots are only apparent, and due to the fact that the large masses of faculæ which are kept in suspense above them are very unstable, and change position with the slightest change in the forces holding them in suspension. Since in these cases we view the spots through the openings of the faculæ situated above them, the slightest motion of these objects produces an apparent motion in the spots, although they have remained motionless. Accordingly, it has been remarked that of all the spots, those which have the greater proper motion are precisely those which have the most faculæ and luminous bridges ; while the other spots in the same regions, but not attended by similar phenomena, are comparatively steady in their movement. These last spots are undoubtedly better adapted than any others to exhibit the rotation of the Sun ; but it is probable that this period of rotation will never be known with accuracy, simply because the solar surface is unstable, and does not rotate uniformly.

The Sun-spots have a remarkable tendency to form into groups of various sizes, but whatever may be the number of spots thus assembled, the group is nearly always composed of two principal spots, to which the others are only accessories. The tendency of the Sun-spots to assemble in pairs is general, and is observed in all latitudes, even among the minute temporary groups formed in the polar regions. Whenever several are situated quite close together, those belonging to the same group can be easily recognized by this character. Whatever may be the position of the axis of the two principal spots of a group when it is first formed, this axis has a decided tendency to place itself parallel to the solar equator, no matter to what latitude the group belongs ; and if it is disturbed from this position, it soon returns to it when the disturbance has ceased.

It is also remarkable that the spots observed at the same time remain in nearly the same parallel of latitude for a greater or less period of time ; but they keep changing their position from year to year, their latitude decreasing with the activity of the solar forces.

Among the Sun-spots, those associated with faculæ form the groups which attain the largest proportions. When such groups acquire an apparent diameter of $1'$ or more, they are plainly visible to the naked eye, since for a spot to be visible to the naked eye on the Sun, it need only subtend an angle of $50''$. I have sometimes seen such groups through a smoky atmosphere, when the solar light was so much reduced that the disk could be observed directly and without injury to the sight.

The largest spot which ever came under my observation was seen during the period from the 13th to the 19th of November, 1870. This spot, which was on the northern hemisphere of the Sun, was conspicuous among the smaller spots constituting the group to which it belonged, and followed them on the east. On November 16th, when it attained its largest size, the diameter of its penumbra occupied fully one-fifth of the diameter of the Sun ; its real diameter being, therefore, not less than 172,000 miles, or nearly 22 times the diameter of the Earth. As the umbra of this spot occupied a little more than one-third of its whole diameter, seven globes like our own, placed side by side on a straight line, could easily have passed through this immense gap. To fill the area of this opening, about 45 such globes would have been needed. This spot was, of course, very easily seen with the naked eye, its diameter being almost eight times that required for a spot to be visible without a telescope.

Ancient historians often speak of obscurations of the Sun, and it has been supposed by some astronomers that this phenomenon might have been due in some cases to the apparition of large spots. A few spots on the surface of the Sun, like that just described, would sensibly reduce its light.

Besides the ordinary Sun-spots already described, others are at times observed on the surface of the Sun, which show some of the same characteristics, but never attain so large proportions. They always appear as if seen through a fog, or veil, between the granulations of the solar surface. On account of their vagueness and ill-defined contours, I have proposed for these objects the term, "*Veiled Spots.*" Veiled spots have a shorter duration than the ordinary spots, the smaller types sometimes forming and vanishing in a few minutes. Some of the larger veiled spots, however, remain visible for several days in succession, and show the characteristics of other spots in regard to the arrangement of their parts.

The veiled spots have no umbra or penumbra, although they are usually accompanied by faculæ resembling those seen near the ordinary spots. They are frequently seen in the polar regions, but are there always of small size and of short duration. The veiled spots are larger, and more apt to arrange themselves into groups, in the regions occupied by the ordinary spots, and it is not rare to observe such spots transform themselves into ordinary spots, and vice versa. The veiled spots, therefore, seem to be ordinary spots filled up, or covered over by the granulations and semi-transparent gases composing the chromospheric layer. That it is so, becomes more evident, from the fact that large Sun-spots in process of diminution are sometimes gradually covered with faint and scattered granules which descend in long, narrow filaments, and become less and less distinguishable as they attain greater depth. This phenomenon, associated with the fact that the luminous bridges seen over the Sun-spots which are closing up are sometimes transformed into branches which show the characteristic structure of the photosphere, goes far to prove that the solar envelopes are mainly composed of an innumerable quantity of radial filaments of varying height.

The group of Sun-spots represented in Plate I., was observed and drawn on June 17th, 1875, at 7h. 30m. A. M. The first traces of this group were seen on June 15th, at noon, and consisted of three small black dots disseminated among the granulations. At that time, no disturbance of the surface was noticeable, and no faculæ were seen in the vicinity of these spots. On June 16th, at 8 o'clock A. M., the three small spots had become considerably enlarged, and, as usual, the group consisted of two principal spots. Between these two spots all was in motion: the granulations, stretched into long, wavy, parallel lines, had somewhat the appearance of a liquid in rapid motion. At 1 o'clock, P. M., on the same day, the group had considerably enlarged; the faculæ, the granulations, and the penumbral filaments being interwoven in an indescribable manner. On the morning of the 17th, these spots had assumed the complicated form and development represented in the drawing ; while at the same time two conspicuous veiled spots were seen on the left hand, at some distance above the group.

Some luminous bridges are visible upon the left hand spot, traversing the penumbra and umbra of this spot in various directions. The umbra of one of the spots is occupied, and partly filled with gray and rosy veils, similar to those above described, and the granulations of the solar surface form a background to the group of spots.

This group of spots was not so remarkable for its size as for its complicated structure. The diameter of the group from east to west was only 2½ minutes of arc, or about 67,000 miles. The upper part of the umbra of the spot situated on the right hand side of the group was nearly 7,000 miles in diameter, or less by 1,000 miles than the diameter of the Earth. Some of the long filaments composing that part of the penumbra, situated on the left hand side of the same spot, were 17,000 miles in length. One of these fiery elements would be sufficient to encircle two-thirds of the circumference of the Earth.

SOLAR PROTUBERANCES.

PLATE II.

THE chromosphere forming the outlying envelope of the Sun, is subject, as has been shown above, to great disturbances in certain regions, causing considerable upheavals of its surface and violent outbursts of its gases. From these upheavals and outbursts of the chromosphere result certain curious and very interesting forms, which are known under the name of "*Solar Protuberances*," "*Prominences*," or "*Flames*."

These singular forms, which could, until recently, be observed only during the short duration of the total eclipses of the Sun, can now be seen on every clear day with the spectroscope, thanks to Messrs. Janssen and Lockyer, to whose researches solar physics is so much indebted.

The solar protuberances, the Sun-spots, and the faculæ to which they are closely related, are confined within the same general regions of the Sun, although the protuberances attain higher heliocentric latitudes.

There is certainly a very close relation between the faculæ and the solar protuberances, since when a group of the faculæ traverses the Sun's limb, protuberances are always seen at the same place. It seems very probable that the faculæ and the protuberances are in the main identical. The faculæ may be the brighter portion of the protuberances, consisting of gases which are still undergoing a high temperature and pressure; while the gases which have been relieved from this pressure and have lost a considerable amount of their heat, may form that part of the protuberances which is only visible on the Sun's limb.

A daily study of the solar protuberances, continued for ten years, has shown me that these objects are distributed on two zones which are equidistant from the solar equator, and parallel with it. The zone arrangement of the protuberances is more easily recognized during the years of minimum solar activity, as in these years the zones are very narrow and widely separated. During these years the belt of protuberances is situated between 40° and 45° of latitude, north and south. In years of great solar activity the zones spread considerably on either side of these limits, especially towards the equator, which they nearly reach, only a narrow belt, usually free from protuberances, remaining between them. Towards the poles the zones do not spread so much, and there the space free from protuberances is considerably greater than it is at the equator.

During years of maximum solar activity, the protuberances, like the Sun-spots and the faculæ, are very numerous, very large, and very complicated—sometimes occupying a great part of the whole solar limb. As many as twenty distinct flames are sometimes observed at one time. In years of minimum solar activity, on the contrary, the prominences are very few in number, and they are of small size; but, as far as my observations go, they are never totally absent.

In general, the solar flames undergo rapid changes, especially those which are situated in the vicinity of Sun-spots, although they occasionally remain unchanged in appearance and form for several hours at a time. The protuberances situated in higher latitudes are less liable to great and sudden changes, often retaining the same form for several days. The changes observed in the protuberances of the equatorial regions are due in part to the comparatively great changes in their position with respect to the spectator, which are occasioned by the rotation of the Sun. This rotation, of course, has a greater angular velocity on the equator than in higher latitudes. In most cases, however, the changes of the equatorial protuberances are too great and too sudden to be thus explained. They are, in fact, due to the greater solar activity developed in the equatorial zones, and wherever spots are most numerous.

The solar protuberances appear under various shapes, and are often so complicated in appearance that they defy description. Some resemble huge clumsy masses having a few perforations on their sides; while others form a succession of arches supported by pillars of different styles. Others form vertical or inclined columns, often surmounted by cloud-like masses, or by various appendages, which sometimes droop gracefully, resembling gigantic palm leaves. Some resemble flames driven by the wind; others, which are composed of a multitude of long and narrow filaments, appear as immense fiery bundles, from which sometimes issue long and delicate columns surmounted by torch-like objects of the most fantastic pattern. Some others resemble trees, or animal forms, in a very striking manner;

while still others, apparently detached from the solar limb, float above it, forming graceful streamers or clouds of various shapes. Some of the protuberances are very massive, while others are so thin and transparent as to form a mere veil, through which more distant flames can easily be seen.

Notwithstanding this variety of form, two principal classes of solar protuberances may be recognized : the cloud-like or quiescent, and the eruptive or metallic protuberances.

The first class, which is the most common, comprises all the cloud-like protuberances resting upon the chromosphere or floating about it. The protuberances of this type often obtain enormous horizontal proportions, and it is not rare to see some among them occupying 20° and 30° of the solar limb. The height attained by protuberances of this class does not correspond in general to their longitudinal extent ; although some of their branches attain considerable elevations. These prominences very seldom have the brilliancy displayed by the other type, and are sometimes so faint as to be seen with difficulty. Although it is generally stated by observers that some of the protuberances belonging to this class are detached from the solar surface, and kept in suspension above the surface, like the clouds in our atmosphere, yet it seems to me very doubtful whether protuberances are ever disconnected from the chromosphere, since, in an experience of ten years, I have never been able to satisfy myself that such a thing has occurrred. Many of them have appeared to me at first sight to be detached from the surface, but with a little patience and attention I was always able to detect faint traces of filamentary elements connecting them with the chromosphere. Quite often I have seen bright protuberances gradually lose their light and become invisible, while soon after they had regained it, and were as clearly visible as before. Observations of this kind seem to show that while the prominences are for the most part luminous, there are also a few which are non-luminous and invisible to the eye. These dark and invisible forms are most generally found in the vicinity of Sun-spots in great activity. When observing such regions with the spectroscope, it is not rare to encounter them in the form of large dark spots projecting on the solar spectrum near the hydrogen lines. On July 28th, 1872, I observed with the spectroscope a dark spot of this kind issuing from the vicinity of a large Sun-spot, and extending over one-fifth of the diameter of the Sun. This object had been independently observed in France a little earlier by M. Chacornac with the telescope, in which it appeared as a bluish streak.

The second class of solar protuberances, comprising the eruptive type, is the most interesting, inasmuch as it conveys to us a conception of the magnitude and violence of the solar forces. The protuberances of this class, which are always intensely bright, appear for the most part in the immediate vicinity of Sun-spots or faculæ. These protuberances, which seem to be due to the outburst of the chromosphere, and to the violent ejection of incandescent gases and metallic vapors from the interior of the Sun, sometimes attain gigantic proportions and enormous heights.

While the spectrum of the protuberances of the cloudy type is simple, and usually composed of four hydrogen lines and the yellow line D^3, that of the eruptive class is very complicated, and, besides the hydrogen lines and D^3, it often exhibits the bright lines of sodium, magnesium, barium, titanium, and iron, and occasionally, also, a number of other bright lines.

The phenomena of a solar outburst are grand and imposing. Suddenly immense and acute tongues and jets of flames of a dazzling brilliancy rise up from the solar limb and extend in various directions. Some of these fiery jets appear perfectly rigid, and remain apparently motionless in the midst of the greatest disorder. Immense straps and columns form and rise in an instant, bending and waving in all sorts of ways and assuming innumerable shapes. Sometimes powerful jets resembling molten metal spring up from the Sun, describing graceful parabolas, while in their descent they form numerous fiery drops which acquire a dazzling brilliancy when they approach the surface.

The upward motion of the protuberances in process of formation is sometimes very rapid. Some protuberances have been observed to ascend in the solar atmosphere at the rate of from 120 to 497 miles a second. Great as this velocity may appear, it is nevertheless insignificant when compared with that sometimes attained by protuberances moving in the line of sight instead of directly upwards. Movements of this kind are indicated by the displacement of the bright or dark lines in the spectrum. A remarkable instance of this kind occurred on the 26th of June, 1874. On that day I observed a displacement of the hydrogen C line corresponding to a velocity of motion of 1,600 miles per second. The mass of hydrogen gas in motion producing such a displacement was, according to theory, moving towards the Earth at this incredible rate, when it instantly vanished from sight as if it had been annihilated, and was seen no more.

Until recently the protuberances had not been observed to rise more than 200,000 miles above the solar surface; but, on October 7th, 1880, a flame, which had an elevation of 80,000 miles when I observed it at 8h. 55m. A. M., had attained the enormous altitude of 350,000 miles when it was observed at noon by Professor C. A. Young. If we had such a protuberance on the Earth, its summit would be at a height sufficient not merely to reach, but to extend 100,000 miles beyond the Moon.

Although the solar protuberances represented in Plate II. have not the enormous proportions attained by some of these objects, yet they are as characteristic as any of the largest ones, and afford a good illustration of the purely eruptive type of protuberances. The height of the largest column in the group equals 4' 43", or a little over 126,000 miles. A large group of Sun-spots was in the vicinity of these protuberances when they were observed and delineated.

TOTAL ECLIPSE OF THE SUN.

PLATE III.

A SOLAR eclipse is due to the passage of the Moon directly between the observer and the Sun. Such an eclipse can only occur at New Moon, since it is only at that time that our satellite passes between us and the Sun. The Moon's orbit does not lie precisely in the same plane as the orbit of the Earth, but is inclined about five degrees to it, otherwise an eclipse of the Sun would occur at every New Moon, and an eclipse of the Moon at every Full Moon.

Since the Moon's orbit is inclined to that of the Earth, it must necessarily intersect this orbit at two opposite points. These points are called the nodes of the Moon's orbit. When our satellite passes through either of the nodes when the Moon is new, it appears interposed to some extent between the Sun and the Earth, and so produces a solar eclipse ; while if it passes a node when the Moon is full, it is more or less obscured by the Earth's shadow, which then produces an eclipse of the Moon. But, on the other hand, when the New Moon and the Full Moon do not coincide with the passage of our satellite through the nodes of its orbit, no eclipse can occur, since the Moon is not then on a line with the Sun and the Earth, but above or below that line.

Owing to the ellipticity of the Moon's orbit, the distance of our satellite from the Earth varies considerably during each of its revolutions around us, and its apparent diameter is necessarily subject to corresponding changes. Sometimes it is greater, sometimes it is less, than the apparent diameter of the Sun. If it is greater at the time of a solar eclipse, the eclipse will be total to a terrestrial observer stationed nearly on the line of the centres of the Sun and Moon, while it will be only partial to another observer stationed further from this line. But the Moon's distance from the Earth may be so great and its apparent diameter consequently so small that even those observers nearest the central line of the eclipse see the border of the Sun all round the black disk of the Moon ; the eclipse is then annular.   Even during the progress of one and the same eclipse the distance of the Moon from the parts of the Earth towards which its shadow is directed may vary so much that, while the eclipse is total to some observers, others equally near the central line, but stationed at a different place, will see it as annular.

The shadow cast by the Moon on the Earth during total eclipses, travels along upon the surface of the Earth, in consequence of the daily movement of rotation of our globe combined with the movements of the Earth and Moon in their orbits.   The track of the Moon's shadow over the Earth's surface has a general eastward course, so that the more westerly observers see it earlier than those east of them.   An eclipse may continue total at one place for nearly eight minutes, but in ordinary cases the total phase is much shorter.

The nodes of the Moon's orbit do not invariably occupy the same position, but move nearly uniformly, their position with regard to the Sun, Earth, and Moon being at any time approximately what it formerly was at a series of times separated by equal intervals from each other.   Each interval comprises 223 lunations, or 18 years, 11 days, and 7 or 8 hours.   The eclipses which occur within this interval are almost exactly repeated during the next similar interval.   This period, called the "Saros," was well known to the ancients, who were enabled by its means to predict eclipses with some certainty.

A total eclipse of the Sun is a most beautiful and imposing phenomenon.   At the predicted time the perfectly round disk of the Sun becomes slightly indented at its western limb by the yet invisible Moon.   This phenomenon is known as the "first contact."

The slight indentation observed gradually increases with the advance of the Moon from west to east, the irregularities of the surface of our satellite being plainly visible on the border of the dark segment advancing on the Sun's disk. With the advance of the Moon on the Sun, the light gradually diminishes on the Earth.   Every object puts on a dull and gloomy appearance, as when night is approaching; while the bright sky, losing its light, changes its pure azure for a livid grayish color.

Two or three minutes before totality begins, the solar crescent, reduced to minute proportions, gives comparatively so little light that faint traces of the Sun's atmosphere appear on the western side behind the dark body of the Moon, whose limb then becomes visible outside of the Sun.   I observed this phenomenon at Creston during the eclipse of 1878.   From 15 to 20 seconds before totality, the narrow arc of the Sun's disk not yet obscured by the Moon seems to break and separate towards the extremities of its cusps, which, thus divided, form independent points of light, which are called *"Baily's beads."* A moment after, the whole solar crescent breaks into numerous beads of light, separated by dark intervals, and, suddenly, they all vanish with the last ray of Sunlight, and totality has begun with the " second contact." This phenomenon of Baily's beads is undoubtedly caused by the irregularities of the Moon's border, which, on reaching the solar limb, divide the thin solar crescent into as many beads of light and dark intervals as there are peaks and ravines seen sidewise on that part of the Moon's limb.

With the disappearance of the last ray of light, the planets and the stars of the first and second magnitude seem to light up and become visible in the sky. The darkness, which had been gradually creeping in with the progress of the eclipse, is then at its maximum. Although subject to great variations in different eclipses, the darkness is never so great as might be expected from the complete obscuration of our luminary, as the part of our atmosphere which is still exposed to the direct rays of the Sun, reflects to us some of that light, which thus diminishes the darkness resulting from the disappearance of the Sun. Usually the darkness is sufficient to prevent the reading of common print, and to deceive animals, causing them to act as if night was really approaching. During totality the temperature decreases, while the humidity of the atmosphere augments.

Simultaneously with the disappearance of Baily's beads, a pale, soft, silvery light bursts forth from behind the Moon, as if the Sun, in disappearing, had been vaporized and expanded in all directions into soft phosphorescent rays and streamers. This pale light is emitted by gases constituting the solar atmosphere surrounding the bright nucleus now obscured by the dark body of our satellite. This solar atmosphere is called *Corona*, from its distant resemblance to the aureola, or glory, represented by ancient painters around the heads of saints.

With the bursting forth of the corona, a very thin arc of bright white light is seen along the Moon's limb, where the solar crescent has just disappeared. This thin arc of light is the reversing layer, which, when observed with the spectroscope at that moment, exhibits bright lines answering to the dark lines of the ordinary solar spectrum. Immediately above this reversing layer, and concentric with it, appears the pink-colored chromospheric layer, with its curiously shaped flames and protuberances. During totality, the chromosphere and protuberances are seen without the aid of the spectroscope, and appear of their natural color, which, although somewhat varying in their different parts, is, on the whole, pinkish, and similar to that of peach-blossoms; yet it is mixed here and there with delicate prismatic hues, among which the pink and straw colors predominate.

The color of the corona seems to vary in every eclipse, but as its tints are very delicate, it may depend, in a great measure, upon the vision of the observer ; although there seems to be no doubt that there are real variations. At Creston, in 1878, it appeared to both Professor W. Harkness and myself of a decided pale greenish hue.

The corona appears under different forms, and has never been observed twice alike. Its dimensions are also subject to considerable variations. Sometimes it appears regular and very little extended, its distribution around the Sun being almost uniform; although in general it spreads a little more in the direction of the ecliptic, or of the solar equator. At other times it appears much larger and more complicated, and forms various wings and appendages, which in some cases, as in 1878, extend to immense distances; while delicate rays radiate in straight or curved lines from the spaces left in the polar regions between the wings. The corona has sometimes appeared as if divided by immense dark gaps, apparently free from luminous matter, and strongly resembling the dark rifts seen in the tails of comets. This was observed in Spain and Sicily during the total eclipse of the Sun in 1870. Different structures, forming wisps and streamers of great length, and interlaced in various ways, are sometimes present in the corona, while faint but more complicated forms, distantly resembling enormous solar protuberances with bright nuclei, have also been observed.

As the Moon continues its eastward progress, it gradually covers the chromosphere and the solar protuberances on the eastern side of the Sun; while, at the same time, the protuberances and the chromosphere on the opposite limb gradually appear from under the retreating Moon. Then, the thin arc of the reversing layer is visible for an instant, and is instantly followed by the appearance of a point of dazzling white light, succeeded immediately by the apparition of Baily's beads on each side, and totality is over, with this third contact. The corona continues to be visible on the eastern side of the Sun for several minutes longer, and then rapidly vanishes.

The thin solar crescent increases in breadth as the Moon advances; while, at the same time, the darkness and gloom spread over nature gradually disappear, and terrestrial objects begin to resume their natural appearance. Finally the limb of the Moon separates from that of the Sun at the instant of " fourth contact," and the eclipse is over.

The phenomena exhibited by the corona in different eclipses are very complex, and, so far, they have not been sufficiently studied to enable us to understand the true nature of the solar atmosphere. From the spectral analysis of the corona, and the phenomena of polarization, it has been learned, at least, that while the matter composing the upper part of the solar atmosphere is chiefly composed of an unknown substance, producing the green line 1474, its lower part is mainly composed of hydrogen gas at different temperatures, a part of which is self-luminous, while the other part only reflects the solar light. But the proportion of the gaseous particles emitting light, to those simply reflecting it, is subject to considerable variations in different eclipses. At present it would seem that in years of great solar disturbances, the particles emitting light are found in greater quantity in the corona than those reflecting it; but further observations will be required to confirm these views.

It is very difficult to understand how the corona, which in certain eclipses extends only one diameter of the Sun, should, in other cases, as in 1878, extend to the enormous distance of twelve times the same diameter. Changes of such magnitude in the solar atmosphere, if due to the operation of forces with which we are acquainted, cannot yet be accounted for by what is known of such forces. Their causes are still as mysterious as those concerned in the production of the monstrous tails displayed by some comets on their approach to the Sun.

Plate 3, representing the total eclipse of the Sun of July 29th, 1878, was drawn from my observations made at Creston, Wyoming Territory, for the Naval Observatory. The eclipse is represented as seen in a refracting telescope, having an aperture of 6⅓ inches, and as it appeared a few seconds before totality was over, and when the chromosphere was visible on the western limb of the Sun. The two long wings seen on the east and west side of the Sun, appeared considerably larger in the sky than they are represented in the picture.

THE AURORA BOREALIS.

PLATE IV.

THE name of Polar Auroras is given to certain very remarkable luminous meteoric phenomena which appear at intervals above the northern or the southern horizons of both hemispheres of the Earth. When the phenomenon is produced in our northern sky, it is called "Aurora Borealis," or "Northern Lights;" and when it appears in the southern sky, it is called "Aurora Australis," or southern aurora.

Marked differences appear in the various auroras observed from our northern latitudes. While some simply consist in a pale, faint luminosity, hardly distinguishable from twilight, others present the most gorgeous and remarkable effects of brightness and colors.

A great aurora is usually indicated in the evening soon after twilight, by a peculiar grayish appearance of the northern sky just above the horizon. The grayish vapors giving that appearance, continuing to form there, soon assume a dark and gloomy aspect, while they gradually take the form of a segment of a circle resting on the horizon. At the same time that this dark segment is forming, a soft pearly light, which seems to issue from its border, spreads up in the sky, where it gradually vanishes, being the brightest at its base. This arc of light, gradually increasing in extent as well as in brightness, reaches sometimes as far as the polar star. On some rare occasions, one or two, and even three, concentric arches of bright light form one above the other over the dark segment, where they appear as brilliant concentric rainbows. While the aurora continues to develop and spread out its immense arc, the border of the dark segment loses its regularity and appears indented at several places by patches of light, which soon develop into long, narrow, diverging rays and streamers of great beauty. For the most part the auroral light is either whitish or of a pale, greenish tint; but in some cases it exhibits the most beautiful colors, among which the red and green predominate. In these cases the rays and streamers, which are usually of different colors, produce the most magnificent effects by their continual changes and transformations.

The brightness and extent of the auroral rays are likewise subject to continual changes. An instant suffices for their development and disappearance, which may be succeeded by the sudden appearance of others elsewhere, as though the original streamers had been swiftly transported to a new place while invisible. It frequently happens that all the streamers seem to move sidewise, from west to east, along the arch, continuing meanwhile to exhibit their various changes of form and color. For a time, these appearances of motion continue to increase, a succession of streamers alternately shooting forth and again fading, when a sudden lull occurs, during which all motion seems to have ceased. The stillness then prevailing is soon succeeded by slight pulsations of light, which seem to originate on the border of the dark segment, and are propagated upwards along the streamers, which have now become more numerous and active. Slow at first, these pulsations quicken by degrees, and after a few minutes the whole northern sky seems to be in rapid vibration. The lively upward and downward movement of these streamers entitles them to the name of "merry dancers" given them in northern countries where they are frequent.

Long waves of light, quickly succeeded by others, are propagated in an instant from the horizon to the zenith; these, in their rapid passage, cause bends and curves in the streamers, which then, losing their original straightness, wave and undulate in graceful folds, resembling those of a pennant in a gentle breeze. Although the coruscations add to the grandeur of the spectacle, they tend to destroy the diverging streamers, which, being disconnected from the dark segment, or torn in various ways, are, as it were, bodily carried up towards the zenith.

In this new phase the aurora is transformed into a glorious crown of light, called the "Corona." From this corona diverge in all directions long streamers of different colors and forms, gracefully undulating in numerous folds, like so many banners of light. Some of the largest of these streamers appear like fringes composed of short transverse rays of different intensity and colors, producing the most fantastic effects, when traversed by the pulsations and coruscations which generally run across these rays during the great auroral displays.

The aurora has now attained its full development and beauty. It may continue in this form for half an hour, but usually the celestial fires begin to fade at the end of fifteen or twenty minutes, reviving from time to time, but gradually dying out. The northern sky usually appears covered by gray and luminous streaks and patches after a great aurora, these being occasionally rekindled, but more often they gradually disappear, and the sky resumes its usual appearance.

The number of auroras which develop a corona near the zenith is comparatively small in our latitudes; but many of them, although not exhibited on so grand a scale, are nevertheless very interesting. On some very rare occasions the auroral display has been confined almost exclusively to the dark segment, which appeared then as if pierced along its border by many square openings, like windows, through which appeared the bright auroral light.

Among the many auroras which I have had occasion to observe, none are more interesting, excepting the type first described, than those which form an immense arch of light spanning the heavens from East to West. This form of aurora, which is quite rare, I last observed on September 12th, 1881. All the northern sky was covered with light vapors, when a small auroral patch appeared in the East at about 20° above the horizon. This patch of light, gradually increasing westward, soon reached the zenith, and continued its onward progress until it arrived at about 20° above the western horizon, where it stopped. The aurora then appeared as a narrow, wavy band of light, crossed by numerous parallel rays of different intensity and color. These rays seemed to have a rapid motion from West to East along the delicately-fringed streamer, which, on the whole, moved southward, while its extremities remained undisturbed. Aside from the apparent displacement of the fringes, a singular vibrating motion was observed in the auroral band, which was traversed by pulsations and long waves of light. The phenomena lasted for about twenty minutes, after which the arch was broken in many places, and it slowly vanished.

The aurora usually appears in the early part of the evening, and attains its full development between ten and eleven o'clock. Although the auroral light may have apparently ceased, yet the phenomenon is not at an end, as very often a solitary ray is visible from time to time; and even towards morning these rays sometimes become quite numerous. On some occasions the phenomenon even continues through the following day, and is manifested by the radial direction of the cirrus-clouds in the heights of our atmosphere. In 1872 I, myself, observed an aurora which apparently continued for two or three consecutive days and nights. In August, 1859, the northern lights remained visible in the United States for a whole week.

The height attained by these meteors is considerable, and it is now admitted that they are produced in the rarefied air of the upper regions of our atmosphere. From the researches of Professor Elias Loomis on the great auroras observed in August and September, 1859, it was ascertained that the inferior part of the auroral rays had an altitude of 46 miles, while that of their summits was 428 miles. These rays had, therefore, a length of 382 miles. From the observation of thirty auroral displays, it has been found that the mean height attained by the summit of these streamers above the Earth's surface was 450 miles.

But if the auroral streamers are generally manifested at great heights in our atmosphere, it would appear from the observations of persons living in the regions where the auroras are most frequent, as also from those who have been stationed in high northern and southern latitudes, that the phenomenon sometimes descends very low. Both Sabine and Parry saw the auroral rays projected on a distant mountain ; Ross saw them almost at sea-level projected on the polar ice ; while Wrangel, Franklin, and others observed similar phenomena. Dr. Hjaltalin, who has lived in latitude 64° 46′ north, and has made a particular study of the aurora, on one occasion saw the aurora much below the summit of a hill 1,600 feet high, which was not very far off.

The same aurora is sometimes observed on the same night at places very far distant from one another. The great aurora borealis of August 28th, 1859, for instance, was seen over a space occupying 150° in longitude—from California to the Ural Mountains in Russia. It even appears now very probable that the phenomenon is universal , on our globe, and that the northern lights observed in our hemisphere are simultaneous with the aurora australis of the southern hemisphere. The aurora of September 2d, 1859, was observed all through North and South America, the Sandwich Islands, Australia, and Africa; the streamers and pulsations of light of the north pole responding to the rays and coruscations of the south pole. Of thirty-four auroras observed at Hobart Town, in Tasmania, twenty-nine corresponded with aurora borealis observed in our hemisphere.

The auroral phenomena, although sometimes visible within the tropics, are, however, quite rare in these regions. For the most part they are confined within certain zones situated in high latitudes north and south. The zone where they are most frequent in our hemisphere forms an ellipse, which has the north pole at one of its foci ; while the other is situated somewhere in North America, in the vicinity of the magnetic pole. The central line of the zone upon which the auroras seem to be most frequent passes from the northern coast of Alaska through Hudson's Bay and Labrador to Iceland, and then follows the northern coast of Europe and Asia. The number of auroras diminishes as the observer recedes from this zone, and it is only in exceptional cases that they are seen near the equator. Near the pole the phenomenon is less frequent than it is in the region described. In North America we occupy a favorable position for the observation of auroras, as we are nearer the magnetic poles than are the Europeans and Asiatics, and we consequently have a greater number of auroras in corresponding latitudes.

The position of the dark auroral segment varies with the place occupied by the observer, and its centre always corresponds with the magnetic meridian. In our Eastern States the auroral segment appears a little to the west of the north point ; but as the observer proceeds westward it gradually approaches this point, and is due north when seen from the vicinity of Lake Winnipeg. At Point Barrow, in the extreme northwest of the United States, the aurora is observed in the east. In Melville Islands, Parry saw it in the south ; while in Greenland it is directly in the west.

It is stated that auroras are more numerous about the equinoxes than they are at any other seasons ; and also, when the earth is in perigee, than when it is in apogee. An examination which I have made of a catalogue by Professor Loomis, comprising 4,137 auroras observed in the temperate zone of our hemisphere from 1776 to 1873, sustains this statement. During this period, one hundred more auroras were recorded during each of the months comprising the equinoxes, than during any other months of the year ; while eighty more auroras were observed when the earth was in perigee, than when it was in apogee. But to establish the truth of this assertion on a solid basis, more observations in both hemispheres will be required.

The aurora is not simply a terrestrial phenomenon, but is associated in some mysterious way with the conditions of the Sun's surface. It is a well-known fact that terrestrial magnetism is influenced directly by the Sun, which creates the diurnal oscillations of the magnetic needle. Between sunrise and two o'clock, the north pole of the needle moves towards the west in our northern hemisphere, and in the afternoon and evening it moves the other way. These daily oscillations of the needle are not uniform in extent ; they have a period of regular increase and decrease. At a given place the daily oscillations of the magnetic needle increase and decrease with regularity during a period which is equal to 10⅓ years. As this period closely coincides with the Sun-spot period, the connection between the variation of the needle and these solar disturbances has been recognized.

Auroral phenomena generally accompany the extraordinary perturbations in the oscillations of the magnetic needle, which are commonly called "magnetic storms," and the greater the auroral displays, the greater are the magnetic perturbations. Not only is the needle subject to unusual displacements during an aurora, but its movements seem to be simultaneous with the pulsations and waving motions of the delicate auroral streamers in the sky. When the aurora sends forth a coruscation, or a streamer in the sky, the magnetic needle responds to it by a vibration. The inference that the auroral phenomena are connected with terrestrial magnetism is further supported by the fact that the centre of the corona is always situated exactly in the direction of that point in the heavens to which the dipping needle is directed.

It has been found that the aurora is a periodical phenomenon, and that its period corresponds very closely with those of the magnetic needle and Sun-spots. The years which have the most Sun-spots and magnetic disturbances have also the most auroras. There is an almost perfect similarity between the courses of the three sets of phenomena, from which it is concluded that the aurora is connected in some mysterious way with the action of the Sun, as well as with the magnetic condition of the earth.

A very curious observation, which has been supposed to have some connection with this subject, was made on Sept. 1st, 1859, by Mr. Carrington and Mr. Hodgson, in England. While these observers, who were situated many miles from one another, were both engaged at the same time in observing the same Sun-spot, they suddenly saw two luminous spots of dazzling brilliancy bursting into sight from the edge of the Sun-spot. These objects moved eastward for about five minutes, after which they disappeared, having then traveled nearly 34,000 miles. Simultaneously with these appearances, a magnetic disturbance was registered at Kew by the self-registering magnetic instruments. The very night that followed these observations, great magnetic perturbations, accompanied by brilliant auroral displays, were observed in Europe. A connection between the terrestrial magnetism and the auroral phenomena is further proved by the fact that, before the appearance of an aurora, the magnetic intensity of our globe considerably increases, but diminishes as soon as the first flashes show themselves.

The auroral phenomena are also connected in some way with electricity, and generate serious disturbances in the electric currents traversing our telegraphic lines, which are thus often rendered useless for the transmission of messages during great auroral' displays. It sometimes happens, however, during such displays, that the telegraphic lines can be operated for a long distance, without the assistance of a battery ; the aurora, or at least its cause, furnishing the necessary electric current for the working of the line. During auroras, the telephonic lines are also greatly affected, and all kinds of noises and crepitations are heard in the instruments.

Two observations of mine, which may have a bearing on the subject, present some interest, as they seem to indicate the action of the aurora on some of the clouds of our atmosphere. On January 6th, 1872, after I had been observing a brilliant aurora for over one hour, an isolated black cumulus cloud appeared at a little distance from the western extremity of the dark auroral segment. This cloud, probably driven by the wind, rapidly advanced eastward, and was soon followed by a succession of similar clouds, all starting from the same point. All these black clouds apparently followed the same path, which was not a straight line, but parallel to and concentric with the border of the dark auroral segment. When the first cloud arrived in the vicinity of the magnetic meridian passing through the middle of the auroral arc, it very rapidly dissolved, and on reaching this meridian became invisible. The same phenomenon was observed with the succession of black clouds following, each rapidly dissolving as it approached the magnetic meridian. This phenomenon of black clouds vanishing like phantoms in crossing the magnetic meridian, was observed for nearly an hour. On June 17th, 1879, I observed a similar phenomenon during a fine auroral display. About midway between the horizon and the polar star, but a little to the west of the magnetic meridian, there was a large black cumulo-stratus cloud which very slowly advanced eastward. As it progressed in that direction, its eastern extremity was dissolved in traversing the magnetic meridian; while, at the same time, several short and quite bright auroral rays issued from its western extremity, which in its turn dissolved rapidly, as if burned or melted away in the production of the auroral flame.

It seems to be a well observed fact, that during auroras, a strong sulphurous odor prevails in high northern latitudes. According to Dr. Hjaltalin, during these phenomena, "the ozone of the atmosphere increases considerably, and men and animals exposed out of doors emit a sulphurous odor when entering a heated room." The Esquimaux and other inhabitants of the northern regions assert that great auroras are sometimes accompanied by crepitations and crackling noises of various sorts. Although these assertions have been denied by several travelers who have visited the regions of these phenomena, they are confirmed by many competent observers. Dr. Hjaltalin, who has heard these noises about six times in a hundred observations, says that they are especially audible when the weather is clear and calm ; but that when the atmosphere is agitated they are not heard. He compares them to the peculiar sound produced by a silk cloth when torn asunder, or to the crepitations of the electric machine when its motion is accelerated. " When the auroral light is much agitated and the streamers show great movements, it is then that these noises are heard at different places in the atmosphere."

The spectrum of the auroral light, although it varies with almost every aurora, always shows a bright green line on a faint continuous spectrum. In addition to this green line I have frequently observed four broad diffused bands of greater refrangibility in the spectra of some auroras. In two cases, when the auroras appeared red towards the west, the spectrum showed a bright red line, in addition to the green line and the broad bands described. These facts evidently show that the light of the aurora is due to the presence of luminous vapors in our atmosphere ; and it may reasonably be supposed that these vapors are rendered luminous by the passage of electric discharges through them.

THE ZODIACAL LIGHT.

PLATE V.

IN our northern latitudes may be seen, on every clear winter and spring evening, a column of faint, whitish, nebulous light, rising obliquely above the western horizon.   A similar phenomenon may also be observed in the east, before day-break, on any clear summer or autumn night.   To this pale, glimmering luminosity the name of " Zodiacal Light" has been given, from the fact that it lies in the zodiac along the ecliptic.

In common with all the celestial bodies, the zodiacal light participates in the diurnal motion of the sky, and rises and sets with the constellations in which it appears.   Aside from this apparent motion, it is endowed with a motion of its own, accomplished from west to east, in a period of a year.   In its motion among the stars, the zodiacal light always keeps pace with the Sun, and appears as if forming two faint luminous wings, resting on opposite sides of this body.   In reality it extends on each side of the Sun, its axis lying very nearly in the plane of the ecliptic.

In our latitudes the phenomena can be observed most advantageously towards the equinoxes, in March and September, when twilight is of short duration.   As we proceed southward it becomes more prominent, and gradually increases in size and brightness.   It is within the tropical regions that the zodiacal light acquires all its splendor : there it is visible all the year round, and always appears very nearly perpendicular to the horizon, while at the same time its proportions and brilliancy are greatly increased.

The zodiacal light appears under the form of a spear-head, or of a narrow cone of light whose base apparently rests on the horizon, while its summit rises among the zodiacal constellations.   In general appearance it somewhat resembles the tail of a large comet whose head is below the horizon.   The most favorable time to observe this phenomenon in the evening, is immediately after the last trace of twilight has disappeared ; and in the morning, one or two hours before twilight appears. When observed with attention, it is seen that the light of the zodiacal cone is not uniform, but gradually increases in brightness inwardly, especially towards its base, where it sometimes surpasses in brilliancy the brightest parts of the Milky-Way. In general, its outlines are vague and very difficult to make out, so gradually do they blend with the sky. On some favorable occasions, the luminous cone appears to be composed of several distinct concentric conical layers, having different degrees of brightness, the inner cone being the most brilliant of all. There is a remarkable distinction between the evening and morning zodiacal light. In our climate, the morning light is pale, and never so bright nor so extended as the evening light.

In general, the zodiacal light is whitish and colorless, but in some cases it acquires a warm yellowish or reddish tint. These changes of color may be accidental and due to atmospheric conditions, and not to actual change in the color of the object. Although the zodiacal light is quite bright, and produces the impression of having considerable depth, yet its transparency is great, since all the stars, except the faint ones, can be seen through its substance.

The zodiacal light is subject to considerable variations in brightness, and also varies in extent, the apex of its cone varying in distance from the Sun's place, from 40 to 90 degrees. These variations cannot be attributed to atmospheric causes alone, some of them being due to real changes in the zodiacal light itself, whose light and dimensions increase or decrease under the action of causes at present unknown. From the discussion of a series of observations on the zodiacal light made at Paris and Geneva, it appears certain that its light varies from year to year, and sometimes even from day to day, independently of atmospheric causes. Some of my own observations agree with these results, and one of them, at least, seems to indicate changes even more rapid. On December 18th, 1875, I observed the zodiacal light in a clear sky free from any vapors, at six o'clock in the evening. At that time, the point of its cone was a little to the north of the ecliptic, at a distance of about 90 degrees from the Sun's place. Ten minutes later, its summit had sunk down 35 degrees, the cone then being reduced to nearly one-half of its original dimensions. Ten minutes later, it had risen 25 degrees, and was then 80 degrees from the Sun's place, where it remained all the evening. On March 22d, 1878, the sky was very clear and the zodiacal light was bright when I observed it, at eight o'clock. At that moment the apex of the cone of light was a little to the south of the Pleiades, but this cone presented an unusual appearance never noticed by me before, its northern border appearing much brighter and sharper than usual, while at the same time its axis of greatest brightness appeared to be much nearer to this northern border than it was to the southern. After a few minutes of observation it became evident that the northern border was extending itself, as stars which were at some distance from it became gradually involved in its light. At the same time that this border spread northward, it seemed to diffuse itself, and after a time the cone presented its usual appearance, having its southern border brighter and better defined than the other. It would have been impossible to attribute this sudden change to an atmospheric cause, since only one of the borders of the cone participated in it, and since some very faint stars near this northern border were not affected in the least while the phenomenon occurred. Besides these observations, Cassini, Mairan, Humboldt, and many other competent observers have seen pulsations, coruscations and flickerings in the light of the cone, which they thought could not be attributed to atmospheric causes. It has also been observed that at certain periods the zodiacal light has shone with unusual intensity for months together.

When this phenomenon is observed from the tropical regions, it is found that its axis of symmetry always corresponds with its axis of greatest brightness, and that both lie in the plane of the ecliptic, which divides its cone into two equal parts. But when the zodiacal light is observed in our latitude, the axis of symmetry does not correspond with the axis of greatest brightness, and both axes are a little to the north of this plane, the axis of symmetry being the farther removed. Furthermore, as already stated, the southern border of the cone always appears better defined and brighter than the corresponding northern margin. It is very probable, if not absolutely certain, that these phenomena are exactly reversed when the zodiacal light is observed from corresponding latitudes in the southern hemisphere, and that there, its axes, both of symmetry and of greatest brightness, appear south of the ecliptic, while the northern margin is the brightest. This seems to be established by the valuable observations of Rev. George Jones, made on board the U. S. steam frigate Mississippi, in California, Japan, and the Southern Ocean. "When I was north of the ecliptic," says this observer, "the greatest part of the light of the cone appeared to the north of this line ; when I was to the south of the ecliptic, it appeared to be south of it ; while when my position was on the ecliptic, or in its vicinity, the zodiacal cone was equally divided by this line."

Besides the zodiacal light observed in the East and West, some observers have recognized an exceedingly faint, luminous, gauzy band, about 10 or 12 degrees wide, stretching along the ecliptic from the summit of the western to that of the eastern zodiacal cone. This faint narrow belt has been called the Zodiacal Band. It has been recognized by Mr. H. C. Lewis, who has made a study of this phenomenon, that the zodiacal band has its southern margin a little brighter and a little sharper than the northern border. This observation is in accordance with similar phenomena observed in the zodiacal light, and may have considerable importance.

In 1854, Brorsen recognized a faint, roundish, luminous spot in a point of the heavens exactly opposite to the place occupied by the Sun, which he has called "Gegenschein," or counter-glow. This luminous spot has sometimes a small nucleus, which is a little brighter than the rest. Night after night this very faint object shifts its position among the constellations, keeping always at 180 degrees from the Sun. The position of the counter-glow, like that of the zodiacal light and zodiacal band, is not precisely on the plane of the ecliptic, but a little to the north of this line. It is very probable that near the equator the phenomenon would appear different and there would correspond with this plane.

There seems to be some confusion among observers in regard to the spectrum of the zodiacal light. Some have seen a bright green line in its spectrum, corresponding to that of the aurora borealis; while others could only see a faint grayish continuous spectrum, which differs, however, from that of a faint solar light, by the fact that it presents a well-defined bright zone, gradually blending on each side with the fainter light of the continuous spectrum. I have, myself, frequently observed the faint continuous spectrum of the zodiacal light, and on one occasion recognized the green line of the aurora; but it might have been produced by the aurora itself, as yet invisible to the eye, and not by the zodiacal light, since, later in the same evening, there was a brilliant auroral display. If it were demonstrated that this green line exists in the spectrum of the zodiacal light, the fact would have importance, as tending to show that the aurora and the zodiacal light have a common origin.

Rev. Geo. Jones describes a very curious phenomenon which he observed several times a little before the moon rose above the horizon. The phenomenon consisted in a short, oblique, luminous cone rising from the Moon's place in the direction of the ecliptic. This phenomenon he has called the Moon Zodiacal Light. In 1874, I had an opportunity to observe a similar phenomenon when the Moon was quite high in the sky. By taking the precaution to screen the Moon's disk by the interposition of some buildings between it and my eye, I saw two long and narrow cones of light parallel to the ecliptic issuing from opposite sides of our satellite. The phenomenon could not possibly be attributed to vapors in our atmosphere, since the sky was very clear at the moment of the observation. Later on, these appendages disappeared with the formation of vapors near the Moon, but they reappeared an hour later, when the sky had cleared off, and continued visible for twenty minutes longer, and then disappeared in a clear sky.

Although the zodiacal light has been studied for over two centuries, no wholly satisfactory explanation of the phenomenon has yet been given. Now, as in Cassini's time, it is generally considered by astronomers to be due to a kind of lens-shaped ring surrounding the Sun, and extending a little beyond the Earth's orbit. This ring is supposed to lie in the plane of the ecliptic, and to be composed of a multitude of independent meteoric particles circulating in closed parallel orbits around the Sun. But many difficulties lie in the way of this theory. It seems as incompetent to explain the slow and rapid changes in the light of this object as it is to explain the contractions and extensions of its cone. It fails, moreover, to explain the flickering motions, the coruscations observed in its light, or the displacement of its cone and of its axes of brightness and symmetry by a mere change in the position of the observer. Rev. Geo. Jones, unable to explain by this theory the phenomena which came under his observation, has proposed another, which supposes the zodiacal light to be produced by a luminous ring surrounding the Earth, this ring not extending as far as the orbit of the Moon. But this theory also fails in many important points, so that at present no satisfactory explanation of the phenomenon can be given.

As the phenomenon is connected in some way with the Sun, and as we have many reasons to believe this body to be always more or less electrified, it might be supposed that the Sun, acting by induction on our globe, develops feeble electric currents in the rarefied gases of the superior regions of our atmosphere, and there forms a kind of luminous ridge moving with the Sun in a direction contrary to the diurnal motion, and so producing the zodiacal light. On this hypothesis, the counter-glow would be the result of a smaller cone of light generated by the solar induction on the opposite point of the Earth.

Plate 5, which sufficiently explains itself, represents the zodiacal light as it appeared in the West on the evening of February 20th, 1876. All the stars are placed in their proper position, and their relative brightness is approximately shown by corresponding variations in size—the usual and almost the only available means of representation. Of course, it must be remembered that a star does not, in fact, show any disk even in the largest telescopes, where it appears as a mere point of light, having more or less brilliancy. The cone of light rises obliquely along the ecliptic, and the point forming its summit is found in the vicinity of the well-known group of stars, called the Pleiades, in the constellation of Taurus, or the Bull.

THE MOON.

PLATE VI.

In its endless journey through space, our globe is not solitary, like some of the planets, but is attended by the Moon, our nearest celestial neighbor. Although the Moon does not attain to the dignity of a planet, and remains a secondary body in the solar system, yet, owing to its proximity to our globe, and to the great influence it exerts upon it by its powerful attraction, it is to us one of the most important celestial bodies.

While the Moon accompanies the Earth around the Sun, it also revolves around the Earth at a mean distance of 238,800 miles. For a celestial distance this is only a trifling one ; the Earth in advancing on its orbit travels over such a distance in less than four hours. A cannon ball would reach our satellite in nine days ; and a telegraphic dispatch would be transmitted there in $1\frac{1}{2}$ seconds of time, if a wire could be stretched between us and the Moon.

Owing to the ellipticity of the Moon's orbit, its distance from the Earth varies considerably, our satellite being sometimes 38,000 miles nearer to us than it is at other times. These changes in the distance of the Moon occasion corresponding changes from 29' to 33' in its apparent diameter. The real diameter of the Moon is 2,160 miles, or a little over one-quarter the diameter of our globe ; our satellite being 49 times smaller than the Earth.

The mean density of the materials composing the Moon is only $\frac{4}{10}$ that of the materials composing the Earth, and the force of gravitation at the surface of our satellite is six times less than it is at the surface of our globe. If a person weighing 150 lbs. on our Earth could be transported to the Moon, his weight there would be only 25 lbs.

The Moon revolves around the Earth in about $27\frac{1}{3}$ days, with a mean velocity of one mile per second, the revolution constituting its sidereal period. If the Earth were motionless, the lunar month would be equal to the sidereal period ; but owing to its motion in space, the Sun appears to move with the Moon, though more slowly, so that after having accomplished one complete revolution, our satellite has yet to advance 2¼ days before reaching the same apparent position in regard to the Earth and the Sun that it had at first. The interval of time comprised between two successive New Moons, which is a little over 29½ days, constitutes the synodical period of the Moon, or the lunar month.

The Moon is not a self-luminous body, but, like the Earth and the planets, it reflects the light which it receives from the Sun, and so appears luminous. That such is the case is sufficiently demonstrated by the phases exhibited by our satellite in the course of the lunar month. Every one is familiar with these phases, which are a consequence of the motion of the Moon around the Earth. When our satellite is situated between us and the Sun, it is New Moon; since we cannot see its illuminated side, which is then turned away from us towards the Sun. When, on the contrary, it reaches that point of its orbit which, in regard to us, is opposite to the Sun's place, it is Full Moon ; since from the Earth we can only see the fully illuminated side of our satellite. Again, when the Moon arrives at either of the two opposite points of its orbit, the direction of which from the Earth is at right angles with that of the Sun, it is either the First or the Last Quarter ; since in these positions we can only see one-half of its illuminated disk.

The curve described by the Moon around the Earth lies approximately in a plane, this plane being inclined about 5° to the ecliptic. Since our satellite, in its motion around us and the Sun, closely follows the ecliptic, which is inclined 23½° to the equator, it results that when this plane is respectively high or low in the sky, the moon is also high or low when crossing the meridian of the observer. In winter that part of the ecliptic occupied by the Sun is below the equator, and, consequently, the New Moons occurring in that season are low in the sky, since at New Moon our satellite must be on the same side of the ecliptic with the Sun. But the Full Moons in the same season are necessarily high in the sky, since a Full Moon can only occur when our satellite is on the opposite side of the ecliptic from the Sun, in which position it is, of course, as many degrees above the equator as the Sun is below. The Full Moon which happens nearest to the autumnal equinox is commonly called the Harvest Moon, from the fact that, after full, its delays in rising on successive evenings are very brief and therefore favorable for the harvest work in the evening. The same phenomenon occurs in every other lunar month, but not sufficiently near the time of

Full Moon to be noticeable. When, in spring, a day or two after New Moon, our satellite begins to show its thin crescent, its position on the ecliptic is north as well as east of that occupied by the Sun ; hence, its horns are nearly upright in direction, and give it a crude resemblance to a tipping bowl, from which many people who are unaware of its cause, and that this happens every year, draw conclusions as to the amount of rain to be expected.

One of the most remarkable features of the Moon's motions is that our satellite rotates on its axis in exactly the same period of time occupied by its revolution around the Earth, from which it results that the Moon always presents to us the same face. To explain this peculiarity, astronomers have supposed that the figure of our satellite is not perfectly spherical, but elongated, so that the attraction of the Earth, acting more powerfully upon its nearest portions, always keeps them turned toward us, as if the Moon were united to our globe by a string. It is not exactly true, however, that the Moon always presents its same side to us, although its period of rotation exactly equals that of its revolution ; since in consequence of the inclination of its axis of rotation to its orbit, combined with the irregularities of its orbital motion about us, apparent oscillations in latitude and in longitude, called librations, are created, from which it results that nearly $\frac{4}{10}$ of the Moon's surface is visible from the Earth at one time or another.

The Moon is a familiar object, and every one is aware that our satellite, especially when it is fully illuminated, presents a variety of bright and dark markings, which, from their distant resemblance to a human face, are popularly known as " the man in the moon." A day or two after New Moon, when the thin crescent of our satellite is visible above the western horizon after sunset, the dark portion of its disk is plainly visible, and appears of a pale, ashy gray color, although not directly illuminated by the Sun. This phenomenon is due to the Earth-shine, or to that portion of solar light which the illuminated surface of our globe reflects to the dark side of the Moon, exactly in the same manner that the Moon-shine, on our Earth, is due to the solar light reflected to our globe by the illuminated Moon.

Seen with a telescope of moderate power, or even with a good opera-glass, the Moon presents a peculiar mottled appearance, and has a strong resemblance to a globe made of plaster of Paris, on the surface of which numerous roundish, saucer-shaped cavities of various sizes are scattered at random. This mottled structure is better seen along the boundary line called the *terminator*, which divides the illuminated from the dark side of the Moon. The line of the terminator always appears jagged, and it is very easy to recognize that this irregularity is due to the uneven and rugged structure of the surface of our satellite.

A glance at the Moon through a larger telescope shows that the bright spots recognized with the naked eye belong to very uneven and mountainous regions of our satellite, while the dark ones belong to comparatively smooth, low surfaces, comparable to those forming the great steppes and plains of the Earth. When examined with sufficient magnifying power, the white, rugged districts of the Moon appear covered over by numerous elevated craggy plateaus, mountain-chains, and deep ravines ; by steep cliffs and ridges ; by peaks of great height and cavities of great depth. This rugged formation, which is undoubtedly of volcanic origin, gives our satellite a desolate and barren appearance. The rugged tract occupies more than one-half of the visible surface of the Moon, forming several distinct masses, the principal of which occupy the south and southwestern part of the disk. That this formation is elevated above the general level is proved by the fact that the mountains, peaks, and other objects which compose it, all cast a shadow opposite to the Sun ; and further, that the length of these shadows diminishes with the elevation of the Sun above the lunar horizon.

Since Galileo's time the surface of the Moon has been studied by a host of astronomers, and accurate maps of its topographical configuration have been made, and names given to all features of any prominence. It may even be said that in its general features, the visible surface of our satellite is now better known to us than is the surface of our own Earth.

One of the most striking and common features of the mountainous districts of the Moon, is the circular, ring-like disposition of their elevated parts, which form numerous crater-like objects of different sizes and depths. Many thousands of crater-like objects are visible on the Moon through a good telescope, and, considering how numerous the small ones are, there is, perhaps, no great exaggeration in fixing their number at 50,000, as has been done by some astronomers. These volcanic regions of the Moon cannot be compared to anything we know, and far surpass in extent those of our globe. The number and size of the craters of our most important volcanic regions in Europe, in Asia, in North and South America, in Java, in Sumatra, and Borneo, are insignificant when compared with those of the Moon. The largest known craters on the Earth give only a faint idea of the magnitude of some of the lunar craters. The great crater Haleakala, in the Sandwich

Islands, probably the largest of the terrestrial volcanoes, has a circumference of thirty miles, or a diameter of a little less than ten
miles.   Some of the great lunar craters, called walled plains, such
as Hipparchus, Ptolemæus, etc., have a diameter more than ten
times larger than that of Haleakala, that of the first being 115 miles
and that of the last 100 miles.   These are, of course, among the
largest of the craters of the Moon, although there are on our satellite a great number of craters above ten miles in diameter.

The crater-forms of the Moon have evidently appeared at different
periods of time, since small craters are frequently found on the walls
of larger ones ; and, indeed, still smaller craters are not rarely seen
on the walls of these last.   The walls of the lunar craters are usually quite elevated above the surrounding surface, some of them
attaining considerable elevations, especially at some points, which
form peaks of great height.   Newton, the loftiest of all, rises at one
point to the height of 23,000 feet, while many others range from
ten to twenty thousand feet in height.   Several craters have their
floor above the general surface—Plato, for instance.   Wargentin
has its floor nearly on a level with the summit of its walls,
showing that at some period of its history liquid lavas, ejected
from within, have filled it to the brim and then solidified.   The
floors of some of the craters are smooth and flat, but in general
they are occupied by peaks and abrupt mountainous masses, which
usually form the centre.   Many of their outside walls are partly or
wholly covered by numerous ravines and gullies, winding down
their steep declivities, branching out and sometimes extending to
great distances from their base.   It would seem that these great
volcanic mouths have at some time poured out torrents of lavas,
which, in their descent, carved their passage by the deep gullies
now visible.   Sometimes, also, the crater slopes are strewn with
debris, giving them a peculiar volcanic appearance.

Notwithstanding their many points of similarity with the volcanoes of the Earth, the lunar craters differ from them in many par-
ticulars, showing that volcanic forces acting on different globes may
produce widely different results.   For example, the floors of terrestrial craters are usually situated at considerable elevations above
the general surface, while those of the lunar craters are generally
much depressed, the height of their walls being only about one-
half the depth of their cavities.   Again, while on the Earth the
mass of the volcanic cones far exceeds the capacity of their openings, on the Moon it is not rare to see the capacity of the crater
cavities exceeding the mass of the surrounding walls.   On the

Earth, the volcanic cones and mouths are comparatively regular and smooth, and are generally due to the accumulation of the ashes and the debris of all kinds which are ejected from the volcanic mouths. On the Moon, very few craters show this character, and for the most part their walls have a very different structure, being irregular, very rugged, and composed of a succession of concentric ridges, rising at many points to great elevations, and forming peaks of stupendous height. Again, many of the larger terrestrial craters have their interior occupied by a central cone, or several such cones, having a volcanic mouth on their summits ; on the Moon such central cones are very rare. Although many of the large lunar craters have their interior occupied by central masses which have been often compared to the central cones of our great volcanoes, yet these objects have a very different character and origin. For the most part, they are mountainous masses of different forms—having very rarely any craters on them—and seem to have resulted from the crowding and lifting up of the crater floor by the phenomena of subsidence, of which these craters show abundant signs. Besides, the terrestrial craters are characterized by large and important lava streams, while on the Moon the traces of such phenomena are quite rare, and when they are shown, they generally differ from those of the Earth by their numerous and complicated ramifications, and also by the fact that many of these lava streamlets take their origin at a considerable distance from the crater slopes, and are grooved and depressed as if the burning liquids which are supposed to have produced them had subsequently disappeared, by evaporation or otherwise, leaving the furrow empty.

The dark spots of the Moon, when viewed through a telescope, exhibit a totally different character, and show that they belong to a different formation from that of the brighter portions. These darker tracts do not seem to have had a direct volcanic origin like the latter, but rather appear to have resulted from the solidification of semi-fluid materials, which have overflowed vast areas at different times. The surface of this system is comparatively smooth and uniform, only some small craters and low ridges being seen upon it. The level and dark appearance of these areas led the ancient astronomers to the belief that they were produced by a liquid strongly absorbing the rays of light, and were seas like our seas. Accordingly, these dark surfaces were called *Maria*, or Seas, a name which it is convenient to retain, although it is well known to have originated in an error. The so-called seas of the Moon are evidently large flat surfaces similar to the deserts, steppes, pampas, and prairies of the Earth in general appearance. The great plains of the Moon are at a lower level than that of the other formation, and that which first attracts the observer's attention is the fact that they are surrounded almost on all sides by an irregular line of abrupt cliffs and mountain chains, showing phenomena of dislocation. This character of dislocation, which is general, and is visible everywhere upon the contours of the plains, seems to indicate that phenomena of subsidence, either slow or rapid, have occurred on the Moon ; while, at the same time, the sunken surfaces were overflowed by a semi-fluid liquid, which solidified afterwards. The evidences of subsidence and overflowing become unmistakable when we observe that, along the borders of the gray plains, numerous craters are more or less embedded in the gray formation, only parts of the summit of their walls remaining visible, to attest that once large craters existed there. The farther from the border of the plain the vestiges of these craters are observed, the deeper they are embedded in the gray formation. That phenomena of subsidence have occurred on a grand scale on the Moon, is further indicated by the fact that the singular systems of fractures called clefts and rifts generally follow closely the outside border of the gray plains, often forming parallel lines of dislocation and fractures. In the interior regions of the gray formation, these fractures are comparatively rare.

The gray, lava-like formation is obviously of later origin than the mountainous system to which belong the embedded craters above described. Its comparatively recent origin might also be inferred from the smallness of its craters and its low ridges. The few large craters observed on this formation evidently belong to the earlier system.

The color of this system of gray plains is far from being uniform. In general appearance it is of a bluish gray, but when observed attentively, large areas appear tinted with a dusky olive-green, while others are slightly tinged with yellow. Some patches appear brownish, and even purplish. A remarkable example of the first case is seen on the surface, which encloses within a large parallelogram the two conspicuous craters, Aristarchus and Herodotus. This surface evidently belongs to a different system from that of the Oceanus Procellarum surrounding it, as, besides its color, which totally differs from that of the gray formation, its surface shows the rugged structure of the volcanic formation.

When the Moon is full, some very curious white, luminous streaks are seen radiating from different centres, which, for the most part, are important craters, occupied by interior mountains. The great crater

Tycho is the centre of the most imposing of the systems of white streaks. Some of the diverging rays of this great centre extend to a distance equal to one-quarter of the Moon's circumference, or about 1,700 miles. The true nature of these luminous streaks is unknown, but it seems certain that they have their origin in the crater from which they diverge. They do not form any relief on the surface, and are seen going up over the mountains and steep walls of the crater, as well as down the ravines and on the floors of craters.

The Moon seems to be deprived of an atmosphere; or, if it has any, it must be so excessively rare that its density is less than $\frac{1}{100}$ of the density of the Earth's atmosphere, since delicate tests afforded by the occultation of stars have failed to reveal its presence. Although no atmosphere of any consequence exists on the Moon, yet phenomena which I have observed seem to indicate the occasional presence there of vapors of some sort. On several occasions, I have seen a purplish light over some parts of the Moon, which prevented well-known objects being as distinctly seen as they were at other times, causing them to appear as if seen through a fog. One of the most striking of these observations was made on January 4th, 1873, on the crater Kant and its vicinity, which then appeared as if seen through luminous purplish vapors. On one occasion, the great crater Godin, which was entirely involved in the shadow of its western wall, appeared illuminated in its interior by a faint purplish light, which enabled me to recognize the structure of this interior. The phenomenon could not be attributed in this case to reflection, since the Sun, then just rising on the western wall of the crater, had not yet grazed the eastern wall, which was invisible. It is not impossible that a very rare atmosphere composed of such vapors exists in the lower parts of the Moon.

If the Moon has no air, and no liquids of any sort, it seems impossible that its surface can maintain any form of life, either vegetable or animal, analogous to those on the Earth. In fact, nothing indicating life has been detected on the Moon—our satellite looking like a barren, lifeless desert. If life is to be found there at all, it must be of a very elementary nature. Aside from the want of air and water to sustain it, the climatic conditions of our satellite are very unfavorable for the development of life. The nights and days of the Moon are each equal to nearly fifteen of our days and nights. For fifteen consecutive terrestrial days the Sun's light is absent from one hemisphere of the Moon; while for the same number of days the Sun pours down on the other hemisphere its light and heat, the effects of which are not in any way mitigated by an atmosphere. During the long lunar nights the temperature must at least fall to that of our polar regions, while during its long days it must be far above that of our tropical zone. It has been calculated that during the lunar nights the temperature descends to 23° below zero, while during the days it rises to 468°, or 256° above the boiling point.

It has been a question among astronomers whether changes are still taking place at the surface of the Moon. Aside from the fact that change, not constancy, is the law of nature, it does not seem doubtful that changes occur on the Moon, especially in view of the powerful influences of contraction and dilatation to which its materials are submitted by its severe alternations of temperature. From the distance at which we view our satellite, we cannot expect, of course, to be able to see changes, unless they are produced on a large scale. Theoretically speaking, the largest telescopes ever constructed ought to show us the Moon as it would appear to the naked eye from a distance of 40 miles ; but in practice it is very different. The difficulty is in the fact that, while we magnify the surface of a telescopic image, we are unable to increase its light; so that, practically, in magnifying an object, we weaken its light proportionally to the magnifying power employed. The light of the Moon, especially near the terminator, where we almost always make our observations, is not sufficiently bright to bear a very high magnifying power, and only moderate ones can be applied to its study. What we gain by enlarging an object, we more than lose by the weakening of its light. Besides, a high magnifying power, by increasing the disturbances generally present in our atmosphere, renders the telescopic image unsteady and very indistinct. On the whole, the largest telescopes now in existence do not show us our satellite better than if we could see it with the naked eye from a distance of 300 miles or more. At such a distance only considerable changes would be visible.

Notwithstanding these difficulties, it is believed that changes have been detected in Linnè, Marius, Messier, and several other craters. An observation of mine seems to indicate that changes have recently taken place in the great crater Eudoxus. On February 20th, 1877, between 9h. 30m. and 10h. 30m., I observed a straight, narrow wall crossing this crater from east to west, a little to the south of its centre. This wall had a considerable elevation, as was proved by the shadow it cast on its northern side. Towards its western end this wall appeared as a brilliant thread of light on the black shadow cast by the western wall of the crater. The first time I had occasion to observe this crater again, after this observation, was a year later, on February 17th, 1878; no traces of the wall were then detected. Many times since I have tried to find this narrow wall again, when the Moon presented the same phase and the same illumination, but always with negative results. It seems probable that this structure has crumbled down, yet it is very singular that so prominent a feature should not have been noticed before.

The " Mare Humorum," or sea of moisture, as it is called, which is represented on Plate VI., is one of the smaller gray lunar plains. Its diameter, which is very nearly the same in all directions, is about 270 miles, the total area of this plain being about 50,000 square miles. It is one of the most distinct plains of the Moon, and is easily seen with the naked eye on the left-hand side of the disk. The floor of the plain is, like that of the other gray plains, traversed by several systems of very extended but low hills and ridges, while small craters are disseminated upon its surface. The color of this formation is of a dusky greenish gray along the border, while in the interior it is of a lighter shade, and is of brownish olivaceous tint. This plain, which is surrounded by high clefts and rifts, well illustrates the phenomena of dislocation and subsidence. The double-ringed crater Vitello, whose walls rise from 4,000 to 5,000 feet in height, is seen in the upper left-hand corner of the gray plain. Close to Vitello, at the east, is the large broken ring-plain Lee, and farther east, and a little below, is a similarly broken crater called Doppelmayer. Both of these open craters have mountainous masses and peaks on their floor, which is on a level with that of the Mare Humorum. A little below, and to the left of these objects, is seen a deeply embedded oval crater, whose walls barely rise above the level of the plain. On the right-hand side of the great plain, is a long *fault*, with a system of fracture running along its border. On this right-hand side, may be seen a part of the line of the terminator, which separates the light from the darkness. Towards the lower right-hand corner, is the great ring-plain Gassendi, 55 miles in diameter, with its system of fractures and its central mountains, which rise from 3,000 to 4,000 feet above its floor. This crater slopes southward towards the plain, showing the subsidence to which it has been submitted. While the northern portion of the wall of this crater rises to 10,000 feet, that on the plain is only 500 feet high, and is even wholly demolished at one place where the floor of the crater is in direct communication with the plain. In the lower part of the *mare*, and a little to the west of the middle line, is found the crater Agatharchides, which shows below its north wall the marks of rills impressed by a flood of lava, which once issued from the side of the crater. On the left-hand side of the plain, is seen the half-demolished crater Hippalus, resembling a large bay, which has its interior strewn with peaks and mountains. On this same side can be seen one of the most important systems of clefts and fractures visible on the Moon, these clefts varying in length from 150 to 200 miles.

ECLIPSES OF THE MOON.

PLATE VII.

SINCE the Moon is not a self-luminous body, but shines by the light which it borrows from the Sun, it follows that when the Sun's light is prevented from reaching its surface, our satellite becomes obscured. The Earth, like all opaque bodies exposed to sunlight, casts a shadow in space, the direction of which is always opposite to the Sun's place. The form of the Earth's shadow is that of a long, sharply-pointed cone, which has our globe for its base. Its length, varying with the distance of the Earth from the Sun, is, on an average, 855,-000 miles, or 108 times the terrestrial diameter. This conical shadow of the Earth, divided longitudinally by the plane of the ecliptic, lies half above and half below that plane, on which the summit of the shadow describes a whole circumference in the course of a year. If the Moon's orbit were not inclined to the ecliptic, our satellite would pass at every Full Moon directly through the Earth's shadow ; but, owing to that inclination, it usually passes above or below the shadow. Twice, however, during each of its revolutions, it must cross the plane of the ecliptic, the points of its orbit where this happens being called nodes. Accordingly, if it is near a node at the time of Full Moon, it will enter the shadow of the Earth, and become either partly or wholly obscured, according to the distance of its centre from the plane of the ecliptic. The partial or total obscuration of the Moon's disk thus produced constitutes a partial or total eclipse of the Moon. The essential conditions for an eclipse of the Moon are, therefore, that our satellite must not only be full, but must also be at or very near one of its nodes.

Although inferior in importance to the eclipses of the Sun, the eclipses of the Moon are, nevertheless, very interesting and remarkable phenomena, which never fail to produce a deep impression on the mind of the observer, inasmuch as they give him a clear insight into the silent motions of the planetary bodies.

At the mean distance of the Moon from the Earth, the diameter of the conical shadow cast in space by our globe is more than twice as large as that of our satellite. But, besides this pure dark shadow of the Earth, its cone is enveloped by a partial shadow called " Penumbra," which is produced by the Sun's light being partially, but not wholly, cut off by our globe.

While the Moon is passing into the penumbra, a slight reduction of the light of that part of the disk which has entered it, is noticeable. As the progress of the Moon continues, the reduction becomes more remarkable, giving the impression that rare and invisible vapors are passing over our satellite. Some time after, a small dark indentation, marking the instant of first contact, appears on the eastern or left-hand border of the Moon, which is always the first to encounter the Earth's shadow, since our satellite is moving from west to east. The dark indentation slowly and gradually enlarges with the onward progress of the Moon into the Earth's shadow, while the luminous surface of its disk diminishes in the same proportion. The form of the Earth's shadow on the Moon's disk clearly indicates the rotundity of our globe by its circular outline. Little by little the dark segment covers the Moon's disk, and its crescent, at last reduced to a mere thread of light, disappears at the moment of the second contact. With this the phase of totality begins, our satellite being then completely involved in the Earth's shadow.

The Moon remains so eclipsed for a period of time which varies with its distance from the Earth, and with the point of its orbit where it crosses the conical shadow. When it passes through the middle of this shadow, while its distance from our globe is the least, the total phase of an eclipse of the Moon may last nearly two hours. The left-hand border of our satellite having gone first into the Earth's shadow, is also the first to emerge, and, at the moment of doing so, it receives the Sun's light, and totality ends with the third contact. The lunar crescent gradually increases in breadth after its exit from the shadow, and finally the Moon recovers its fully illuminated disk as before, at the moment its western border leaves the Earth's shadow. Soon after, it passes out of the penumbra, and the eclipse is over. In total eclipses, the interval of time from the first to last contact may last 5h. 30m, but it is usually shorter.

Soon after the beginning of an eclipse, the dark segment produced by the Earth's shadow on the Moon's disk generally appears of a dark grayish opaque color, but with the progress of the phenomenon, this dark tint is changed into a dull reddish color, which, gradually increasing, attains its greatest intensity when the eclipse is total. At that moment the color of the Moon is of a dusky, reddish, coppery hue, and the general features of the Moon's surface are visible as darker and lighter tints of the same color. It sometimes happens, however, that our satellite does not exhibit this peculiar coppery tint, but appears either blackish or bluish, in which case it is hardly distinguishable from the sky.

It is very rare for the Moon to disappear completely during totality, and even when involved in the deepest part of the Earth's shadow, our satellite usually remains visible to the naked eye, or, at least, to the telescope. This phenomenon is to be attributed to the fact that the portion of the solar rays which traverse the lower strata of our atmosphere are strongly refracted, and bend inward in such a manner that they fall on the Moon, and sufficiently illuminate its surface to make it visible. The reddish color observed is caused by the absorption of the blue rays of light by the vapors which ordinarily saturate the lower regions of our atmosphere, leaving only red rays to reach the Moon's surface. Of course, these phenomena are liable to vary with every eclipse, and depend almost exclusively on the meteorological conditions of our atmosphere.

In some cases the phase of totality lasts longer than it should, according to calculation. This can be attributed to the fact that the Earth is enveloped in a dense atmosphere, in which opaque clouds of considerable extent are often forming at great elevations. Such strata of clouds, in intercepting the Sun's light, would have, of course, the effect of increasing the diameter of the Earth's shadow, in a direction corresponding to the place they occupy, and, if the Moon were moving in this direction, would increase the phase of total obscuration.

The eclipses of the Moon, like those of the Sun, as shown above, have a cycle of 18 years, 11 days and 7 hours, and recur after this period of time in nearly the same order. They can, therefore, be approximately predicted by adding 18y. 11d. 7h. to the date of the eclipses which have occurred during the preceding period. During this cycle 70 eclipses will occur—41 being eclipses of the Sun and 29 eclipses of the Moon. At no time can there ever be more than seven eclipses in a year, and there are never less than two. When there are only two eclipses in a year, they are both eclipses of the Sun.

Although the number of solar eclipses occurring at some point or other of the Earth's surface is greater than that of the eclipses of the Moon, yet at any single terrestrial station the eclipses of the Moon are the more frequent. While an eclipse of the Sun is only visible on a narrow belt, which is but a very small fraction of the hemisphere then illuminated by the Sun, an eclipse of the Moon is visible from all the points of the Earth which have the Moon above their horizon at the time. Furthermore, an eclipse of the Sun is not visible at one time over the whole length of its narrow tract, but moves gradually from one end of it to the other ; while, on the contrary, an eclipse of the Moon begins and ends at the very same instant for all places from which it can be seen, but, of course, not at the same local time, which varies with the longitude of the place.

The partial eclipse of the Moon, represented on Plate VII., shows quite plainly the configuration of our satellite as seen with the naked eye during the eclipse, with its bright and dark spots, and its radiating streaks. This eclipse was observed on October 24th, 1874.

THE PLANETS.

AROUND the Sun circulate a number of celestial bodies, which are called " *Planets.*" The planets are opaque bodies, and appear luminous because their surfaces reflect the light they receive from the Sun.

The planets are situated at various distances from the Sun, and revolve around this body in widely different periods of time, which are, however, constant for each planet, so far as ascertained, and doubtless are so in the other cases.

The ideal line traced in space by a planet in going around the Sun, is called *the orbit* of the planet ; while the period of time employed by a planet to travel over its entire orbit and return to its starting point, is called *the sidereal revolution, or year* of the planet. The dimensions of the orbits of the different planets necessarily vary with the distance of these bodies from the Sun, as does also the length of their sidereal revolution.

The distance of a planet from the Sun does not remain constant, but is subject to variations, which in certain cases are quite large. These variations result from the fact that the planetary orbits are not perfect circles having the Sun for centre, but curves called " *Ellipses*," which have two centres, or foci, one of which is always occupied by the Sun. This is in accordance with Kepler's first law.

The ideal point situated midway between the two foci is called *the centre of the ellipse, or orbit ;* while the imaginary straight line which passes through both foci and the centre, with its ends at opposite points of the ellipse, is called " *the major axis* " of the orbit. It is also known as " *the line of the apsides.*" The ideal straight line which, in passing through the centre of the orbit, cuts the major axis at right angles, and is prolonged on either side to opposite points on the ellipse, is called " *the minor axis* " of the orbit.

When a planet reaches that extremity of the major axis of its orbit which is the nearest to the Sun, it is said to be in its " *perihelion ;*" while, when it arrives at the other extremity, which is farthest from this body, it is said to be in its " *aphelion.*" When a planet reaches

either of the two opposite points of its orbit situated at the extremities of its minor axis, it is said to be at its *mean distance* from the
Sun.

The rapidity with which the planets move on their orbits varies
with their distance from the Sun ; the farther they are from this
body, the more slowly they move.   The rapidity of their motion is
greatest when they are in perihelion, and least when they are in
aphelion, having its mean rate when these bodies are crossing either
of the extremities of the minor axes of their orbits.

The imaginary line which joins the Sun to a planet at any point
of its orbit, and moves with this planet around the Sun, is called
" *the radius vector*."   According to Kepler's second law, whatever
may be the distance of a planet from the Sun, the radius vector
sweeps over equal areas of the plane of the planet's orbit in equal
times.

There is a remarkable relation between the distance of the
planets from the Sun and their period of revolution, in consequence
of which the squares of their periodic times are respectively equal to
the cubes of their mean distances from the Sun.   From this third
law of Kepler, it results that the mere knowledge of the mean distance of a planet from the Sun enables one to know its period of
revolution, and *vice versa.*

The orbit described by the Earth around the Sun in a year, or
the apparent path of the Sun in the sky, is called " *the ecliptic*."   Like
that of all the planetary orbits, the plane of the ecliptic passes
through the Sun's centre.   The ecliptic has a great importance in
astronomy, inasmuch as it is the fundamental plane to which the
orbits and motions of all planets are referred.

The orbits of the larger planets are not quite parallel to the
ecliptic, but more or less inclined to this plane ; although the inclination is small, and does not exceed eight degrees.   On account of
this inclination of the orbits, the planets, in accomplishing their revolutions around the Sun, are sometimes above and sometimes below
the plane of the ecliptic.   A belt extending 8° on each side of the
ecliptic, and, therefore, 16° in width, comprises within its limits
the orbits of all the principal planets.   This belt is called " *the
Zodiac*."

Since all the planets have the Sun for a common centre, and have
their orbits inclined to the ecliptic, it follows that each of these
orbits must necessarily intersect the plane of the ecliptic at two opposite points situated at the extremities of a straight line passing
through the Sun's centre.   The two opposite points on a planetary

orbit where its intersections with the ecliptic occur, are called " *the Nodes,*" and the imaginary line joining them, which passes through the Sun's centre, is called " the line of the nodes." The node situated at the point where a planet crosses the ecliptic from the south to the north, is called " *the ascending node,*" while that situated where the planet crosses from north to south, is called " *the descending node.*"

The planets circulating around the Sun are eight in number, but, beside these, there is a multitude of very small planets, commonly called "asteroids," which also revolve around our luminary. The number of asteroids at present known surpasses two hundred, and constantly increases by new discoveries. In their order of distance from the Sun the principal planets are : Mercury, Venus, Earth, Mars, Jupiter, Saturn, Uranus and Neptune. The orbits of the asteroids are comprised between the orbits of Mars and Jupiter.

When the principal planets are considered in regard to their differences in size, they are separated into two distinct groups of four planets each, viz.: the small planets and the large planets. The orbits of the small planets are wholly within the region occupied by the orbits of the asteroids, while those of the large planets are wholly without this region.

When the planets are considered in regard to their position with reference to the Earth, they are called " inferior planets " and " superior planets." The inferior planets comprise those whose orbits are within the orbit of our globe ; while the superior planets are those whose orbits lie beyond the orbit of the Earth.

Since the orbits of the inferior planets lie within the orbit of the Earth, the angular distances of these bodies from the Sun, as seen from the Earth, must always be included within fixed limits ; and these planets must seem to oscillate from the east to the west, and from the west to the east of the Sun during their sidereal revolution. In this process of oscillation these planets sometimes pass between the Earth and the Sun, and sometimes behind the Sun. When they pass between us and the Sun they are said to be in "inferior conjunction," while, when they pass behind the Sun, they are said to be in "superior conjunction." When such a planet reaches its greatest distance, either east or west, it is said to be at its greatest elongation east or west, as the case may be, or in quadrature.

The superior planets, whose orbits lie beyond that of the Earth and enclose it, present a different appearance. A superior planet never passes between the Earth and the Sun, since its orbit lies beyond that of our globe, and, therefore, no inferior conjunction of such a planet can ever occur. When one of these planets passes beyond the Sun, just opposite to the place occupied by the Earth, the planet is said to be in "conjunction;" while, when it is on the same side of the Sun with our globe, it is said to be in "opposition." While occupying this last position, the planet is most advantage-ously situated for observation, since it is then nearer to the Earth. The period comprised between two successive conjunctions, or two successive oppositions of a planet, is called its "synodical period." This period differs for every planet.

It is supposed that all the planets rotate from west to east, like our globe; although no direct evidence of the rotation of Mercury Uranus, and Neptune has yet been obtained, it is probable that these planets rotate like the others. It results from the rotation of the planets that they have their days and nights, like our Earth, but differing in duration for every planet.

The axes of rotation of the planets are more or less inclined to their respective orbits, and this inclination varies but little in the course of time. From the inclination of the axes of rotation of the planets to their orbits, it results that these bodies have seasons like those of the Earth; but, of course, they differ from our seasons in duration and intensity, according to the period of revolution and the inclination of the axis of each separate planet.

THE PLANET MARS.

PLATE VIII.

MARS is the fourth of the planets in order of distance from the sun; Mercury, Venus and the Earth being respectively the first, second and third.

Owing to the great eccentricity of its orbit, the distance of Mars from the Sun is subject to considerable variations. When this planet is in its aphelion, its distance from the Sun is 152,000,000 miles, but at perihelion it is only 126,000,000 miles distant, the planet being therefore 26,000,000 miles nearer the Sun at perihelion than at aphelion. The mean distance of Mars from the Sun is 139,000,-000 miles. Light, which travels at the rate of 185,000 miles a second, occupies 12½ minutes in passing from the Sun to this planet.

While the distance of Mars from the Sun varies considerably, its distance from the Earth varies still more. When Mars comes into opposition, its distance from our globe is comparatively small, especially if the opposition occurs in August, as the two planets are then as near together as it is possible for them to be, their distance apart being only 33,000,000 miles. But if the opposition occurs in February, the distance may be nearly twice as great, or 62,000,000 miles. On the other hand, when Mars is in conjunction in August, the distance between the two planets is the greatest possible, or no less than 245,-000,000 miles; while, when the conjunction occurs in February, it is only 216,000,000 miles. Hence the distance between Mars and the Earth varies from 33 to 245 millions of miles; that is, this planet may be 212 million miles nearer to us at its nearest oppositions than at its most distant conjunctions.

From these varying distances of Mars from the Earth, necessarily result great variations in the brightness and apparent size of the planet, as seen from our globe. When nearest to us it is a very conspicuous object, appearing as a star of the first magnitude, and approaching Jupiter in brightness; but when it is farthest it is much reduced, and is hardly distinguishable from the stars of the second and even third magnitude. In the first position, the apparent diameter of Mars is 26″, in the last it is reduced to 3″ only.

The orbit of Mars has the very small inclination of 1° 51′ to the plane of the ecliptic. The planet revolves around the Sun in a period of 687 days, which constitutes its sidereal year, the year of Mars being only 43 days less than two of our years.

Mars travels along its orbit with a mean velocity of 15 miles per second, being about $\frac{8}{10}$ of the velocity of our globe in its orbit. The synodical period of Mars is 2 years and 48 days, during which the planet passes through all its degrees of brightness.

Mars is a smaller planet than the Earth, its diameter being only 4,200 miles, and its circumference 13,200 miles. It seems well established that it is a little flattened at its poles, but the actual amount of this flattening is difficult to obtain. According to Prof. Young, the polar compression is $\frac{1}{219}$.

The surface of this planet is a little over $\frac{28}{100}$ of the surface of our globe, and its volume is 6½ times less than that of the Earth. Its mass is only about $\frac{1}{10}$, while its density is about ¾ that of the Earth. The force of gravitation at its surface is nearly ¾ of what it is at the surface of our globe.

The planet Mars rotates on an axis inclined 61° 18′ to the plane of its orbit, so that its equator makes an angle of 28° 42′ with the same plane. The period of rotation of this planet, which constitutes its sidereal day, is 24 h. 37 m. 23 s.

The year of Mars, which is composed of 669⅔ of these Martial days, equals 687 of our days, this planet rotating 669⅔ times upon its axis during this period. But owing to the movement of Mars around the Sun, the number of solar days in the Martial year is only 668⅔, while, owing to the same cause, the solar day of Mars is a little longer than its sidereal day, and equals 24 h. 39 m. 35 s.

The days and nights on Mars are accordingly nearly of the same length as our days and nights, the difference being a little less than three-quarters of an hour. But while the days and nights of Mars are essentially the same as ours, its seasons are almost twice as long as those of the Earth. Their duration for the northern hemisphere, expressed in Martial days, is as follows: Spring, 191; Summer, 181; Autumn, 149; Winter, 147. While the Spring and Summer of the northern hemisphere together last 372 days, the Autumn and Winter of the same hemisphere last only 296 days, or 76 days less. Since the summer seasons of the northern hemisphere correspond to the winter seasons of the southern hemisphere, and vice versa, the northern hemisphere, owing to its longer summer, must accumulate a larger quantity of heat than the last. But on Mars, as on the Earth, there is a certain law of compensation resulting from the eccentricity of the planet's orbit, and from the fact that the middle of the summer of the southern hemisphere of this planet, coincides with its perihelion. From the greater proximity of Mars to the Sun at that time, the southern hemisphere then receives more heat in a given time than does the northern hemisphere in its summer season. When everything is taken into account, however, it is found that the southern hemisphere must have warmer summers and colder winters than the northern hemisphere.

Seen with the naked eye, Mars appears as a fiery red star, whose intensity of color is surpassed by no other star in the heavens. Seen through the telescope, it retains the same red tint, which, however, appears less intense, and gradually fades away toward the limb, where it is replaced by a white luminous ring.

Mars is a very difficult object to observe, the atmosphere surrounding it being sometimes so cloudy and foggy that the sight can hardly penetrate through its vapors. When this planet is observed under favorable atmospheric conditions, and with sufficient magnifying power, its surface, which is of a general reddish tint, is found to be diversified by white, gray and dark markings. The dark markings, which are the most conspicuous, almost completely surround the planet. They are of different forms and sizes, and very irregular, as can be seen on Plate VIII., which represents one of the hemispheres of this planet. Many of them, especially those situated in the tropical regions of the planet, form long narrow bands, whose direction is in the main parallel to the Martial equator.

The dusky spots differ very much, both from one another and in their several parts, as regards intensity of shade. Some appear almost black, while others which appear grayish, are so faint, that they can seldom be seen. In the southern hemisphere, the darkest part of the spots is generally found along their northern border; especially where there are deep indentations.

Some observers have described these spots as being greenish or bluish, but I have never been able to see the faintest trace of these colors in them, except when they were observed close to the limb, and involved in the greenish tinted ring which is always to be seen there. It is probably an effect of contrast, since green and red are complementary colors, and since this greenish tinge around the limb covers all kinds of spots, whether white or dark. When such dark spots, involved in the greenish tint, are carried by the rotation towards the centre of the disk, they no longer show this greenish color. To me, these spots have always appeared dark, and of such tints as would result from a mixture of white and black in different proportions ; except that on their lighter portions they show some of the prevalent reddish tint of the Martial surface. It is to be remarked that in moments of superior definition of the telescopic image, the intensity of darkness of all the spots is considerably increased—some of them appearing almost perfectly black.

The markings on the surface of Mars are now tolerably well known—especially those of its southern hemisphere, which, owing to the greater proximity of the planet to our globe when this hemisphere is inclined towards the earth, have been better studied. Those of the northern hemisphere are not so well known, since when this hemisphere is inclined towards us, the distance of Mars from the Earth is 26,000,000 miles greater, so that the occasions for observing them are not so favorable.

Several charts of Mars are in existence, but as the same nomenclature has not been employed in all of them, some confusion has arisen in regard to the names given to the most remarkable features of the planet's surface.   In order to give clearness to the subject, it will be necessary here to give a brief description of the principal markings represented on Plate VIII.   In this the nomenclature will be employed which has been adopted by the English observers in the fine chart of Mr. Nath. Green.   The large dark spot represented on the left-hand side of the plate is called De La Rue Ocean. The dark oval spot, isolated in the vicinity of the centre of the disk, is called Terby Sea ; while the dark, irregular form on the right, near the border, represents the western extremity of Maraldi Sea.

The dusky spots of Mars seem to be permanent, and to form a part of the general surface of the planet. That several among them, at least, are permanent, is proved by the fact that they have been observed in the same position, and with the same general form, for over two centuries.   Yet, if we are to depend upon the drawings made fifty years ago by Beer and Maedler, it would seem that the permanency of some of them does not exist, since a very large spot represented by these astronomers on their chart of Mars is not visible now.   This object, which, on their map, has its middle at 270°, should be precisely under the prominent dark oval spot called Terby Sea, seen near the centre of the picture, and would extend down almost as far as the northern limb. This can hardly be attributed to an error of observation, since these observers were both careful, and had great experience in this class of work. It is a very singular fact that, at the very same place where Maedler represented the spot in question, I found a conspicuous dark mark on December 16, 1881, which was certainly not visible in 1877, during one of the most favorable oppositions which can ever occur. The object, · which is still visible (Feb., 1882), consists of an isolated spot situated a little to the north of Terby Sea. During the memorable opposition of 1877, I investigated thoroughly the markings of Mars, and made over 200 drawings of its disk, 32 of which represent the Terby Sea; but this isolated spot was not to be seen, unless it be identified with the faint mark, represented on the plate, which occupied its place. There cannot be the slightest doubt that a change has occurred at that place. Changes in the markings have also been suspected on the other hemisphere of the planet.

The well-known fact that the continents, and especially the mountainous and denuded districts of our globe, reflect much more light than the surfaces covered by water, has led astronomers to suppose that the dark spots on Mars are produced by a liquid strongly absorbing the rays of light, like the liquids on the surface of the Earth. According to this theory the dark spots observed are supposed to be lakes, seas, and oceans, similar to our own seas and oceans, while the reddish and whitish surfaces separating these dark spots, are supposed to be islands, peninsulas, and continents. This supposition seems certainly to have a great deal of probability in its favor, although some of the lighter markings may have a different origin, and perhaps be due to vegetation ; but no observer has yet seen in them any of the changes which ought to result from change of seasons. Some of the changes in the dark spots might also be attributed to the flooding or drying up of marshes and low land. The change which I have observed lately might be attributed to such a cause, especially as my observation was made shortly after the spring equinox of the northern hemisphere of Mars, which occurred on December 8th.

Besides the dark spots just described, there are markings of a different character and appearance. Among the most conspicuous are two very brilliant white oval spots, which always occupy opposite sides of the planet. These two bright spots, which correspond very closely with the poles of rotation of Mars, have been called "polar spots."

On account of the inclination of the axis of rotation of this planet to the ecliptic, it is rare that both of these spots are visible on the disk at the same time ; and when this occurs, they are seen considerably foreshortened, as they are then both on the limb of the planet.

Usually only one spot is visible, and it appears to its best advantage when the region to which it belongs attains its maximum of inclination towards the Earth.

The polar spots change considerably in size, as they do also in form. Sometimes they occupy nearly one-third of the disk, as is proved by many of my observations ; while at other times they are so much reduced as to be totally invisible. It is to be remarked that the reduction of these spots generally corresponds with the summer seasons, and their enlargement with the winter seasons of the hemispheres to which they respectively belong. From these well-observed facts it would appear that a relation exists between the temperature of the two hemispheres of Mars and the variations of the white spots observed at its poles. A similar relation is known to exist on our globe between the progress of the seasons and the melting away and the accumulation of snow in the polar regions. Astronomers have been led, accordingly, to attribute the polar spots of Mars, with all their variations, to the alternate accumulation and melting of snows. On this account, the polar spots of Mars are sometimes also called " snow-spots."

Errors have certainly been made by astronomers in some of their observations of the so-called polar snow-spots, other objects occupying their place having been mistaken for them. A regular series of observations on this planet, which I have now continued for seven years, has revealed the fact that during the winter seasons of the southern hemisphere of Mars, the polar spots are most of the time invisible, being covered over by white, opaque, cloud-like forms, strongly reflecting light. In 1877, during more than a month, I, myself, mistook for the polar spots such a canopy of clouds, which covered at least one-fifth of the surface of the whole disk. I only became aware of my error when the opaque cloud, beginning to dissolve at the approach of the Martial summer, allowed the real polar spot to be seen through its vapors, as through a mist at first, and afterwards with great distinctness. In this particular case, the snow-spot was considerably smaller than the cloudy cap which covered it, and it is to be remarked that it was not situated at the centre of this cloudy cap, but was east of that centre ; a fact which may account for the so-called polar spots not being always observed on exactly opposite sides of the disk. From my observations of 1877, 1878 and 1880, it appears that at the approach of the autumnal equinox of the southern hemisphere of Mars, large, opaque masses, like cumulus clouds in form, began to gather in the polar regions of that hemisphere, and continued through autumn and winter, dissolving only at the approach of spring. These clouds, which varied in form and extent, were very unsteady at first, but as the winter drew nearer they enlarged and became more permanent, covering large surfaces for months at a time.

That the large white spots under consideration are real clouds in the atmosphere of Mars, and are not due to a fall of snow, is proved by the fact that these spots covered both seas and continents with equal facility, even in the equatorial regions of the planet. Snow, of course, could not cover the seas of Mars, unless these were all frozen over, even in the equatorial zones ; therefore, if the dark spots of Mars are assumed to be due to water, these large white spots cannot well be ascribed to snow.

The real polar spots of Mars seem to be in relief on the surface of the planet, since the southern spot often appeared slightly shaded on the side opposite to the Sun during my observations in 1877. In certain cases, when they are on or very near the limb, they have been observed, both by others and by myself, to project from the disk slightly.

The polar spots of Mars are doubtless composed of a material which, like our snow or ice, melts under the rays of the Sun ; although it seems difficult to admit that the Martial snow is identical with our terrestrial snow, and that it melts at a like temperature. The south polar spot of Mars entirely disappeared from sight in its summer season in 1877, although the planet receives less than one-half as much heat as we receive from the Sun ; yet on our globe the arctic or antarctic ices and snow are perpetual—never melting entirely. An important fact disclosed by the melting away of the southern polar spot is, that in melting it is always surrounded with a very dark surface, which takes the place of the melted portion of the spot, as observed by myself in 1877-'78. When the polar spot had entirely disappeared, its place was occupied by a very dark spot. Now, if the polar spot is really ice, and the dark spots are actual seas, this polar spot must be situated in mid-ocean, since, on melting away, it is replaced by a dark spot. If the polar spots are composed of a white substance melting under the rays of the Sun, as seems altogether probable, its melting point must be above that of terrestrial snow.

Many of the dark spots of Mars, and especially those whose northern border forms an irregular belt upon the equatorial regions of this planet, are bordered on that side by a white luminous belt, following all their sinuosities. These white borders are variable. Sometimes they are very prominent and intensely bright, especially at some points, which occasionally almost equal the polar spots in brilliancy; while at other times they are so faint, that they can hardly be distinguished, or are even invisible; although the atmosphere is clear and the dark spots appear perfectly well defined. While these white borders were invisible, I have sometimes watched for several hours at a time to see if I could detect any traces of them in places where they usually appear the most prominent, but generally without success. On a few occasions, however, I had the good fortune to see some of these spots forming gradually in the course of one or two hours, at places where nothing of them could be seen before.

These whitish fringes forming and vanishing along the coasts of the Martial seas have been very little studied by astronomers. From my observations made during the last seven years, it appears very probable that this belt and its white spots are mainly due to the condensation of vapors around, and over high peaks, and extensive mountain chains, forming the Martial sea-coasts, as the Andes and Rocky Mountains form the sea-coasts of the Pacific Ocean. These high mountains on Mars, condensing the vapors into fogs or clouds above them, or at their sides, as often happens in our mountainous districts, would certainly suffice to produce the phenomena observed. Some of the highest peaks among these mountain chains may even have their summits covered with perpetual snow, or some substance partaking of the nature of snow. The temporary visibility and invisibility of the white spots seen on Mars, as well as the rapid transformations they sometimes undergo, may be explained as caused by clouds having a high reflective power and a liability to form and disappear quickly.

The assumption that these irregular whitish bands and spots are formed by the condensation of vapors on mountain chains, and elevated table lands, is supported by my observations made in 1877 and 1879. When such white spots were traversing the terminator at sunrise, they very often projected far into the night side, thus indicating that they were at a higher level than that of the general surface. Indentations in the terminator, corresponding to large dark spots crossing its line, also clearly indicated the depression of the dark spots below the general surface. The highest mountainous districts thus observed on Mars, are situated between 60° and 70° of south latitude, towards the western extremity of Gill Land. The mountain chain, which almost completely forms the surface of this land, is so elevated at some points, that they not only change the form of the terminator when they are seen upon it, but also the limb of the planet, as seen by myself. They then appear so brilliant, that the principal summit among them has been mistaken by several observers for the polar spot itself, as proved by the wrong position assigned to it on their drawings. It seems probable that this high peak, which appears always white, is constantly covered with snow, or the similar · material replacing it on Mars. This high region is situated between longitudes 180° and 190°.

The highest mountainous parts belonging to the hemisphere represented on Plate VIII., which are nearly always more or less visible as whitish spots and bands, form a coast line along the northern (lower) border of De La Rue Ocean. This great spot, which is not so simple as it has been represented by observers, is in fact divided by two narrow isthmuses, one in the north, the other in the east, both joining, in the interior of the great ocean, a peninsula heretofore known as Hall Island. Upon the south-eastern extremity of this peninsula, a white spot, called Dawes Ice Island, was observed in 1865, but it soon disappeared, and was after that seen only now and then. It is very probable that this so-called Ice Island was due to clouds forming around the summit of some high peak of this peninsula.

On the opposite hemisphere to that represented on Plate VIII., the white fringes bordering the dark spots are much more conspicuous than they are on this side. On the eastern side of a remarkable dark spot called Kaiser Sea, they are very bright, and almost always present, although they vary considerably, both in brightness and in extent. To the south of Kaiser Sea, they are very conspicuous on the eastern border of Lockyer Land, forming an elevated and deeply indented coast-line along Lambert Sea. There the white spots never disappear entirely, being always visible on the north side, where they turn westward along Dawes' Ocean—the mountain chain attaining there its greatest altitude. Very frequently Lockyer Land, which seems to be a vast plateau, appears throughout white and brilliant, this occurring usually towards the sunrise or sunset of that region, probably from the condensation of vapors and the formation of fogs, but generally this whiteness gradually disappears with the progress of the sun above this plateau. Inside of the great continents of Mars these temporary white spots are not so frequent, but when visible they occupy always the same positions—a fact which probably indicates that they occupy the culminating points of these continents. One of these temporary white spots inside of the continents is represented on Plate VIII., on the left-hand side, below De La Rue Ocean, on Maedler Continent.

Although large, opaque, cumulus-shaped, cloud-like forms are seen in the polar regions of Mars, such forms are very seldom seen in the tropical zones, or, at least, it appears so, from the fact that my observations, continued during the last seven years, have disclosed no real opaque cloudy forms there.   Although the Martial sky is frequently overcast by dense vapors or thick fogs in these regions, yet no real opaque clouds were ever seen ; the most prominent among the dusky spots being faintly visible through the vapory veil, when they approached the centre of the disk.

Besides these phenomena, which prove that Mars is surrounded by an atmosphere having a great deal of similarity to our own, a further proof is afforded by the fact that the dark spots, which appear sharply defined and black when they are seen near the centre, become less and less visible as they advance towards the limb, and are totally invisible before they reach it.   Moreover, the spectroscope also indicates the existence of an atmosphere, and even the presence of watery vapor in it.   A very curious state of the Martial atmosphere is revealed by my observations of 1877-'78.   During eight consecutive weeks, from December 12th to February 6th, a whole hemisphere of the planet—precisely that represented on Plate VIII.— was completely covered by dense vapors, or a thick fog which barely allowed the dark spots to be seen through it, even when they were in the centre of the disk. The opposite hemisphere of Mars appeared just as clear and calm as possible ; there all the spots and their minutest details could be seen, and when the planet was observed at the proper time, the line separating the foggy from the clear side was plainly visible.

The reddish tint observed on the continents of Mars has been supposed by some astronomers to be the real color of the atmosphere of this planet.   But, for many reasons, this explanation is not acceptable.   Besides the fact that the border of the planet appears white, while it should be more red than the other part, owing to the greater depth of atmosphere there presented to us, the polar spots, the white bands along the sea-coasts, and the cloud-like forms appear perfectly white, not the slightest tint of red being visible on them, as would be the case if these objects were seen through an atmosphere tinted red.   Other astronomers have supposed that the vegetation of this planet has a reddish color ; but this is not supported by observation. It has been again supposed, with much more probability, that the surface of Mars is composed of an ochreous material which gives the planet its predominant ruddy color.

Until lately Mars was supposed to be without a satellite, but in August, 1877, Professor Hall, of the Washington Observatory, made one of the most remarkable discoveries of the time, and found two satellites revolving around this planet. These satellites are among the smallest known heavenly bodies, their diameter having been estimated at from 6 to 10 miles for the outer satellite, and from 10 to 40 miles for the inner one.

The most extraordinary feature of these bodies is the proximity of the inner satellite to the planet, and the consequent rapidity of its motion. The distance of the inner satellite from the centre of Mars is about 6,000 miles, and from surface to surface it is less than 4,000 miles, or a little more than the distance from New York to San Francisco. The shortest period of revolution of any satellite previously known, is that of the inner satellite of Saturn, which is a little more than 22½ hours ; but the inner satellite of Mars accomplishes its revolution in 7h. 38m., or in 17 hours less than the period of rotation of the planet upon its axis. The period of revolution of the outer satellite is greater, of course, and equals 30h. 7m.

From this rapidity of motion of the inner satellite of Mars, a very curious result follows, which at first sight may appear in contradiction with the fact that this body has a direct motion, like that of all the planets of the solar system, and moves around Mars from west to east. While the outer satellite of this planet, in company with all the stars and planets, rises in the east and sets in the west, the inner satellite, on the contrary, rises in the west and sets in the east. Since the period of rotation of Mars is greater than is the period of revolution of this satellite, it necessarily follows that this last body must constantly be gaining on the rotation, and, consequently, that the satellite sets in the east and rises in the west, compassing the whole heavens around Mars three times a day, passing through all its phases in 11 hours, each quarter of this singular Moon lasting less than 3 hours.

It has been shown above that Mars has many points of resemblance to the Earth. It has an atmosphere constituted very nearly like ours ; it has fogs, clouds, rains, snows, and winds. It has water, or at least some liquids resembling it ; it has rivers, lakes, seas and oceans. It has also islands, peninsulas, continents, mountains and valleys. It has two Moons, which must create great and rapid tides in the waters of its seas and oceans. It has its days and nights, its warm and cold seasons, and very likely its vegetation, its prairies and forests, like the Earth. On the other hand, its year and seasons are double those of the Earth, and its distance from the Sun is greater.

Is this planet, which is certainly constituted very nearly like our globe, and seems so nearly fitted for the wants of the human race, inhabited by animals and intelligent beings?

To answer this question, either in the negative or in the affirmative, would be to step out of the pure province of science, and enter the boundless domain of speculation, since no observer has ever seen anything indicating that animal life exists on Mars, or on any other planet or satellite. So far as observation goes, Mars seems to be a planet well suited to sustain animal life, and we may reason from analogy that if animal life can exist at all outside of the Earth, Mars must have its flora and fauna ; it must have its fishes and birds, its mammalia and men ; although all these living beings must inevitably be very different in appearance from their representatives on the Earth, as can easily be imagined from the differences existing between the two planets. Although all this is possible, and even very probable, yet it must be remembered that we have not the slightest evidence that it is so ; and until we have acquired this evidence, we may only provisionally accept this idea as a pleasing hypothesis, which, after all, may be wrong and totally unfounded.

THE PLANET JUPITER.

PLATE IX.

JUPITER, the giant of the planetary world, is the fifth in order of distance from the Sun, and is next to Mars, our ruddy neighbor. To the naked eye, Jupiter appears as a very brilliant star, whose magnitude, changing with the distance of this planet from the Earth, sometimes approaches that of Venus, our bright morning and evening star.

The mean distance of Jupiter from the Sun is 475,000,000 miles, but owing to the eccentricity of its orbit, its distance varies from 452 to 498 millions of miles. The distance of this planet from the Earth varies still more. When nearest to our globe, or in opposition, its distance is reduced to 384,000,000 miles, and its apparent diameter increased to 50″; while when it is farthest, or in conjunction, its distance is increased to 567,000,000 miles, and its apparent diameter reduced to 30″; Jupiter being thus 183,000,000 miles nearer our globe while in opposition than when it is in conjunction.

This planet revolves around the Sun in 11 years, 10 months and 17 days, or in only 50 days less than 12 terrestrial years. Such is the year of this planet. The plane of its orbit is inclined 1° 19′ to the ecliptic. No planet, except Uranus, has an orbit exhibiting a smaller inclination. The planet advances in its orbit at the mean rate of 8 miles a second; which is a little less than half the orbital velocity of the Earth.

Jupiter is of enormous proportions. Its equatorial diameter measures 88,000 miles, and its circumference no less than 276,460 miles, these dimensions being 11 times greater than those of the Earth. This planet, notwithstanding its huge size, rotates on its axis in not far from 9h. 55m. 36s., which period constitutes its day. Owing, however, to the changeable appearance of its surface, this period cannot be ascertained with very great exactitude. In consequence of its rapid rotation, the planet is far from spherical, its polar diameter being shorter than the equatorial by about $\frac{1}{16}$, or 5,500 miles. Its surface is 124 times the surface of the earth; while its volume is 1,387 times as great. If Jupiter occupied the place of our satellite in the sky, it would appear 40 times as large as the Moon appears to us, and would cover a surface of the heavens 1,600 times that covered by the full Moon, and would subtend an angle of 21°. Jupiter's mass does not correspond with its great bulk, and is only $\frac{1}{1047}$ of the mass of the Sun, and 310 times the mass of the earth; its density being only $\frac{1}{4}$ of that of our globe. The force of gravitation at the surface of this planet is over $2\frac{1}{2}$ times what it is on the Earth, so that a terrestrial object carried to the surface of Jupiter would weigh over two and a half times as much as on our globe.

Observed with a telescope, even of moderate aperture, Jupiter, with its four attending satellites and its dazzling brilliancy, appears as one of the most magnificent objects in the sky. The general appearance of the disk is white; but unlike that of Mars, it is brightest towards its central parts, and a little darker around the limb, especially on the side opposite to the Sun. Although an exterior planet, and so far from us, Jupiter shows faint traces of phases when observed near its quadratures, but this gibbosity of its disk is very slight, and is indicated only by a kind of penumbral shadow on the limb.

When observed with adequate power, the disk of Jupiter is found to be highly diversified. The principal features consist of a series of alternate light and dark streaks or bands, disposed most of the time parallel with the Jovian equator. These bands differ from each other in intensity as well as in breadth; those near the equator being usually much more prominent than those situated in higher latitudes north and south.

The equatorial zone of Jupiter is occupied most of the time by a broad, prominent belt 20° or 30° wide, limited on each side by a very dark narrow streak. Between these two dark borders, but seldom occupying the whole space between them, appears an irregular white belt, apparently composed of dense masses of clouds strongly reflecting the Sun's light, some of these cloudy masses being very brilliant. The spaces left between the cloudy belt and the dark borders, usually exhibit a delicate pink or rosy color, which produces a very harmonious effect with the varying grayish and bluish shades of some of the belts and streaks seen on the disk. Quite often the cloudy belt is broken up, and consists of independent cloudy masses, separated by larger or smaller intervals, these intervals disclosing the rosy background of this zone.

On each side of the equatorial belt there is usually a broad whitish belt, succeeded by a narrow gray band; the space left on each hemisphere between these last bands and the limb being usually occupied by two or three alternate white and gray bands. A uniform gray segment usually forms a sort of polar cap to Jupiter.

When observed under very favorable conditions, all the lighter belts appear as if composed of masses of small cloudlets, resembling the white opaque clouds seen in our atmosphere. This, as already stated, is particularly noticeable on the equatorial belt. It is not unusual, when Jupiter is in quadrature, to see some of the most conspicuous white spots casting a shadow opposite to the Sun; a fact which sufficiently indicates that these spots are at different levels. They probably form the summits of vast banks of clouds floating high up in the atmosphere of Jupiter.

What we see of Jupiter is chiefly a vaporous, cloudy envelope. If our sight penetrates anywhere deeper into the interior, it can only be through the narrow fissures of this envelope, which appear as gray or dark streaks or spots. That most of the visible surface of Jupiter is simply a cloudy covering, is abundantly proved by the proper motion of its spots, which sometimes becomes very great.

In periods of calm, very few changes are noticeable in the markings of the planet, except, perhaps, some slight modifications of form in the cloudy, equatorial belt which, in general, is much more liable to changes than the other belts. But the Jovian surface is not always so tranquil, great changes being observed during the terrific storms which sometimes occur on this mighty planet, when all becomes disorder and confusion on its usually calm surface; and nothing on the Earth can give us a conception of the velocity with which some of its clouds and spots are animated. New belts quickly form, while old ones disappear. The usual parallelism of the belts no more exists. Huge, white, cumulus-like masses advance and spread out, the rosy equatorial belt enlarges sometimes to two or three times its usual size, and occupies two-thirds, or more, of the disk, the rosy tint spreading out in a very short time. At times very dark bands extending across the disk are transformed into knots or dark spots, which encircle the planet with a belt, as it were, of jet black beads. Sometimes, also, a secondary but narrower rosy belt forms either in the northern or the southern hemisphere, and remains visible for a few days or for years at a time.

On May 25, 1876, I witnessed one of the grandest commotions which can be conceived as taking place in an atmosphere. All the southern hemisphere of Jupiter, from equator to pole, was in rapid motion, the belts and spots being transported entirely across the disk, from the eastern to the western limb, in one hour's time, during which the equatorial belt swelled to twice its original breadth, towards the south.

Now, when one stops for a moment to think what is signified by that motion of the dark spots across the little telescopic disk of Jupiter in an hour's time, he may arrive at some conception of the magnitude of the Jovian storms, compared with those of our globe. The circumference of Jupiter's equator, as stated above, is 276,460 miles; half this number, or 138,230 miles, represents the length of the equatorial line seen from the Earth. Now, after taking into account the rotation of the planet, which somewhat diminishes the apparent motion, we arrive at the astonishing result that the spots and markings were carried along by this Jovian storm, at the enormous rate of 110,584 miles an hour, or over 30.7 miles a second. On our globe, a hurricane or tornado, which blows at the rate of 100 miles an hour, sweeps everything before it. What, then, must be expected from a velocity over 1,105 times as great? Enormous as this motion may appear, its occurrence cannot be doubted, since it is disclosed by direct observation.

The surface of Jupiter, it would seem, has its periods of calm and activity like that of the Sun, although it is not yet known, as it is for the latter, that they recur with approximate regularity.

My observations of this planet, which embrace a period of ten years, seem to point in that direction, for they show, at least, that Jupiter has its years of calm and its years of disturbances. The year 1876 was a year of extraordinary disturbance on Jupiter. Changes in the markings were going on all the time, and no one form could be recognized the next day, or even sometimes the next hour, as shown above. The cloudy envelope of the planet was in constant motion, the equatorial belt, especially, showing the signs of greatest disturbance, being, for the most part, two or three times as wide as in other years. After 1876 the calm was very great on the planet, only a slight change now and then being noticeable, the same forms being recognized day after day, month after month, and even year after year. In one case the same marking has been observed for seventeen consecutive months, and in another for twenty-eight months. This state of quietude lasted until October, 1880, when considerable commotion occurred on the northern hemisphere, where large round black spots, somewhat resembling the Sun-spots, formed in the cloudy atmosphere, and finally changed, towards the end of December, into a narrow pink belt, which still exists.

The most curious marking ever seen on Jupiter is undoubtedly the great Red Spot, observed on the southern hemisphere of this planet for the last three years. This interesting object, seen first in July, 1878, disappeared for a time, reappeared on September 25 of the same year, and has remained visible until now. When seen by me in September, it was much elongated, and sharply pointed on one side, like a spear-head, but it subsequently acquired an irregular form, with short appendages protruding from its northern border. At first, the changes were great and frequent, but at length it acquired the regular oval form, which, with but slight modifications, it has retained until now. During the month of November, 1880, I noticed two small black specks upon this Red Spot, and they were seen again in January of the succeeding year, by Mr. Alvan Clark, Jr. When the spot had attained its oval shape, it appeared part of the time surrounded with a white luminous ring of cloudy forms which, however, was changing more or less all the time, being sometimes invisible. The color of this curious spot is a brilliant rosy red, tinged with vermilion, and altogether different in shade from the pinkish color of the equatorial belt. The size of the spot varies, but of late its changes have been slight. Its longer diameter may be estimated at 8,000 miles, and the shorter at 2,200 miles. The Red Spot is represented on Plate IX. with its natural color, and as it appears at the moments most favorable for observation. In ordinary cases its color does not appear so brilliant, but paler.

It is difficult to account for the color of the equatorial belt and that of the Red Spot; but it is known, at least, that the material to which they are due cannot be situated at the level of the general surface visible to us, and especially that of the cloudy forms of the equatorial zone. Undoubtedly the red layer lies deeper than the superficial envelope of the planet, although it does not seem to be very deeply depressed.

Jupiter is attended by four satellites, which revolve around the planet at various distances, and shine like stars of the 6th and 7th magnitude. It is said that under very favorable circumstances, and in a very clear sky, the satellites can be seen with the naked eye, but this requires exceptionally keen eyes, since the glare of the planet is so strong as to overpower the comparatively faint light of the satellites. However, I myself have sometimes seen, without the aid of the telescope, two or three of the satellites' as a single object, when they were closely grouped on the same side of Jupiter.

The four moons of Jupiter are all larger than our Moon, except the first, which has about the same diameter. They range in size from 2,300 to 3,400 miles in diameter, the third being the largest;

the determination of their diameter is by no means accurate, however, as it is difficult to measure such small objects with precision.
Their mean distance from the centre of Jupiter varies from 267,000
to 1,192,000 miles, the first satellite, the nearest to the planet,
being a little farther from Jupiter then our satellite is from us.   The
four satellites revolve around the planet in orbits whose planes have
a slight inclination to the equator of Jupiter, and consequently to the
ecliptic.   The diameter of the largest satellite is nearly half that of
the Earth, or 3,436 miles; while its volume is five times that of our
Moon.   The period of revolution of these satellites varies from 1d.
18h. for the first, to 16d. 16h. for the last.

Owing to the slight inclination of the plane of their orbits to that
of the planet, the three first satellites, and generally the fourth,
pass in front of the disk and also through the shadow of the planet
at every revolution, and are accordingly eclipsed.   Their passages
behind Jupiter's disk are called occultations; those in front of it,
transits.   The eclipses, the occultations and the transits of the moons
of Jupiter are interesting and important phenomena ; the eclipses
being sometimes observed for the rough determination of longitudes
at sea.

The satellites in transit present some curious phenomena.   When
they enter the disk, they appear intensely luminous upon its grayish border ; but as they advance, they seem by degrees to lose
their brightness, until they finally become undistinguishable from
the luminous surface of Jupiter.   It sometimes happens, however,
that the first, the third and the fourth satellites, after ceasing to
appear as bright spots, continue to be visible as dark spots upon
the bright central portions of the planet's disk ; but in these cases
their disks appear smaller than the shadows they cast.   Undoubtedly these satellites have extensive atmospheres, since they sometimes pass unperceived across the central parts of Jupiter, this being
probably when their atmospheres are condensed into clouds, strongly reflecting light ; while when these clouds are absent, we can see
their actual surface, with traces of the dark spots upon them similar
to those on Mars.

From the variation in the brightness of these satellites, which is
said to be always observed in the same part of their orbit, William
Herschel was led to suppose that these bodies, like our Moon,
rotate upon their axes in the same period in which they move round
the planet, so that they always present the same face to Jupiter ;
but these conclusions have been denied.   From my observations
it is apparent, however, that the light reflected by them varies in

intensity as well as in color. But this is rather to be attributed to the presence of an atmosphere surrounding these bodies, which when cloudy reflects more light than when clear, with corresponding changes in the color of the light.

The satellites in transit are sometimes preceded or followed, according to the position of the Sun, by a round black spot having about the same size as the satellite itself. This black spot is the shadow of the satellite cast on the vapory envelope of Jupiter, similar to the shadow cast by the Moon on the Earth, during eclipses of the Sun ; in fact, all the Jovian regions traversed by these shadows have the Sun totally eclipsed. Sometimes it happens that the shadow appears elliptical. This occurs either when it is observed very near the limb, or when entering upon a round, cloud-like spot. This effect is attributable to the perspective under which the shadow is seen on the spherical globe or spot.

The proper motion of the satellites in the Jovian sky is much more rapid than that of the Moon in our sky. During one Jovian day of ten hours, the first satellite advances 84° ; the second, 42° ; the third, 20° and the fourth, 9°. The first satellite passes from New Moon to its first quarter in a little more than a Jovian day, while the fourth occupies ten such days in attaining the same phase.

In density, as well as in physical constitution, Jupiter differs widely from the interior planets, and especially from the Earth; and, as has been shown, it is surrounded by a dense, opaque, cloudy layer, which is almost always impenetrable to the sight, and hides from view the nucleus, which we may conceive to exist under this vaporous envelope. In 1876, the year of the great Jovian disturbances, I observed frequently in the northern hemisphere of the planet a very curious phenomenon, which seems to prove that its cloudy envelope is at times partially absent in some places, its vapors being apparently either condensed, or transported to other parts of its surface, and that, therefore, a considerable part of the real globe of the planet was visible at these places. The phenomenon consisted in the deformation of the northern limb, which had a much shorter radius on all of this hemisphere situated northward of the white belt which adjoins the equatorial zone. The deformation of the limb on both sides, where it passed from a longer to a shorter radius, was abrupt, and at right angles to the limb, forming there a step-like indentation which was very prominent. The polar segment having a smaller radius, appeared unusually dark, and was not striped, as usual, but uniform in tint throughout. On September 27th, the third satellite passed over this dark segment, and emerged from the western border, a little below the place where the limb was abruptly deformed, as above described. When the satellite had fully emerged from this limb, it was apparent that if the portion of the limb having a longer radius had been prolonged a little below, and as far as the satellite, it would have enclosed it within its border, and thus retarded the time of emersion. The depth of deformation of the limb was accordingly greater than the diameter of the third satellite, and certainly more than 4,000 miles. That the phenomenon was real, is proved by the fact that the egress of this satellite occurred at least four minutes sooner than the time predicted for it in the American Ephemeris. Other observations seem to point in the same direction, since some of the satellites which were occulted have been seen through the limb of Jupiter by different astronomers, as if this limb was sometimes semi-transparent. Another observation of mine seems to confirm these conclusions. On April 24th, 1877, at 15h. 25m. the shadow of the first satellite was projected on the dark band forming the northern border of the equatorial belt, the shadow being then not far from the east limb. Close to this shadow, and on its western side, it was preceded by a secondary shadow, which was fainter, but had the same apparent size. This round dark spot was not the satellite itself, as I had supposed at first, since this object was yet outside of the planet, on the east, and entered upon it only at 16h. 4m. I watched closely this strange phenomenon, and at 16h. 45m., when the shadow had already crossed about ¾ of the disk, it was still preceded by the secondary, or mock shadow, as it may be called; the same relative distance having been kept all the while between the two objects, which had therefore traveled at the same rate. It is obvious that this dark spot could not be one of the planet's markings, since the shadow of the first satellite moves more quickly on the surface of Jupiter than a spot on the same surface travels by the effect of rotation, so that in this case the shadow would soon have passed over this marking, and left it behind, during the time occupied by the observation. From these observations it seems very probable that Jupiter has a nucleus, either solid or liquid, which lies several thousand miles below the surface of its cloudy envelope. It is also probable that the uniformly shaded dark segment seen in 1876, was a portion of the surface of this nucleus itself. When the cloudy envelope is semi-transparent at the place situated on a line with an occulted satellite and the eye of an observer, this satellite may accordingly remain visible for a time through the limb, as shown by observation. The phenomenon of the mock shadow may also be attributed to a similar cause, where semi-transparent vapors receive the shadow of a satellite at their surface, while at the same time part of this shadow, passing through the semi-transparent vapors, may be seen at the surface of the nucleus, or of a layer of opaque clouds situated at some distance below the surface.

Some astronomers are inclined to think that Jupiter is at a high temperature, and self-luminous to a certain extent. If this planet is self-luminous to any degree, we might expect that some light would be thrown upon the satellites when they are crossing the shadow cast into space by the planet; but when they cross this shadow they are totally invisible in the best telescopes, a proof that they do not receive much light from the non-illuminated side of Jupiter. It would, indeed, seem probable that some of the intensely white spots occasionally seen on the equatorial belt of the planet are self-luminous in a degree, yet not enough to render the satellites visible while they are immersed in Jupiter's shadow. It does not seem impossible that the planet should have the high temperature attributed to it, when we remember the terrific storms observed in its atmosphere, which, owing to the great distance of Jupiter from the Sun, do not seem to be attributable to this body, but rather to some local cause within the envelope of the planet.

Astronomy, which is a science of observation, is naturally silent with regard to the inhabitants of Jupiter. If there are any such inhabitants, they are confined to the domain of conjecture, under the dense cloudy envelope of the planet. The conditions of habitability on Jupiter must differ very widely from those of our globe. Comparatively little direct light from the Sun reaches the surface of the globe of Jupiter, except that which passes through the narrow openings forming the dark clouds. All the rest of the planet's surface, being covered perpetually by opaque clouds, receives only diffused light. On Jupiter there are practically no seasons, since its axis is nearly perpendicular to its orbit. The force of gravity on the surface of Jupiter being more than double what it is on the Earth, living bodies would there have more than double the weight of similar bodies on the Earth. Furthermore, Jupiter only receives 0.011 of the light and heat which we receive from the Sun; and its year is nearly equal to 12 of our years. If there are living beings on Jupiter, they must, then, be entirely different from any known to us, and they may have forms never dreamed of in our most fantastic conceptions.

The two round black spots represented towards the central parts of Plate IX. are the shadows of the first and second satellite; while the two round white spots seen on the left of the disk, are the satellites themselves, as they appeared at the moment of the observation.   The first satellite and its shadow are the nearest to the equator ; while the second satellite and its shadow are higher, the last being projected on the Great Red Spot.*   The row of dark circular spots represented on the northern, or lower hemisphere, when they first appeared, had some resemblance to Sun-spots without a penumbra, with bright markings around them, resembling faculæ. These round spots subsequently enlarged considerably, until they united along the entire line, encircling the planet, and finally forming a narrow pink belt, which is still visible.

* *Note.*—By an accidental error in enlarging the original drawing, the satellites and shadows appear in Plate IX. of double their actual size.   The error is one easy of mental correction.

THE PLANET SATURN.

PLATE X.

SATURN, which is next to Jupiter in order of distance from the Sun, while not the largest, is certainly the most beautiful and interesting of all the planets, with his grand and unique system of rings, and his eight satellites, which, like faithful servants, attend the planet's interminable journey through space.

Seen with the naked eye, Saturn shines in the night like a star of the first magnitude, whose dull, soft whiteness is, however, far from attaining the brilliancy of Venus or Jupiter, although it sometimes approaches Mars in brightness. Saturn hardly ever exhibits the phenomenon of scintillation, or twinkling, a peculiarity which makes it easily distinguishable among the stars and planets of the heavens.

The synodical period of Saturn occupies 1 year and 13 days, so that every 378 days, on an average, this planet holds the same position in the sky relatively to the Sun and the Earth.

The mean distance of Saturn from the Sun is a little over 9½ times that of our globe, or 872,000,000 miles. Owing to the orbital eccentricity, this distance may increase to 921,000,000 miles, when the planet is in aphelion ; or decrease to 823,000,000 miles, when it is in perihelion ; Saturn being therefore 98,000,000 miles nearer to the Sun when in perihelion than in aphelion. If gravitation were free to exert its influence alone, Saturn would fall into the Sun in 5 years and 2 months.

The distance of Saturn from the Earth varies, according to the position of the two planets in their respective orbits. At the time of opposition, when the Earth lies between the Sun and Saturn, this distance is smallest ; while, on the contrary, at the time of conjunction, when the Sun lies between the Earth and Saturn, it is greatest. Owing, however, to the eccentricity of the orbits of Saturn and our globe, and the inclination of their planes to each other, and owing also to the variable heliocentric longitude of the perihelion, the distance of the two planets from each other at their successive conjunctions and oppositions is rendered extremely variable. At present it is when the oppositions of Saturn occur in December that this planet comes nearest to us ; while when the conjunctions take place in June, the distance of Saturn from the Earth is the greatest possible. In the former case the distance of the planet from our globe is only 730,000,000 miles ; while in the last it is 1,014,000,000 miles, the difference between the nearest and farthest points of Saturn's approach to us being no less than 284,000,000 miles, or over three times the mean distance of the Sun from the Earth.

From the great variations in the distance of Saturn from the Earth, necessarily result corresponding changes in the brightness and apparent diameter of this body. When it is farthest from us, its angular diameter measures but 14" ; while, when it is nearest, it measures 20".

The orbit of Saturn is inclined 2°30′ to the ecliptic, and its eccentricity, which equals 0,056, is over three times that of the Earth's orbit.

This planet revolves around the Sun in a period of 29 years and 5½ months, or 10,759 terrestrial days, which constitutes its sidereal year. The extension of the immense curve forming the orbit of this planet, is no less than 5,505,000,000 miles, which is traversed by the planet with a mean velocity of a little less than 6 miles per second, or three times less than the motion of our globe in space.

The real dimensions of the globe of Saturn are not yet known' with accuracy, and the equatorial diameter has been variously estimated by observers, at from 71,000 to 79,000 miles. If we adopt the mean of these numb:rs, 75,000 miles, the circumference of the Saturnian equator would measure 235,620 miles, or 9½ times the circumference of our globe ; the surface of Saturn would be 86 times, and its volume over 810 times that of the Earth.

However great the volume of Saturn, its mass is proportionally small, being only 90 times greater than that of our globe ; the mean density of the materials composing this planet being less than that of cork, and only 0.68 the density of water. The force of gravitation at the surface of Saturn is greater, by a little over $\frac{1}{6}$, than it is at the surface of the Earth ; a body falling in a vacuum at its surface, would travel 17.59 feet during the first second.

From observations of markings seen on the surface of Saturn, and from the study of their apparent displacements on the disk, William Herschel found that the planet rotated upon its axis in 10h. 16m. 0.24s. Since Herschel's determination, new researches have been made, and lately, Professor Hall, noticing a bright spot, followed it for nearly a month, observing its transits across the central meridian of the disk. From these observations he has obtained for the rotation period 10h. 14m. 23.8s., a result which agrees very closely with that obtained 82 years earlier by Herschel, considering the fact that the markings from which the period of rotation is ascertained are not fixed on the planet, but are always more or less endowed with proper motion. The velocity of rotation at the equator is 21,538 miles per hour, or nearly 6 miles per second.

The axis of rotation of Saturn is inclined 64° 18′ to the plane of the orbit, so that its equator makes an angle of 25° 42′ with the same plane. The seasons of this planet therefore present greater extremes of temperature than those of the Earth, but not quite so great variations as the seasons of Mars.

The globe of Saturn is not a perfect sphere, but its figure is that of an oblong spheroid, flattened at the poles. The polar compression of Saturn is greater than that of any other planet, surpassing even that of Jupiter. Though not yet determined with a great degree of accuracy, the compression is known to be between $\frac{1}{9}$ and $\frac{1}{10}$ of the equatorial diameter; that is, a flattening of about 3,894 miles, at each pole, the polar diameter being 7,788 miles shorter than the equatorial.

The internal condition of the planet Saturn, whether solid, liquid or gaseous, cannot be discovered from the examination of its surface, as its globe is enwrapped in a dense opaque layer of vapors and cloud-like forms, through which the sight fails to penetrate. The appearance of this vapory envelope is like that of *cumulus* clouds, and one of its characteristics is to arrange itself into alternate bright and dark parallel belts, broader than those seen on Jupiter, and also more regular and dark. These belts, which are parallel to the equator of the planet, vary in curvature with the inclination of its axis of rotation to the line of sight.

The belts of Saturn, like those of Jupiter, are not permanent, but keep changing more or less rapidly. Sometimes they have been observed to be quite numerous; while at other times they are few. Occasionally conspicuous white or dark spots are seen on the surface, although the phenomenon is quite rare. It is from the observation of such spots that Saturn's period of rotation has been determined, as stated above. The equatorial zone of Saturn always appears more white and brilliant than the other parts, as it also appears more mottled and cloud-like. In late years the globe has been characterized, and much adorned, by a pale pinkish tint on its equatorial belt, resembling that of Jupiter, but somewhat fainter. On either side of the equatorial belt there is a narrower band, upon which the mottled appearance is visible. Below these, one or two dark belts, separated by narrow white bands, are usually seen ; but, of late, the bands have been less numerous, being replaced in high latitudes by a dark segment, which forms a polar cap to Saturn. The globe of Saturn does not anywhere appear perfectly white, and when compared with its ring, it looks of a smoky yellowish tint, which becomes an ashy gray on its shaded parts. It usually appears darker near the limb than in its central portions ; although on some occasions I have seen portions of the limb appear brighter, as if some white spots were traversing it.

Some observers have seen the limb deformed and flattened at different places, and W. Herschel even thought such a deformation to be a permanent feature of this globe, which he termed diamond-shaped, or " square shouldered." But this was evidently an illusion, since the planet's limb usually appears perfectly elliptical, although it occasionally appears as if flattened at some points, especially where it comes in apparent contact with the shadow cast by the globe on the ring, as observed by myself many times. But with some attention, it is generally found that this deformation is apparent rather than real, and is caused by the passage of some large dark spots over the limb, which is thus rendered indistinguishable from the dark background upon which it is projected.

What distinguishes Saturn from all known planets, or heavenly bodies, and makes it unique in our universe, is the marvelous broad flat ring which encircles its equator at a considerable distance from it. With a low magnifying power this flat ring appears single, but when carefully examined with higher powers, it is found to consist of several distinct concentric rings and zones, all lying nearly in the same plane with the planet's equator.

At first sight only two concentric rings are recognized, the *outer* and the *middle*, or *intermediary*, which are separated by a wide and continuous black line, called the *principal division*. This line, and indeed all the features of the surface of the rings are better seen, and appear more prominent on that part of the ring on either side called the *ansa*, or handle. Besides these two conspicuous rings, a third, of very dark bluish or purplish color, lies between this middle ring, to which it is contiguous, and the planet. This inner ring, which is quite wide, is called the *gauze* or *dusky ring*. Closer examination shows that the outer ring is itself divided by a narrow, faint, grayish line called the *pencil line*, which, from its extreme faintness, is only visible on the ansæ. Moreover, the middle ring is composed of three concentric zones, or belts, which, although not' apparently divided by any interval of space, are distinguished by the different shadings of the materials composing them. The outer zone of this compound middle ring is, by far, the brightest of all the system of rings and belts, especially close to its external border, where, on favorable occasions, I have seen it appear on the ansæ as if mottled over, and covered throughout with strongly luminous cloud-like masses. On the ansæ of the double outer ring, similar cloudy forms have also been seen at different times. The second zone of the middle ring is darker than the first, the innermost being darker still. All the characteristic points which have thus been described, are shown in Plate X.

Although suspected in 1838, the dusky ring was not recognized before 1850, when G. P. Bond discovered it with the 15-inch refractor of the Cambridge Observatory. It was also independently discovered the same year in England by Dawes and Lassell. The dusky ring differs widely in appearance and in constitution from the other rings, inasmuch as these last are opaque, and either white or grayish, while the former is very dark, and yet so transparent that the limb of the planet is plainly seen through its substance. On particularly favorable occasions, the appearance of this ring resembles that of the fine particles of dust floating in a ray of light traversing a dark chamber. Whatever may be the material of which this ring is composed, it must be quite rarefied, especially towards its inner border, which appears as if composed of distinct and minute particles of matter feebly reflecting the solar light. That the inner part of the dusky ring is composed of separate particles, is proved by the fact that the part of the ring which is seen in front of the globe of Saturn has its inner border abruptly deflected and curved inward on entering upon the disk, causing it to appear considerably narrower than it must be in reality, a peculiarity which is shown in the Plate. This phenomenon may be attributed to an effect of irradiation, due to the strong light reflected by the central parts of the ball, which so reduces the apparent diameter of the individual particles that they become invisible to us, especially those near the inner border, which are more scattered and less numerous than elsewhere.

The dusky ring, which was described by Bond, Lassell and other astronomers as being equally transparent throughout all its width, has not been found so by mè in later years. The limb of the planet, seen by these observers through the whole width of the dusky ring in 1850, could not be traced through its outer half by myself in 1872 and 1874, and this with the very same instrument used by Bond in his observations of 1848 and 1850. Moreover, I have plainly seen that its transparency was not everywhere equal, but greatest on the inner border, from which it gradually decreases, until it becomes opaque, as proved by the gradual loss of distinctness of the limb, which vanishes at about the middle of the dusky ring. These facts, which have been well ascertained, prove that the particles composing this ring are not permanently located, and are undergoing changes of relative position. It will be shown that the surface of the other rings is also subject to changes, which are sometimes very rapid.

The globe of Saturn is not self-luminous, but opaque. It shines by the solar light, as is proved by the shadow it casts opposite the Sun upon the ring. Although receiving its light from the Sun, Saturn does not exhibit any traces of phases, like the other planets nearer to the Sun, owing to its great distance from the Earth. When near its quadratures, however, the limb opposite to the Sun appears much darker, and shows traces of twilight. As far as can be ascertained, the rings, with the exception of the inner one, are opaque, as proved by the strong shadow which they cast on the globe of Saturn.

The shadows cast by the planet on the ring, and by the ring on the planet, are very interesting phenomena, inasmuch as they enable the astronomer to recognize the form of the surface which receives them. The shadow cast by the ring on the ball is not quite so interesting as the other, although it has served to prove that the surface of this globe is not smooth, as is likewise suggested by its mottled appearance. I have sometimes found, as have also other observers, that the outline of this shadow upon the ball was irregular and indented, an observation which proves either that the surface of the ball is irregular, or that the border of the ring casting the shadow was jagged. The shadow of the globe on the rings has much more interest, as it enables us to get at some knowledge of the form of the surface of the rings, which otherwise is very difficult to discover, owing to the oblique position in which we always see them.

In general, the shadow of the ball on the middle ring has its outline concave towards the planet; while on the outer ring it is usually slanting, and at a greater distance from the limb than on the middle, and dusky rings. This form of the shadow evidently proves that the middle ring stands at a higher level than the two others, especially towards its outer margin. The system seems to increase gradually in thickness from the inner border of the dusky ring to the vicinity of the outer margin of the middle ring, after which it rapidly diminishes on this border, while the surface of the outer ring is almost level.

But this surface is by no means fixed, as its form sometimes changes, as proved by my observations and those of others. As may be noticed on Plate X., the outline of the shadow of the planet on the rings is strongly deviated towards the planet, near the outer margin of the middle ring; the notch indicating an abrupt change of level, and a rise of the surface at that point. Some observers have endeavored to explain these deviations by the phenomena of irradiation, from which it would follow that the maximum effect of deviation should be observed where the ring is the brightest, which does not accord with observation ; as the deepest depression in the shadow is not to be found usually at the brightest part, which is towards the outer border of the middle ring, but occurs near its centre. From these observations it is undoubtedly established that the surface of the rings is far from being flat throughout, and is, besides, not permanent, but changes, as would, for instance, the surface of a large mass of clouds seen from the top of a high mountain. In general, the system is thickest not very far from the outer border of the intermediary ring.

Some interesting phenomena which I had occasion to observe before and after the passage of the Sun through the plane of the rings, on February 6th, 1878, conclusively show that the surface of this system cannot be of a uniform level, but must be thicker towards the outer border of the middle ring, thence gradually sloping towards the planet. Many of my observations irresistibly lead to this conclusion. As it would, however, be out of place to have them recorded here in detail, I will simply give one of the most characteristic among them.

From December 18th, 1877, when the Sun was about 41' above the plane of the rings, to February 6th, 1878, the day of its passage through their plane, the illuminated surface of this system gradually decreased in breadth with the lowering of the Sun, until it was lost sight of, February 5th, on the eve of the passage of the Sun through their plane. The phenomenon in question consisted in the gradual invasion of their illuminated surface by what appeared to be a black shadow, apparently cast by the front part of the outer portion of the middle ring the nearest to the Sun. On January 25th, when the elevation of the Sun above the plane of the rings was reduced to 15', the shadow thus cast had extended so far on their surface that it reached the shadow cast by the globe on the opposite part of the

ring in the east, and accordingly the remaining portion of the illuminated surface of the eastern ansa then appeared entirely disconnected from the ball, by a large dark gap, corresponding in breadth
to that of the globe's shadow on the rings. On February 4th, when
the Sun was only 5′ above the plane of the rings, their illuminated
and only visible surface was reduced to a mere thread of light, which
on the 5th appeared broken into separate points. It is evident that
the phenomenon was not caused by the obliquity of the ring as seen
from our globe, since the elevation of the Earth above the plane of
the rings—which on December 18th was 3° 20′—was still 1° 20′ on the
4th of February. In ordinary circumstances, when the Sun is a little more elevated, and the rings seen at this last angle, they appear
quite broad and conspicuous, and even the dark open space separating
the dusky ring from the planet is perfectly visible on the ansæ, where
the Earth's elevation above their plane is reduced to 40′. It is also
evident that the phenomenon was not to be attributed to the reduction of the light which they received from the Sun, although the illumination in February might be expected to be comparatively feeble,
since the Sun then shone upon the rings so obliquely; yet (on the supposition that their surface is flat) they should have been illuminated
throughout, and if not very brightly, sufficiently so, at least, to make
them visible and as bright as was the narrow thread of light observed on the 4th of February. The phenomenon actually observed
may be explained most readily by assuming, as other phenomena also
indicate, that the surface of the ring is not flat, but more elevated
towards, or in the vicinity of its outer border, from which place it
slopes inwardly towards the planet. On this assumption, it is evident that the elevated part of the ring the nearest to the Sun would
cast a shadow, which, with the increasing obliquity of the Sun, would
gradually cover the whole surface comprised within the elevated
part, and thus become invisible to us. Several observations made
by Bond and other observers undoubtedly show the same phenomenon, and do not seem to be intelligible on any other supposition.
From my observations made in 1881 it would appear, however, that
the opposite surfaces of the rings do not exactly correspond in form,
but this may not be a permanent feature, as the surface of this system is subject to changes, as already shown.

The dimensions of the rings are great, the diameter of the outer
one being no less than 172,982 miles, the distance from the centre
of the globe to the outer border of the system being, therefore,
86,491 miles. The breadth of the outer ring is 9,941 miles ; that of
the principal division, 2,131 miles ; that of the middle ring, 19,902

miles, and that of the dusky ring, 8,772 miles. The breadth of all the rings taken together is, therefore, 40,746 miles. The interval between the surface of Saturn and the inner border of the dusky ring is 7,843 miles.

The thickness of the system of rings has been variously estimated by astronomers, on account of the great difficulties attending its determination. While Sir John Herschel estimated it at more than 250 miles, G. P. Bond reduces it to 40 miles. Both of these numbers are evidently too small, as so slight a thickness cannot explain the observed phenomenon of the shadow cast by a portion of the ring on its own surface, when the Sun is very low in its horizon, as shown above.

The plane of the system of rings is inclined 27° to the planet's orbit, and is parallel, or at least very nearly so, with the equator of the planet, passing, therefore, through its centre, and dividing its globe into northern and southern hemispheres. Seen from the Earth, a portion of the ring always appears projected in front of the planet, thus concealing a small part of its globe, while the opposite portion passes behind the globe, which hides it from sight.

As the plane of the ring is not affected by the motion of the planet around the Sun, but always remains parallel to itself, it follows that as Saturn advances in its orbit the rings must successively present themselves to us under various angles of inclination, appearing, therefore, more or less elliptical, and presenting two maxima and two minima of inclination in the course of one of its revolutions. As the revolution of Saturn is accomplished in 29½ years, the maxima and the minima must recur every 14 years and 9 months; the maxima being separated from the minima by an interval of 7 years and 4½ months.

When Saturn arrives at the two opposite points of its orbit, where the major axis of its ring is at right angles to the line joining its centre to that of the Sun, the ring, which is then viewed at an inclination of 27°, the greatest angle at which it can ever be seen, has reached its maximum opening, the smaller diameter of its ellipse being then about half that of the larger. At this moment the outer ring projects north and south beyond the globe, which is then completely enclosed in its ellipse. The maximum opening of the northern surface of the ring takes place, at present, when Saturn arrives in longitude 262°, in the constellation Sagittarius, and that of the southern surface when it arrives in longitude 82° in the constellation Taurus. When, on the contrary, Saturn reaches the two opposite points of its orbit, where the plane of its ring is parallel to the line joining its centre to that of the Sun, the opening vanishes, as only the thin edge of the ring is then presented to the Sun and receives its light, the rest being in darkness. At this moment the ring disappears, except in the largest telescopes, where it is seen as an exceedingly thin thread of light; and the Saturnian globe, having apparently lost its ring, appears solitary in the sky, like the other planets. The disappearance of the ring from this cause occurs now when Saturn arrives at 90° from either of the positions of maximum inclination, that is, in longitude 352° in the constellation Pisces, and in longitude 172° in the constellation Leo.

When the planet is in any other position than one of these last two, either the northern or the southern surface of the ring is illuminated by the Sun, while the opposite surface is in the night, and does not receive any direct sunlight. At the time of the passage of the plane of the ring through the Sun's centre, a change takes place in the illumination of the ring. If it is the northern surface which has received the rays of the Sun during the previous half of the Saturnian year, at the moment the plane has passed the centre of the Sun, the southern surface, after having been buried in darkness for 14¾ years, sees the dawn of its long day of the same length. Such a phenomenon will not occur until 1892, when the passage of the Sun from the northern to the southern side of the ring will close in twilight the day commenced in 1878.

Aside from the periodic disappearance of the ring, resulting from the passage of the Sun through its plane, the ring may also disappear from other reasons. Just before or just after the time of the passage of the Sun through the plane of the ring, the Earth and the Sun may occupy such positions, that while the one is north of the plane of the ring, the other is south of it, or vice versa, in which event the ring becomes invisible, because its dark and non-illuminated surface is presented to us. The ring may also become invisible to us when the Earth passes through its plane.

Since the distance from Saturn to the Sun is to the distance of the Earth from this last body as 9.54 is to 1; and since the circumference of a circle increases in the same proportion as its radius, it follows that the diameter of the Earth's orbit projected on the orbit of Saturn would occupy only $\frac{1}{30}$ part of the latter, or about 12° 2', this being 6° 1' on either side of the nodes of the rings. To describe such an arc on its orbit, it takes Saturn almost 360 days on an average, or almost a complete year; the Earth describing therefore almost a whole revolution around the Sun during the time it takes Saturn to advance 12° 2' on its orbit. Then, when Saturn occupies a position comprised within an arc 6° 1' from either side of the nodes of its ring, the Earth, by its motion, is liable to encounter the plane of the ring, when therefore it will only present its thin edge to us, and becomes invisible. At least one such encounter is unavoidable within the time during which Saturn occupies either of these positions on its orbit ; while three frequently happen, and two are possible.

The natural impression received by looking at the rings, while seeing the ponderous globe of Saturn enclosed in its interior, is that this gigantic, but very delicate structure, in order to avoid destruction, must be endowed with a swift movement of rotation on an axis perpendicular to its plane, and that the centrifugal force thence arising counterbalances the powerful attraction of the planet, and thus keeps the system in equilibrium.

Theoretically, the rotation of the rings is admitted by every astronomer, as being an essential condition to the existence of the system, which otherwise, it is thought, would fall upon the planet. Although the rotation of the rings seems so probable that it is theoretically considered as certain, yet its existence has not been satisfactorily demonstrated by direct observation, which alone can establish it on a firm basis as a matter of scientific knowledge.

The determination of the period of rotation of the rings, which is supposed to be 10h. 32m. 15s., rests only on the observations of W. Herschel, made in 1790, from the apparent displacement of irregularities on the ring ; but his results have been contradicted by other observations, and even by those of Herschel himself, made in later years.

Although the system of rings is very nearly concentric with the globe of Saturn, yet the coincidence is not considered as mathematically exact. It seems to have been satisfactorily demonstrated by direct observations that the centre of gravity of the system oscillates around that of the planet, thus describing a minute orbit. This peculiarity is in accordance with theory, which has shown it to be essential to the stability of the system.

Besides its system of rings, which makes Saturn the most remarkable planet of the solar system, this globe is attended by eight satellites, moving in orbits whose planes very nearly coincide with the plane of the rings, except that of the most distant one, which has an inclination of about 12° 14'. In the order of their distance from the planets, the satellites of Saturn are as follows :   Mimas, Enceladus, Tethys, Dione, Rhea, Titan, Hyperion and Iapetus.   The three first satellites are nearer to Saturn than the Moon is to the Earth ; while Iapetus, the farthest, is 9½ times the distance of our satellite from us.   All the satellites, with the exception of the farthest, move more rapidly around Saturn than the Moon moves around the Earth ; while Iapetus, on the contrary, takes almost three times as long to make one revolution.

The period of revolution of the four inner satellites is accomplished in less than three days, that of Mimas being only a little more than 22 hours.   From such swiftness of motion, it is easily understood how short must be the intervals between the different phases of these satellites.   Mimas, for instance, passes from New Moon to First Quarter in less than 6 hours.

The distance of the nearest satellite from the planet's surface is 84,000 miles, and its distance from the outer ring only 36,000 miles. It is difficult to determine the diameter of objects so faint and distant as are some of these satellites, but the diameter of Titan, the largest of all, is pretty well known, and estimated to be $\frac{1}{16}$ the diameter of the planet, or more than half the diameter of our globe.

Iapetus is subject to considerable variations in brilliancy, and as the maxima and minima always occur when this satellite occupies the same parts of its orbit, it was conjectured by W. Herschel that, like our Moon, it turns once upon its axis during each of its revolutions about the planet.   It has been shown by my observations, that Iapetus attains its maximum brightness a little before it reaches its greatest western elongation, and its minimum on the opposite side.

As the planes of the orbits of the satellites are inclined to the planet's orbit, it follows that their transits, occultations and eclipses, are only possible when Saturn is near its equinoxes.   Passages of the satellites and their shadows across the disk, although rare, have been observed, and they somewhat resemble the phenomena exhibited by the satellites of Jupiter in transit.   When the Earth is very near the plane of the rings, the satellites, except the farthest, appear to be in a straight line nearly coincident with the plane of the rings, and are seen occasionally moving along the thin edge of the rings, appearing as luminous beads moving on a thread of light.

Owing to the considerable inclination of the axis of rotation of Saturn to its orbit, the seasons of this planet must have greater extremes of temperature than those of the Earth.   As the year of Saturn consists of 25,217 Saturnian days, each season, on the average, is composed of 6,304 Saturnian days.

To an observer on Saturn, the immense arches formed by its rings would appear as objects of great magnificence, spanning the sky like soft colorless rainbows. Moreover, the eight moons, several of which are always visible, would be of the highest interest, with their swift motions and rapid phases. Mimas, traveling in its orbit at the rate of 16' of arc per minute of time, moves over a space equal to the apparent diameter of our Moon in two minutes, or at the rate of 16° an hour.

Owing to the globular form of Saturn, the rings would be invisible in latitudes situated above 65° from its equator, and their apparent form and breadth would naturally vary with the latitude. At 63° only a very small portion of the outer ring would be visible above the equatorial horizon, where it would appear as a small segment of a circle. At 62° the principal division would just graze the horizon. At 46° the outer portion of the dusky ring would become visible, while at 35° its inner edge would appear above the horizon. From 65° of latitude down to the equator, the arches of the rings would be seen more and more elevated above the equatorial horizon, but at the same time that they are seen higher up, their apparent breadth gradually diminishes, owing to the effect of foreshortening, and at the equator itself the system would only present its thin edge to view.

During the summer seasons of either hemisphere of Saturn, the surface of the rings turned towards such hemisphere, being fully illuminated by the Sun, is visible from these regions. In the day time its light must be feeble and similar to the light reflected by our Moon during sunshine; but at night the system would display all its beauty, and the different rings, with their divisions and their various reflective powers, must present a magnificent sight.

During the nights of the long winter seasons on Saturn, on the contrary, the surface of the rings turned towards the hemisphere undergoing winter, receives no light from the Sun, and is invisible, or very nearly so, except towards morning and evening, when it may be faintly illuminated by the secondary light which it receives from the illuminated globe of Saturn. Although dark and invisible, the rings may make their form apparent at night by the absence of stars from the region which they occupy in the sky. Again, in other seasons, the days present very curious phenomena. In consequence of the diurnal rotation of the planet, the Sun seems to move in circular arcs, which, owing to the inclination of Saturn's axis, are more or less elevated above its horizon, according to the position of the planet in its orbit. As such arcs described by the Sun in the sky of Saturn are liable to encounter the rings, the Sun in passing behind them becomes eclipsed. It must be a magnificent

spectacle to witness the gradual disappearance of the fiery globe behind the outer ring, and its early reappearance, but for a moment
only, through the narrow gap of the principal division; to see it vanish again behind the middle ring, to reappear a little later through the
semi-transparent dusky ring, but very faint and red colored at first;
and then, gradually brighten up, and finally emerge in all its beauty
from the inner edge of the dusky ring.

It is in latitude 23° that the rings produce the most prolonged
eclipses of the Sun.   During a period equivalent to ten of our terrestrial years, such eclipses continually succeed each other with but
very short periods of interruption; and even during a long series of
rotations of Saturn, the Sun remains completely invisible in those
regions where the apparent arcs which it describes coincide with
the arcs of the rings.   In neighboring latitudes, the eclipses of the
Sun, although still frequent, would have a shorter and shorter duration as the observer should travel north or south.   These eclipses
of the Sun must produce a partial darkness of the regions involved
in the shadow of the rings, which may be compared to the darkness
produced on our globe by a total eclipse of the Sun.   The frequent
recurrence of these eclipses, and their comparatively long duration
in some regions, must still further reduce the duration of the short
Saturnian days.

The globe of Saturn, as already shown, casts a shadow on the
rings, which, according to the position of the planet in its orbit,
either extends across their whole breadth, or covers only a part of
their surface.   The shadow on the rings rising in the east after sunset, ascends to the culminating point of their arcs in the sky, in 2h.
34m., and as rapidly descends on the western horizon, to disappear
with sunrise.   This shadow, when projected on the rings in the sky,
must be hardly distinguishable from the dark background of the
heavens, except from the absence of stars in the regions which it
occupies.   It must appear as a large dark gap, separating the rings
into two parts, and constantly moving from east to west.   Possibly
the refraction of the solar rays, in passing through Saturn's atmosphere, may cast some colored light on the rings, similar to that
observed on the Moon during its eclipses.

An observer on the rings would behold phenomena still more
curious, a long day of 14¾ years being followed by a long night of
14¾ years.   The long days of Saturn's rings are, however, diversified by numerous eclipses of the Sun, which regularly occur every
10¼ hours; the phenomenon being due to the interposition of the
globe of Saturn between the rings and the Sun.   These eclipses.

produce partial obscurations of their surface, lasting from 1½ to 2 hours at a time.   Although the surface of the rings never receives direct sunlight during their long nights, yet they are not plunged all the time in total darkness, as they receive some reflected light from that part of the globe of Saturn which is illuminated by the Sun.   To the supposed observer on the rings, during every 10¼ hours, the immense globe would exhibit continually changing phases. At first he would see a point of light rapidly ascending from the horizon, and appearing under the form of a half crescent of considerable radius; 5⅛ hours later, the crescent having gradually increased, would appear as a half circle, covering ⅛ of the visible heavens, its surface being more than 20,000 times as large as the surface of the Moon.   Upon this brilliantly illuminated semi-circle would be projected the shadows of the rings, appearing as black belts separated by a narrow luminous band.

It is very difficult for one to conceive how such a delicate structure, as the system of rings appears to be, can keep together in equilibrium and avoid destruction from the powerful attraction of the planet on one side and the disturbing influence of the satellites on the other.   To explain it, several hypotheses have been advanced. The rings were first supposed to be solid, and upon this supposition Laplace determined the necessary conditions for their equilibrium; the most important of which require that the cross section of the rings should be an ellipse of irregular curvature, and having its major axis directed towards the centre of the planet, and also that the system should rotate upon an axis perpendicular to the plane of the rings.   This theory was superseded by another, which supposed the rings to be fluid.   This one was soon rejected for a third, assuming the system to be composed of vapors or gases; and more recently, all these theories were considered untenable, and replaced by a fourth, which supposes the system of rings to be made up of a congregation of innumerable small, independent bodies, revolving around Saturn in concentric zones.   Naturally, such a divergence of opinion can only result from our comparative ignorance of the subject, and sufficiently indicates our inability to explain the phenomena; and it must be admitted that, so far, nothing is certainly known about this strange system.   We shall probably remain in the same uncertainty until the rotation of the rings is ascertained by direct observations.   It is pretty certain, however, that none of these theories account for the observed phenomena in their details, although a partial explanation may be obtained by borrowing something from each hypothesis.

It has been conjectured, and a theory has been advanced, that the breadth of the whole ring system is gradually increasing inwards, and that it will come in contact with the planet in about 2,150 years ; but the question seems to have been settled in the negative by the elaborate measurements of the English observers. It is likely that the increase is only in the defining power of the instruments.

COMETS.

PLATE XI.

AMONG the celestial phenomena, none are more interesting than those mysterious apparitions from the depths which unexpectedly display their strange forms in our familiar constellations, through which they wander for a time, until they disappear like phantoms.

A comet, with its luminous diffused head, whence proceeds a long vapory appendage gradually fading away in the sky, presents an extraordinary aspect, which may well astonish and deeply impress the observer. Although these visitors from infinite space do not now inspire dread, as in by-gone times, yet, owing to the mystery in which the phenomenon is still involved, the apparition of a large comet, even in our days, never fails to create a profound sensation, and in some cases that unconscious fear which results from the unknown.

The effect of such a spectacle largely depends upon its rarity ; but since the telescope has been applied to the sounding of the heavens, it has been found that the appearance of comets is by no means an unusual occurrence. If so few comets, comparatively, are seen, it is because most of them are telescopic objects, and are therefore invisible to the naked eye. Most of the telescopic comets are not only too faint to be perceived by the unaided eye, but are insignificant objects, even when observed through the largest telescopes.

It was Kepler's opinion that comets are as numerous in the sky as fishes are in the ocean. Undoubtedly the number of these bodies must be great, considering that we can only see them when they come into the neighborhood of the Earth, and that many even here remain invisible, or at least pass unperceived. That many of them have passed unperceived heretofore, is proved by the fact that the number of those observed becomes greater every year, with the increase of the number of instruments used in their search. The number of comets observed with the naked eye during historic times is nearly 600, and that of telescopic comets, which, of course, all belong to the last few centuries, is more than 200, so that we have a total number of about 800 comets of which records have been kept. From theoretical considerations, Lambert and Arago estimated their entire number at several millions, but such speculations have generally no real value, since they cannot be established on a firm basis.

Comets remain visible for more or less time, according to their size and the nature and position of their orbits, but in general, the large ones can be followed with the telescope for several months after they have become invisible to the naked eye. The comet of 1861, for example, remained telescopically visible for a year, and that of 1811, for 17 months after disappearing from ordinary sight.

While a comet remains visible, it appears to revolve daily about us like the stars in general ; but it also moves among the constellations, and from this movement its orbit may be computed like that of a planet. From the apparent diurnal motion of a comet with the heavens, result the changes of position which it seems to undergo in the course of a night. The direction of the head and tail of a comet, of course, has only changed in regard to the horizon, but not in regard to the sky, in which they occupy very nearly the same position throughout a given night, and even for many nights in succession.

The movements of the comets in their orbits are, like those of the planets, in accordance with Kepler's laws, the Sun occupying one of the foci of the orbit they describe ; but the orbits of comets differ, however, in several points from those of the planets. Their eccentricity is always great, being sometimes apparently infinite, in which case the orbit is said to be parabolic, or hyperbolic; but the smallness of the portion of a cometary orbit which can ordinarily be observed, makes it difficult to determine this with certainty. Again, while the planetary orbits are usually near the plane of the ecliptic, those of comets frequently have great inclinations to that plane, and even when the inclination is less than 90°, the comet may have a retrograde movement, or, in other words, a movement contrary to the course in which all the planets revolve about the Sun.

Notwithstanding these differences between the elements of the orbits of the comets and those of the planets, the fact that each has the Sun in one focus indicates that the body moving in it is a member of the solar system, either for the time, or permanently, according to the nature of its orbit.

A distinction may accordingly be made between the comets which are permanent members of our solar system and those which

are only accidental or temporary visitors. Those moving in elliptical orbits around the Sun, like the planets, and therefore having a
determinate period of revolution, from which the time of their successive returns may be predicted, are permanent members of our
system, and are called periodic comets. All comets moving in para-
bolical or hyperbolical curves, are only temporary members of the
solar system, being apparently strangers who have been diverted
from their courses by some disturbing influence. No comet is classed
as periodical which does not follow a perceptibly elliptical orbit. Any
comet passing around the Sun at the mean distance of the Earth
from this body, with a velocity of 26 miles per second, will fly off
into infinite space, to return to us no more.

The time of revolution of the different periodic comets thus far
observed varies greatly, as do also the distances to which they recede from the Sun at aphelion. Whilst the period of revolution of
Encke's comet, the shortest thus far known, is only $3\frac{1}{2}$ years, that of
the comet of 1844, II., is 102,000 years ; and whilst the orbit of the
first is comprised within the orbit of Jupiter, that of the last extends
to a distance equal to 147 times the distance of Neptune from the
Sun. But so vast an orbit cannot be accurately determined from
the imperfect data at our disposal.

The periodic comets are usually divided into two classes. The
comets whose orbits are within the orbit of Neptune are called interior comets, while those whose orbits extend beyond that of Neptune are called exterior comets. The known interior periodic comets are twelve in number, while, including all the cases in which
there is some slight evidence of elliptic motion, the number of exterior comets observed is six or seven times as great. The periodic
comets of short period are very interesting objects, inasmuch as by
their successive returns they afford an opportunity to calculate their
motions and to observe the physical changes which they undergo
in their intervals of absence.

From observation of the periodic comets, it has been learned
that the same comet never presents twice the same physical appearance at its different returns, its size, shape and brilliancy varying so
greatly that a comet can never be identified by its physical characters alone. It is only when its elements have been calculated, and
are found to agree with those of a cometary orbit previously known,
that the two comets can be identified one with the other. There
are reasons to believe that, in general, comets decrease in brightness and size at each of their successive returns, and that they are
also continually losing some of their matter as they traverse their
orbits.

When very far away from us, all comets appear nearly alike, consisting of a faint nebulosity, of varying dimensions. When a comet first appears in the depths of space, and travels towards the Sun, it generally resembles a faint, uniformly luminous nebulosity, either circular or slightly elongated in form. As it approaches nearer to the Sun, a slight condensation of light appears towards its centre, and as it draws still nearer, it becomes brighter and brighter, and in condensing forms a kind of diffused luminous nucleus. At the same time that the comet acquires this concentration of light, the nebulosity gradually becomes elongated in the direction of the Sun. These effects generally go on increasing so long as the comet is approaching the Sun ; the condensation of light sometimes forms a bright nucleus, comparable to a very brilliant star, while the elongation becomes an immense appendage or tail. When the comet has passed its perihelion and recedes from the Sun, the inverse phenomena are observed ; the comet, decreasing in brightness, gradually loses its nucleus and tail, resumes its nebulous aspect, and finally vanishes in space, to appear again in due course, if it chance to be a periodic comet. While all comets become brighter in approaching the Sun, they do not all, however, develop a large tail, some of them showing only a slight elongation.

When a comet is first discovered with the telescope at a great distance from the Sun, it is difficult to predict whether it will become visible to the naked eye, or will remain a telescopic object, as it is only in approaching the Sun that these singular bodies acquire their full development. Thus, Donati's comet, whose tail became so conspicuous an object at its full appearance in 1858, remained two months after its discovery by the telescope without any indication of a tail. The comet of Halley, which before and after its return in 1759, remained five years inside of the orbit of Saturn, showed not the least trace of its presence during the greater part of this time. Nothing but calculation could then indicate the position in the sky of this invisible object, which was so prominent when it approached the Sun.

Another curious phenomenon exhibited by comets, and first noticed by Valz, is that in approaching the Sun the nebulosity composing these bodies contracts, instead of dilating, as would be naturally supposed from the greater amount of solar heat which they must then receive. In receding from the Sun, on the contrary, they expand gradually. As comets approach the Sun, the tail and nucleus are developed, while the nebulosity originally constituting these comets contracts, as if its material had been partly consumed in this development. In a certain sense it may be said that the comets are partly created by the Sun; in more exact terms, the changes of form which they undergo are induced by the Sun's action upon them at different distances and under varying conditions. Moreover, they are rendered visible by its influence, without which they would pass unperceived in our sky. When a comet disappears from view, it is not because its apparent diameter is so much reduced by the distance that it vanishes, but rather on account of the diminution of its light, both that which it receives from the Sun, and its own light; these bodies being in some degree self-luminous, as will be shown below.

The large comets, such as can be seen with the naked eye, always show the following characteristics, on examination with the telescope. A condensation of light resembling a diffused star forms the brightest part of the comet, this condensation being situated towards the extremity the nearest to the Sun. It is this starlike object which is called the *nucleus*. The nucleus seems to be entirely enclosed in a luminous vapory envelope of the same general texture, called the *coma*. This envelope, which is quite variable in brightness and form, is brightest next to the nucleus, and gradually fades away as it recedes from it. The *nucleus* and the *coma*, considered as a whole, constitute the *head* of a comet. From the head of a comet proceeds a long trail of pale nebulous light, which usually grows wider, but fainter, as it recedes from the nucleus, and insensibly vanishes in the sky. This delicate appendage, or tail, as it is commonly called, varies very much in size and shape, not only in different comets, but in the very same comet, at different times. Its direction is generally opposite to that of the Sun from the head of the comet.

The nuclei vary very much in brightness, in size and in shape; and while in some telescopic comets they are either absent or barely distinguishable as a small condensation of light, in bright comets they may become plainly visible to the naked eye, and they sometimes even surpass in brightness the most brilliant stars of the heavens. But whatever may be the size of cometary nuclei, they are subject to sudden and rapid changes, and vary from day to day. Sometimes they appear exceedingly brilliant and sharply outlined, while at other times they are so dim and diffused that they are hardly distinguishable from the coma of which they seem then to form a part.

From my observations upon the comets which have appeared since the year 1873, it is apparent that the changes in the nucleus, coma and tail, are due to a solar action, which contracts or expands these objects in such a manner that the nuclei become either bright and star-like, or dim and diffused, in a very short time. I had excellent opportunity, especially in the two large comets of 1881, to observe some of these curious changes, a description of which will give an idea of their extent and rapidity. On July 2d, 1881, at 9 o'clock, the nucleus of comet 1881, III., which is represented on Plate XI., appeared sharply defined, bright and considerably flattened cross-wise; but half an hour later it had considerably enlarged and had become so diffused that it could hardly be distinguished from the coma, with which it gradually blended. It is perhaps worth mention that, at the time this last observation was made, an aurora borealis was visible. This comet 1881, III., underwent other very important changes of its nucleus, coma and tail. On June 25th, the nucleus, which was bright and clearly defined, was ornamented with four bright diverging conical wings of light, as shown on Plate XI. On the 26th these luminous wings had gone, and the nucleus appeared one-third smaller. On the 28th it had enlarged, but on the 29th its shape was considerably altered, the nucleus extending in one direction to three or four times its diameter on previous nights, and being curved, so as to resemble a comma. On the 6th of July the nucleus of this comet showed the greatest disturbances. The nucleus, which had appeared perfectly round on the evening of the 5th, was found much elongated at 10 o'clock on the 6th, forming then a straight, acute, and well-defined wedge of light, inclined upwards to the left. The length of the nucleus, at this time, was three or four times its ordinary diameter. At the same time rapid changes occurred ; the strangely shaped nucleus soon became unsteady, extending and contracting alternately, and varying greatly in brightness. At 10h. 45m., the elongated nucleus, then gently curved, took the shape of a succession of luminous knots, which at times became so brilliant and distinct that they seemed to be about to divide and form separate nuclei; but such a separation did not actually occur, at least while I was observing. While these important changes were going on in the comet, a bright auroral arch appeared in the north, which lasted only a short time. On July 7th, the sky being cloudy, no observations were made, but on the 8th I observed the comet again. The nucleus had then resumed its circular form, but it was yet very unsteady, being sometimes small, bright and sharp, while a few seconds later it appeared twice as large, but dim in outlines; and sometimes an ill-defined secondary nucleus appeared at its centre. On several occasions the nucleus appeared as if it were double, one nucleus being apparently projected partly upon the other.

The nuclei of comets are sometimes very small, and in other cases very large. Among those which have been measured, the nucleus of the comet of 1798, I., was only 28 miles in diameter, but that of Donati's comet, in 1858, was 5,600 miles, and that of the comet of 1845 was 8,000 miles in diameter.

The coma of comets is found to be even more variable than the nucleus. The changes observed in the coma are generally in close connection with those of the nucleus and tail, the same perturbations affecting simultaneously the whole comet. While the coma of the comet of 1847 was only 18,000 miles in diameter, that of Halley's comet, in 1835, was 357,000 miles, and that of the comet of 1811 was 1,125,000 miles in diameter. In general, as already stated, the coma of a comet decreases in size in approaching the Sun. That of Encke's comet, which, on October 9th, 1838, had a diameter of 281,000 miles, gradually decreased at a daily mean rate of 4,088 miles in going towards the Sun; so that, on December 17th, when the distance of the comet from the Sun was more than four times less than it was on the first date, its diameter was reduced to 3,000 miles.

The form of the coma, in that part which is free from the tail, is in general a portion of a circle, but is sometimes irregular, with its border deformed. Thus, the border of the coma of Halley's comet was depressed at one point towards the Sun. I observed a similar phenomenon in Coggia's comet, with the great refractor of the Harvard College Observatory, on July 13th, 1874, when its border appeared deeply depressed on the side nearest to the Sun, as if repelled by this body. The coma of comet 1881, III., showed also very sigular outlines on the nights of the 25th and 26th of June, when its border was so deeply depressed that the coma appeared as if it were double. Luminous rays and jets often radiate from the nucleus across the coma, and describe graceful lateral curves, falling backwards and gradually fading away into the tail, of which they then form a part. The rays and jets emitted by the nucleus seem at first to obey the solar attraction and travel towards the Sun; but they are soon repelled, and move backward towards the tail. It is a mystery, as yet unexplained, how these cometary jets, which at first seem to obey to the laws of attraction, are compelled to retreat apparently by superior opposing forces. Among the forces of nature, we know of no other than those of an electrical sort, which would act in a similar manner; but this explanation would require us to assume some direct electrical communication between the comet and the Sun. Considering the distance between the two bodies, and the probable absence or great tenuity of the gaseous material in interstellar space, such an assumption is a difficult one.

Under the action of the solar forces, the coma also very frequently forms itself into concentric luminous arcs, separated by comparatively dark intervals. These luminous semi-circles vary in number, but sometimes there are as many as four or five at a time. All great comets show these concentric curves more or less, but sometimes only a portion is visible, the rest of the coma having a different structure. When great comets approach near the Sun, their coma is generally composed of two distinct parts, an inner and an outer coma, the inner one being due to the luminous jets issuing from the nucleus, which, never extending very far, form a distinct, bright zone within the fainter exterior coma.

The tails of comets, which are in fact a prolongation of the coma, are likewise extremely variable in form. They are sometimes straight like a rod; again, are curved like a sabre, or even crooked like an S, as was that of the comet of 1769. They are also fan-shaped, pointed, or of the same width throughout. Many of these appendages appear longitudinally divided through their middle by a narrow, darkish rift, extending from the nucleus to the extremity. This peculiarity appears in the comet shown on Plate XI. Sometimes the dark rift does not commence near the nucleus, but at some distance from it, as I observed in the case of comet 1881, III., on June 26th. This dark rift is not a permanent feature of a comet's tail, but may be visible one day and not at all the next. Comet 1881, III., which had shown a dark rift towards the end of June, did not exhibit any such rift during July and August, when, on the contrary, its tail appeared brighter in the middle. Coggia's comet, which showed so prominent a dark rift in July, 1874, had none on June 10th. On the contrary, the tail was on that date very bright along its middle, as also along each of its edges.

The tail of a comet does not invariably point directly away from the Sun, as above mentioned, and sometimes the deviation is considerable ; for instance, the tail of the comet of 1577 deviated 21° from the point opposite to the Sun.

In general, the tail inclines its extremity towards the regions of space which it has just left, always presenting its convex border to the regions towards which it is moving. It is also a remarkable fact that this convex border, moving first in space, always appears brighter and sharper than the opposite one, which is often diffused. From these peculiarities it would seem that in moving about the Sun the comets encounter some resistance to their motion, from the medium through which they pass, and that this resistance is sufficient to curve their tails away from the course in which they move, and to crowd their particles together on the forward side. It is especially when they approach their perihelion, and move more rapidly on a curve of a shorter radius, that the comets' tails show the greatest curvature, unless their position in regard to the observer prevents their being advantageously seen. The tail of Donati's comet presented a fair illustration of this peculiarity, its curvature having augmented with the velocity of the comet's motion about the Sun. But possibly this phenomenon has another cause, and may be found rather in the solar repulsion which acts on comets and is not instantaneously propagated throughout their mass.

Although, in general, comets have but one tail, it is not very rare to see them with multiple tails. The comets of 1807 and 1843 had each a double tail; Donati's comet, in 1858, showed several narrow, long rectilinear rays, issuing from its abruptly curved tail. The comet of 1825 had five branches, while that of 1744 exhibited no less than six distinct tails diverging from the coma at various angles. In general character the multiple and single tails are similar. When a comet has two tails, it is not rare for the second to extend in the general direction of the Sun, as was the case with the great comet of 1881, III., represented on Plate XI. From July 14th to the 21st it exhibited quite an extended conical tail, starting obliquely downwards from the right side of the coma, and directed towards the Sun. From the 24th of July to the 2d of August this secondary tail was exactly opposite in its direction from that of the primary tail, and gave to the head a very elongated appearance. Comet 1881, IV., also exhibited a secondary appendage, not directed towards the Sun, but making an angle of about 45° with the main tail.

These cometary appendages sometimes attain prodigious dimensions. The comets of 1680 and 1769 had tails so extended that, after their heads had set under the horizon, the extremities of these immense appendages were still seen as far up as the zenith. In a single day the tail of the comet of 1843 extended 100°, and it was thrust from the comet "as a dart of light" to the enormous distance of 48,500,000 miles, and yet of this immense appendage nothing was left on the following day. The tail of Donati's comet, in 1858, attained a real length of 42,000,000 miles, while that of the great comet of 1843 had the enormous length of 200,000,000 miles. If this last comet had occupied the position of the Sun, which it approached very nearly for a moment, the extremity of its tail would have extended 60,000,000 miles beyond the orbit of Mars.

In some cases the tails of comets have been seen undulating and vibrating in a manner similar to the undulations and coruscations of light characteristic of some auroras.   Many observers report having seen such phenomena.   The comet of 1769 was traversed by luminous waves and pulsations, comparable to those seen in the aurora borealis.   I myself observed these curious undulations in Coggia's comet in 1874, while the head of this object was below the horizon. For an hour the undulations rapidly succeeded each other, and ran along the whole length of the tail.

Some of the brightest comets have shone with such splendor that they could be observed easily in full sunshine.   Many comets, such as those of 1577 and 1744, have equaled Sirius and Venus in brilliancy.   The great comet of 1843, which suddenly appeared in our sky, was so brilliant that it was seen by many observers at noon time, within a few degrees from the Sun.   I remember that I myself saw this remarkable object in the day time, with a number of persons, who were gazing at the wonderful apparition.   So brilliant was this comet, that besides its nucleus and head, a portion of its tail was also visible in the day time, provided the observer screened his eyes from the full sunlight by standing in the shadow of some building.

Of all the bodies revolving around the Sun, none have been known to approach so near its surface as did the comet of 1843. When it arrived at perihelion, the distance from the centre of its nucleus to the surface of the Sun's photosphere was only 96,000 miles, while the distance from surface to surface was less than 60,000 miles.   This comet, then, went through the solar atmosphere, and in traversing it with its tremendous velocity of 366 miles per second, may very possibly have swept through some solar protuberances, many of which attain much higher elevations than that at which the comet passed.   The comet of 1680 also approached quite near the surface of the Sun, and near enough to encounter some of the high solar protuberances, its distance at perihelion being about two-thirds of the Moon's distance from the Earth.   The rapidity of motion of the comet of 1843 was such, when it approached the Sun, that it swept through all that part of its orbit which is situated north of the plane of the ecliptic in a little more than two hours, moving in this short time from one node to the other, or 180°.

But if some comets have a very short perihelion distance, that of others is considerable.   Such a comet was that of 1729, whose perihelion distance was 383,000,000 miles, the perihelion point being situated between the orbits of Mars and Jupiter.

While some comets come near enough to the Sun at perihelion to be volatilized by its intense heat, others recede so far from it at aphelion that they may be said to be frozen. The shortest cometary aphelion distance known is that of Encke's comet, whose greatest distance from the sun is 388,000,000 miles. But that of the comet of 1844 is 406,000,000,000 miles from the Sun. The comets of 1863 and 1864 are so remote in space when they reach their aphelion points that light, with its velocity of 185,500 miles a second, would require 171 days in the first case, and 230 in the last, to pass from them to the Earth.

The period of revolution of different comets also varies immensely. While that of Encke's comet is only 3½ years, that of comet 1864, II., is 280,000 years.

Among the periodic comets of short period, some have exhibited highly interesting phenomena. Encke's comet, discovered in 1818, is remarkable for the fact that its period of revolution diminishes at each of its successive returns, and consequently this comet, with each revolution, approaches nearer and nearer to the Sun. The decrease of the period is about 2½ hours at each return. Although the decrease is small, if it go on in future as it does at present, the inevitable consequence will be that this comet will finally fall into the Sun. This curious phenomenon of retardation has been attributed by astronomers to the existence of a resisting medium filling space, but so rare and ethereal that it does not produce any sensible effect on the movements of the planets. But some other causes may retard this comet, as similar retardations have not been observed in the case of other periodic comets of short period. These, however, are not so near to the Sun, and perhaps our luminary may be surrounded by matter of extreme tenuity, which does not exist at a greater distance from it.

Another of the periodic comets which has exhibited a very remarkable phenomenon of transformation is Biela's comet, which divided into two distinct parts, moving together in the same direction. When this comet was first detected at its return in 1845, it presented nothing unusual, but in the early part of 1846 it was noticed by several astronomers to be divided into two parts of unequal brightness, forming thus a twin comet. At its next return in 1852, the two sister comets were still traveling in company, but their distance apart, which in 1846 was 157,000 miles, had increased to 1,500,000 miles. · At the two next returns in 1859 and 1865, their position not being very favorably situated for observation, the comets were not seen. In 1872 the position should have been favorable for observation, and they were consequently searched for, but in vain ; neither comet was found. An astronomer in the southern hemisphere, however, found a comet on the track of Biela's, but calculation has shown that the two objects are probably not identical, since this comet was two months behind the computed position for Biela's. It will be shown in the following chapter that our globe probably crossed the orbit of Biela's comet on November 27th, 1872, and the phenomena resulting from this passage will be there described.

It is seen from these observations that comets may be lost or dissipated in space by causes entirely unknown to us. Biela's comet is not the only one which has been thus disintegrated. Ancient historians speak of the separation of large comets into two or more parts. In 1661 Hevelius observed the apparent division of the comet of that year and its reduction to fragments. The return of this comet, calculated for 1790, was vainly waited for ; the comet was not seen.

Other comets, whose periods of revolution were well known, have disappeared, probably never to return. Such is Lexell's comet, whose period was $5\frac{6}{10}$ years ; also De Vico's comet, both of which are now lost. It is supposed that Lexell's comet, which passed twice very near the giant planet Jupiter, had its orbit changed from an ellipse to a parabola, by the powerful disturbing influence of this planet, and was thus lost from our system. Several other comets, in traveling over their different orbits, have approached near enough to Saturn, Jupiter and the Earth to have their orbits decidedly altered by the powerful attraction of these bodies.

But since comets are liable to pass near the planets, and several have orbits which approach that of the Earth, it becomes important for us to know whether an encounter of such a body with our globe is possible, and what would then be the result for us. Although that knowledge would not enable us to modify the possibilities of an encounter, yet it is better to know the dangers of our navigation through space than to ignore them. This question of a collision of the Earth with a comet has been answered in different ways, according to the ideas entertained in regard to the mass of these bodies. While some have predicted calamities of all kinds, such as deluges, conflagrations, or the reduction of the Earth to incandescent gases, others have asserted that it would produce no more effect than does a fly on encountering a railroad train. In our days astronomers entertain very little fears from such an encounter, because the probabilities of danger from an occurrence of this sort are very slight, the mass of an ordinary comet being so small compared with that of our globe. We know with certainty that the Earth has never had an encounter with a comet *by which it has been transformed into gases*, at least within the several millions of years during which animal and vegetable life have left their marks upon the stony pages of its history, otherwise these marks would not now be seen. If, then, such an accident has not happened during this long period, the chances for its occurring must be very small, so small indeed that they might almost be left out of the question. It is true that our globe shows signs of great perturbations of its surface, but we have not the slightest proofs that they resulted from an encounter with a celestial body. It seems very probable that our globe passed through the tail of the comet of 1861, before it was first seen on June 29th ; but nothing unusual was observed, except perhaps some phosphorescent light in the atmosphere, which was afterwards attributed to this cause.

The density and mass of comets must be comparatively very small. Their tails consist of matter of such extreme tenuity that it affects but very little the light of the small stars over which they pass. The coma and nucleus, however, are not quite so transparent, and may have greater masses. On several occasions I have seen the light of stars reduced by the interposition of cometary matter, comet 1881, III., presenting remarkable cases of this sort. On July 8th, at 10h. 50m., several small stars were involved in this comet, one of which passed quite near the nucleus through the bright inner coma. At that time the comet was greatly disturbed, its nucleus was contracting and enlarging rapidly, and becoming bright and again faint in an instant. Every time that the nucleus grew larger, the star became invisible, but reappeared the moment the nucleus was reduced in size. This phenomenon could not be attributed to an atmospheric effect, since, while the nucleus was enlarging, a very small inner nucleus was visible within the large diffused one, the matter of which had apparently spread over the part of the coma in which the star was involved, making it invisible.

That the mass of comets is small, is proved by the fact that they have sometimes passed near the planets without disturbing them in any sensible manner. Lexell's comet, which in 1770 remained four months very near Jupiter, did not affect in the least the orbits, or the motions of its satellites. The same comet also came within less than 1,500,000 miles from the Earth, and on this occasion it was calculated that its mass could not have been the $\frac{1}{5000}$ part of that of our globe, since otherwise the perturbations which it would have caused in the elements of the Earth's orbit would have been sensible. There was, however, no change. If this comet's mass had been equal to that of our globe, the length of our year would have been increased by 2h. 47m. The comet of 1837 remained four days within 3,500,000 miles of the Earth, with no sensible effect.

It seems quite difficult to admit that the denser part of a comet forming the nucleus is solid, as supposed by some physicists, since it is so rapidly contracted and dilated by the solar forces, while the comet is yet at a too great distance from the Sun to allow these effects to be attributed to solar heat alone. This part of a comet, as indeed the other parts, seems rather to be in the gaseous than in the solid state ; the changes observed in the intensity of its light and in its structure may be conceived as due to some solar action partaking of the nature of electricity.

It has been a question whether comets are self-luminous, or whether they simply reflect the solar light. When their light is analyzed by the spectroscope, it is found that the nucleus of a comet generally gives a continuous spectrum, while the coma and tail give a spectrum consisting of several bright diffused bands. The spectrum given by the nucleus is rarely bright enough to allow the dark lines of the solar spectrum to be discerned upon it ; but such lines were reported in the spectrum of comet 1881, III., a fact proving that this nucleus at least reflected some solar light. The nucleus of a comet may be partly self-luminous, and either solid, liquid, or composed of incandescent gases submitted to a great pressure. As to the coma and tail, they are evidently gaseous, and partly, if not entirely, self-luminous, as is proved by the band spectrum which they give. The position of these bands, moreover, indicates that the luminous gases of which they are composed contain carbon. The phenomena of polarization, however, seem to prove that these parts of comets also reflect some solar light.

No theory so far proposed, to explain comets and the strange phenomena they exhibit, seems to have been successful in its attempts, and the mystery in which these bodies have been involved from the beginning of their apparition, seems to be now nearly as great as ever. It has been supposed that their tails have no real existence, but are due to an optical illusion. Prof. Tyndall has endeavored to explain cometary phenomena by supposing these bodies to be composed of vapors subject to decomposition by the solar radiations, and thus made visible, the head and tail being an actinic cloud due to such decompositions. According to this view, the tails of comets would not consist of matter projected into space, but simply of matter precipitated by the solar rays in traversing the cometary nebulosity. The endeavor has also been made to explain the various phenomena presented by comets by an electrical action of the Sun on the gases composing these objects. Theories taking this as a base seem to us to be more likely to lead to valuable results. M. Faye, who has devoted much time and learning to this subject, assumes a real repulsive force of the Sun, acting inversely to the square of the distance and proportionally to the surface, and not to the mass as attraction does. He supposes, however, that this repulsive force is generated by the solar heat, and not by electricity. Prof. Wm. Harkness says that many circumstances seem to indicate that the comets' tails are due, in a great measure, to electrical phenomena.

The fact that the tails of comets are better defined and brighter on the forward side, associated with the other fact that they curve the most when their motion is most rapid, sufficiently indicates that these appendages are material, and that they either encounter some resistance from the medium in which they move, or from a solar repulsion. The phenomena of condensation and extension, which I have observed in the comets of 1874 and 1881, added to the curious behavior exhibited by the jets issuing from the nucleus, seem to indicate the action of electrical forces rather than of heat. The main difficulty encountered in the framing of a theory of comets consists in explaining how so delicate and extended objects as their tails seem to be, can be transported and whirled around the Sun at their perihelion with such an enormous velocity, always keeping opposite to the Sun, and, as expressed by Sir John Herschel, "in defiance of the law of gravitation, nay, even of the received laws of motion."

To consider the direction of the comets' tails as an indirect effect of attraction, seems out of the question ; the phenomenon of repulsion so plainly exhibited by these objects seems to point to a positive solar repulsion, as alone competent to produce these great changes. The repulsive action of the Sun on comets' tails might be conceived, for instance, as acting in a manner similar to that of a powerful current of wind starting from the Sun, and constantly changing in direction, but always keeping on a line with the comet. Such a current, acting on a comet's tail as if it were a pennant, would drive it behind the nucleus just as observed. If it could once be ascertained that the great disturbances on comets correspond with the magnetic disturbances on our globe and with the display of the auroral light, the electric nature of the forces acting so strangely on the comets would be substantially demonstrated. I have shown that some of the great disturbances observed in the comets of 1874 and 1881 have coincided with auroral displays, and it will be shown hereafter that similar displays have also coincided with the passage of meteoric showers through our atmosphere. Whether these simultaneous phenomena were simple coincidences having no connection, or whether they are the result of a common cause, can only be ascertained by long continued future observations.

SHOOTING-STARS AND METEORS.

PLATE XII.

WHILE contemplating the heavens on a clear moonless night, we occasionally witness the sudden blazing forth of a star-like meteor, which glides swiftly and silently across some of the constellations, and as suddenly disappears, leaving sometimes along its track a phosphorescent trail, which remains visible for a while and gradually vanishes. These strange apparitions of the night are called *Falling* or *Shooting-stars*.

There is certainly no clear night throughout the year during which some of these meteors do not make their appearance, but their number is quite variable. In ordinary nights only four or five will be observed by a single person in the course of an hour ; but on others they are so numerous that it becomes impossible to count them. When the falling stars are only a few in number, and appear scattered in the sky, they are called *Sporadic Meteors*, and when they appear in great numbers they constitute *Meteoric Showers* or *Swarms*.

Probably there is no celestial phenomenon more impressive than are these wonderful pyrotechnic displays, during which the heavens seem to break open and give passage to fiery showers, whose luminous drops describe fantastic hieroglyphics in the sky. While observing them, one can fully realize the terror with which they have sometimes filled beholders, to whom it seemed that the stability of the universe had come to an end, and that all the stars of the firmament were pouring down upon the Earth in deluges of fire.

The ancients have left record of many great meteoric displays, and the manner in which they describe them sufficiently indicates the fear caused by these mysterious objects. Among the many meteoric showers recorded by ancient historians may be mentioned one observed in Constantinople, in the month of November, 472, when all the sky appeared as if on fire with meteors. In the year 599, meteors were seen on a certain night flying in all directions like fiery grasshoppers, and giving much alarm to the people. In March, 763, "the stars fell suddenly, and in such crowded number that people were much frightened, and believed the end of the world had come." On April 10th, 1095, the stars fell in such enormous quantity from midnight till morning that they were as crowded as are the hail stones during a severe storm.

In modern times the fall of the shooting-stars in great number has been frequently recorded. One of the most remarkable meteoric showers of the eighteenth century occurred on the night of. November 13th, 1799, and was observed throughout North and South America and Europe. On this memorable night thousands of falling stars were seen traversing the sky between midnight and morning. Humboldt and Boupland, then traveling in South America, observed the phenomena at Cumana, between two and five o'clock in the morning. They saw an innumerable number of shooting-stars going from north to south, appearing like brilliant fire-works. Several of these meteors left long phosphorescent trails in the sky, and had nuclei whose apparent diameter, in some cases, surpassed that of the Moon.

The shower of November 13th, 1833, was still more remarkable for the great number of meteors which traversed the heavens, and was visible over the whole of North and South America. On that occasion the falling stars were far too numerous to be counted, and they fell so thickly that Prof. Olmsted, of New Haven, who observed them carefully, compared their number at the moment of their maximum fall to half that of the flakes of snow falling during a heavy storm. This observer estimated at 240,000 the number of meteors which must have traversed the heavens above the horizon during the seven hours while the display was visible.

In the years 1866, 1867 and 1868, there were also extraordinary meteoric displays on the night of November 13th. It was on the last mentioned date that I had the opportunity to observe the remarkable shower of shooting-stars of which I have attempted to represent all the characteristic points in Plate XII. My observations were begun a little after midnight, and continued without interruption till sun-rise. Over three thousand meteors were observed during this interval of time in the part of the sky visible from a northern window of my house. The maximum fall occurred between four and five o'clock, when they appeared at a mean rate of 15 in a minute.

In general, the falling stars were quite large, many being supe-

rior to Jupiter in brightness and apparent size, while a few even surpassed Venus, and were so brilliant that opaque objects cast a strong
shadow during their flight. A great many left behind them a luminous train, which remained visible for more or less time after the
nucleus had vanished. In general, these meteors appeared to move
either in straight or slightly curved orbits ; but quite a number
among them exhibited very extraordinary motions, and followed
very complicated paths, some of which were quite incomprehensible.

While some moved either in wavy or zig-zag lines, strongly
accentuated, others, after moving for a time in a straight line, gradually changed their course, curving upward or downward, thus
moving in a new direction. Several among them, which were apparently moving in a straight line with great rapidity, suddenly
altered their course, starting at an abrupt angle in another direction, with no apparent slackening in their motion. One of them,
which was a very conspicuous object, was moving slowly in a
straight course, when of a sudden it made a sharp turn and continued to travel in a straight line, at an acute angle with the first,
retreating, and almost going back towards the regions from which
it originally came. As nearly all the meteors which exhibited these
extraordinary motions left the trace of their passage in the sky by a
luminous trail, it was easily ascertained that these appearances were
not deceptive. On one occasion I noticed that the change of direction in the orbit corresponded with the brightening up of the meteor
thus disturbed in its progress.

Among these meteors, some traveled very slowly, and a few
seemed to advance as if by jerks, but in general they moved very
rapidly. One of the meteors thus appearing to move by jerks left a
luminous trail, upon which the various jerks seemed to be left impressed by a succession of bright and faint spaces along the train.
Some of the largest meteors appeared to rotate upon an axis as
they advanced, and most of these revolving meteors, as also a great
number of the others, seemed to explode just before they disappeared, sending bright fiery sparks of different colors in all directions, although no sound was at any time heard. The largest and
most brilliant meteor observed on that night appeared at 5h. 30m.,
a little before sunrise. It was very bright, and appeared considerably larger than Venus, having quite a distinct disk. This meteor
moved very slowly, leaving behind a large phosphorescent trail,
which seemed to issue from the inside of the nucleus as it advanced.
For a moment the train increased in size and brightness close to
the nucleus, which then appeared as an empty transparent sphere,

sprinkled all over with minute fiery sparks ; the nucleus then suddenly burst out into luminous particles, which immediately vanished, only the luminous trail of considerable dimensions being left.

Many of the trails thus left by the meteors retained their luminosity for several minutes, and sometimes for over a quarter of an
hour.   These trails slowly changed their form and position; but it
is perhaps remarkable that almost all those which I observed on
that night assumed the same general form—that of an open, irregular ring, or horse-shoe, somewhat resembling the letter C.   This
ring form was subsequently transformed into an irregular, roundish
cumulus-like cloud.   The trail left by a very large meteor, which
I observed on the evening of September 5th, 1880, also exhibited
the same general character of transformation.

While I was observing a long brilliant trail left by a meteor
on the night of November 13th, 1868, it was suddenly crossed by
another bright shooting-star.   The latter apparently went through
the luminous substance forming the trail, which was suddenly altered
in form, and considerably diminished in brightness simultaneously
with this passage, although electrical action at some distance might
perhaps as well explain the sudden change observed.

In the majority of cases the meteors appeared white; but many,
especially the largest, exhibited a variety of brilliant colors, among
which the red, blue, green, yellow and purple were the most common.   In general the trails exhibited about the same color as the
nucleus, but much fainter, and they were usually pervaded by a
greenish tint.   In some instances the trails were of quite a different
color from the nucleus.

The luminous cloud observed at 5h. 30m. on the morning of November 14th, 1868, after having passed through the series of transformations above described, remained visible for a long while after
sunrise, appearing then as a small cirrus cloud, exactly similar in
appearance to the hundreds of small cirrus clouds then visible in the
sky, which had probably the same meteoric origin.   For over three
hours after sunrise, these cirrus clouds remained visible in the sky,
moving all together with the wind in the high regions of the atmosphere.

Although Plate XII. is intended to represent all the characteristics exhibited by the meteors observed on that night, every form
represented having been obtained by direct observation, yet the
number is much greater than it was at any single moment during
the particular shower of 1868.   As regards number, the intention
was to give an idea of a great meteoric shower, such as that of 1833,

for instance. Although many of the falling stars seem to be close to the Earth's surface, yet this is only an effect of perspective due to their great distance, very few of these meteors ever coming into the lower regions of our atmosphere at all.

The phenomena exhibited during other great meteoric showers have been similar to those presented by the shower just described, the only differences consisting in variations of size and brightness in the meteors, and also in the trails, which sometimes are not so numerous as they were in 1868.

While some shooting-stars move so rapidly that they can hardly be followed in their orbits, others move so slowly that the sight can easily follow them, and even remark the peculiarities of their movements, some remaining visible for half a minute. Some of the falling stars move at the rapid rate of 100 miles a second, but others only 10 miles a second, and even less. In general, they move about half as fast again as the Earth in its orbit. The arcs described by the meteors in the sky are variable. While some extend 80° and even 100°, others are hardly half a degree in length. While some shooting-stars are so faint that they can hardly be seen through the largest telescopes, others are so large and brilliant that they can be seen in the day-time. In general, a shooting-star of average brightness resembles a star of the third or fourth magnitude.

Whatever may be the origin of the shooting-stars, they are, when we see them, not in the celestial spaces, like the planets, the comets, or the stars, but in our atmosphere, through which they travel as long as they remain visible. The height at which they appear and disappear is variable, but in general they are about 80 miles above the surface of our globe when they are first seen, and at about 55 miles when they disappear. In many cases, however, they have been observed at greater elevations, as also at smaller. A meteor simultaneously observed at two different stations first appeared at the height of 285 miles, and was last seen at 192 miles above the Earth's surface; but in rare cases the falling stars have been seen below a layer of clouds completely covering the sky. I myself saw one such shooting-star a few years since. The fact that the meteors are visible at so great elevations, proves that our atmosphere extends much farther than was formerly supposed, although at these great heights it must be extremely rarefied, and very different from what it is in its lower regions.

There is a remarkable difference between the sporadic meteors seen in the sky on every night, and the meteoric showers observed only at comparatively rare intervals. While the first appear from different points in the sky and travel in all directions, being perfectly independent, the meteors of a shower all come from the same point of the heavens, from which they apparently diverge in all directions. This point of divergence of the meteors is called the *radiant point* of the shower. Although the meteors seem to diverge in all directions from the radiant point, yet they all move in approximately parallel lines, the divergence being an effect of perspective.

Whatever may be the position of the radiant point in the constellations, it remains as fixed in the sky as the stars themselves, and participates with them in the apparent motion which they undergo by the effect of the diurnal motion, and thus rises and sets with the constellation to which it belongs. This fact is sufficient to prove that the orbits of these meteors are independent of the Earth's motion, and that consequently they do not originate in our atmosphere. It has been shown by Encke that the radiant point of the meteoric shower of November 13th is precisely the point towards which our globe moves in space on November 13th; a tangent to the Earth's orbit would pass through this radiant point.

The meteoric showers are particularly remarkable, not merely because of the large number of meteors which are visible and the fact that they all follow a common orbit, but chiefly because they have a periodic return, either after an interval of a year, or after a lapse of several years. At the beginning of the present century only two meteoric showers were known, those of August 10th and of November 13th, and their periodicity had not yet been recognized, although it had begun to be suspected. It was only in 1836 that Quetelet and Olbers ventured to predict the reappearance of the November meteors in the year 1867. Having made further investigations, Prof. Newton, of Yale College, announced their return in the year 1866. In both of these years, as also in 1868, the meteors were very numerous, and were observed in Europe and in America on the night of November 13th. The predictions having thus been fulfilled, the periodicity of the meteors was established. Since then, other periodic showers have been recognized, although they are much less important in regard to number than those of August and November, except that of November 27th, which exhibited so brilliant a display in Europe in 1872. These successive appearances have established the main fact that meteoric showers are more or less visible every year when the Earth occupies certain positions in its orbit.

The meteoric shower of the 10th of August has its radiant point situated in the vicinity of the variable star Algol, in the constellation Perseus, from which its meteors have received the name of Perseids. Although varying in splendor, this meteoric swarm never fails to make its appearance every year. The Perseids move through our atmosphere at the rate of 37 miles per second. The shower usually lasts about six hours.

The meteoric shower of November 13th has its radiant point situated in the vicinity of the star Gamma, in the constellation Leo, from which its meteors have been called Leonids. But while the August meteors recur regularly every year, with slight variations, the shower of November does not occur with the same regularity. During several years it is hardly noticeable, and is even totally absent, while in other years it is very remarkable. Every 33 years an extraordinary meteoric shower occurs on the 13th of November, and the phenomenon is repeated on the two succeeding years at the same date, but with a diminution in its splendor at each successive return. The Leonids move in an opposite direction to that of the Earth, and travel in our atmosphere with an apparent velocity of 45 miles per second, this being about the maximum velocity observed in falling stars. But when the motion of our globe is taken into account, and a deduction is made of the 18 miles which it travels per second, it is found that these meteors move at an actual mean rate of 27 miles a second.

In a meteoric shower the stars do not fall uniformly throughout the night, there being a time when they appear in greater numbers. Usually it is towards morning, between 4 and 6 o'clock, that the maximum occurs. The probable cause of this phenomenon will be explained in its place hereafter.

The orbits of the meteoric showers are not all approximately in the same plane, like those of the planets, but rather resemble those of comets, and have all possible inclinations to the ecliptic. Like the comets, too, the different meteoric showers have either direct or retrograde motion.

The shooting-stars were formerly considered as atmospheric meteors, caused by the combustion of inflammable gases generated at the surface of the Earth, and transported to the high regions of our atmosphere by their low specific gravity. But the considerable height at which they usually appear, the great velocity of their motion, the common orbit followed by the meteors of the same shower, and the periodicity of their recurrence, do not permit us now to entertain these ideas, or to doubt their cosmical origin. But what is their nature?

It is now generally admitted that innumerable minute bodies, moving in various directions around the Sun, are scattered in the interplanetary spaces through which our globe travels. It has been supposed that congregations of such minute bodies form elliptical rings, within which they are all moving in close parallel orbits around the Sun. On the supposition that such rings intersect the orbit of the Earth at the proper places, it was practicable to account for the shooting-stars by the passage through our atmosphere of the numerous minute cosmical bodies composing the rings, and the Leonid and Perseid showers were so explained. But when the elements of the orbits of these two last swarms came to be better known, and were compared with those of other celestial bodies, it was found necessary to alter this theory.

It had for a long while been suspected that some kind of relation existed between the shooting-stars and the comets. This idea, vaguely formulated by Kepler more than two centuries ago, more clearly expressed by Chladni, and still more by Mr. Grey, before the British Association, at Liverpool, in 1855, has recently received a brilliant confirmation by the researches of Professor Schiaparelli, Director of the Observatory of Milan. A thorough investigation of the orbits of the August and November meteors led Schiaparelli to the discovery of a remarkable relation between meteoric and cometary orbits. By comparing the elements of these meteoric orbits with those of comets, he found a very close resemblance between the orbit of the August meteors and that of the comet 1862, III.; and again between the orbit of the November meteors and that of Tempel's comet, 1866, I. These resemblances were too striking to be the result of mere chance, and demonstrated the identity of these cometary orbits with those of the Perseid and Leonid showers. In accordance with these new facts, it is now admitted that the meteoric showers result from the passage of our globe through swarms of meteoric particles following the orbits of comets, which intersect the orbit of the Earth.

Professor Schiaparelli has attempted to show how these meteoric swarms were originally scattered along the orbits of comets, by supposing these bodies to originate from nebulous masses, which, in entering the sphere of attraction of the Sun, are gradually scattered along their orbits, and finally form comets followed by long trails of meteoric particles.

It has been shown that in approaching the Sun the comets become considerably elongated, their particles being disseminated over immense distances by the solar repulsion. It seems probable that, owing to its feeble attractive power, the nucleus is incompetent to recall the scattered cometary particles and retain them in its grasp when they are relieved from the solar repulsion, so that they remain free from the nucleus, although they continue to move along its orbit. It is supposable that these cometary particles will scatter more and more in course of time. Forming at first an elongated meteoric cloud, they will finally spread along the whole orbit, and thus form a ring of meteoric particles. Since our globe constantly moves in its orbit and daily occupies a different position, it follows that at any point where such a cometary orbit happens to cross that of the Earth, our globe will necessarily encounter the cometary particles as a shower of meteors. This encounter will take place at a certain time of the year, either yearly, if they form a continuous ring, or after a succession of years, if they simply form an elongated cloud. Such meteoric clouds or rings would not be visible in ordinary circumstances, even through the largest telescopes, except on penetrating the upper regions of our atmosphere, when they would appear as showers of falling stars. It is supposed that in penetrating our atmosphere, even in its most rarefied regions, these meteors are heated by the resistance offered by the air to their motion, first becoming luminous and then being finally vaporized and burnt before they can reach the surface of the Earth.

The orbit of the comet of 1862, III., which so closely corresponds with that of the Perseid meteors, is much more extended than that of Tempel's comet corresponding with that of the Leonids. While the first extends far beyond the orbit of Neptune, the latter only goes a little beyond that of Uranus. The former orbit makes a considerable angle with the plane of the Earth's orbit, but the latter is much nearer to parallelism with it. The period of revolution of the first is 108 years, and that of the last about 33¼ years.

From the fact that the Perseid shower occurs yearly on the 10th of August, when the Earth crosses the orbit of the comet of 1862, III., it is supposed that the cometary particles producing this shower are disseminated along the whole orbit, and form a ring encircling the Sun and Earth. To explain the yearly variations in the number of the shooting-stars observed, these particles are supposed to be unequally distributed over the orbit, being more crowded at one place than they are at another. In order to explain the meteoric shower of Leonids, which appears in all its splendor every 33 years, and then with diminished intensity for two successive years, after which it is without importance, it is supposed that the cometary particles of the comet of 1866, I., have not as yet spread all along the orbit, a sufficient time not having been allowed, but form an elongated meteoric cloud, more dense in its front than in its rear part. From these considerations it has been supposed also that the comet of 1866, I., is of a more recent date than that of 1862, III. While Tempel's comet makes its revolution around the Sun in about 33 years, this meteoric cloud, which has the same period and returns to the same point of its orbit every 33 years, encounters our globe for three successive years. The first year we are passing through its densest parts, and the two following years in less and less crowded parts, from which result the observed phenomena. An idea of the extent of this meteoric cloud may be formed from the fact that, with its cometary velocity of motion, it takes this cloud three years at least to cross the Earth's orbit. From recent researches it would appear that the Leonid cloud is not single, but that at least two others of smaller importance exist, and have periods of $33\frac{1}{4}$ years.

Biela's comet, which was divided into two parts in 1846, is another of the few comets whose orbit approaches that of the Earth. Possessing this knowledge, and knowing then the close connection existing between meteors and comets, astronomers supposed that there were sufficient reasons to expect a meteoric shower when this comet was passing near the Earth. They consequently expected a meteoric display in 1872, when our globe was to cross its orbit. Their anticipation was plainly fulfilled, and on the night of November 27th, 1872, a splendid meteoric display, having its radiant point in the constellation Andromeda, was observed in Europe, and also in America, but the meteors seen here were not so numerous as in Europe. Other meteoric showers of less importance, such as that of April 20th, for instance, have also been identified with cometary orbits, so that now no doubt seems to remain as to the identity of cometary particles and shooting-stars.

The fact that the maximum number of meteors is always observed in the morning hours, supports the hypothesis of the cosmic origin of the shooting-stars, since the regions of the Earth where it is morning are precisely those fronting the regions towards which our globe is moving in space, and accordingly encounter more directly the meteors moving in their orbit. The greater abundance of falling stars at that time may thus be accounted for.

The number of meteors penetrating our atmosphere must be very great; there is not an hour and probably not a minute during which none fall. From various considerations, some astronomers have estimated at from 65,000,000,000 to 146,000,000,000 the total number of shooting-stars yearly penetrating in our atmosphere. The actual number is undoubtedly great, yet the fact that the meteors are rarely seen through the telescope while employed in observing various celestial objects, does not indicate that they are so numerous as these figures imply. It is only occasionally that one is seen traversing the field of the instrument. Even when the sky is observed with a low power eye-piece for several hours in succession, many nights may pass without disclosing one, although an observer, sweeping the sky more freely with the naked eye, may often perceive four or five during an ordinary night.

About the true nature of these bodies nothing is known with certainty. From spectrum analysis it seems to be established that most of them contain sodium and magnesium, while a few indicate the presence of strontium and iron, and in some rare cases there are traces of coal-gas. Some of the nuclei give a continuous spectrum, and others a spectrum of lines. The trail always gives a spectrum of bright lines which indicates its gaseous state. The traces of coal-gas rarely seen in meteors are, however, of great importance, as it identifies them more closely with the comets, which generally show a similar spectrum. The continuous spectra exhibited by some nuclei would indicate that they are incandescent and either solid or liquid; but it is difficult to conclude from their spectra what is their true nature, since we do not know exactly what part the terrestrial atmosphere may play in producing the results.

The mass of the shooting-stars is not known with certainty, but the fact that during great meteoric showers, none are seen to reach the surface of the Earth, all being consumed in a few seconds, sufficiently indicates that it must be very small. It has been calculated that those equal to Venus in apparent size and brilliancy may weigh several pounds, while the faint ones would weigh only a few grains.

If the shooting-stars have even such a mass as that here attributed to some of them, the extraordinary motions which I have described above seem to be unaccountable. The change of direction of a heavy mass moving swiftly cannot be sudden. The semi-circular, the wavy and the angular orbits observed could not be described, it would seem, by such a mass animated with a great velocity. Although the meteors are said to be ignited by the transformation of part of their progressive motion into molecular motion, yet it is not observed that the velocity of the falling stars diminishes when they are about to disappear. The luminous trails they leave in the atmosphere do not appear to be endowed with any motion, but remain for a time in their original positions. These facts are apparently opposed to the hypothesis that such meteors have any appreciable mass. The extraordinary motions exhibited by some meteors seem to indicate that some unsuspected force resides in these bodies, and causes them to deviate from the laws of ordinary motion.

Although it is very probable that the ordinary shooting-stars have no appreciable mass, yet it is known that very heavy meteoric masses sometimes fall at the surface of the Earth. Such falls are generally preceded by the sudden apparition in the sky of a large, and usually very brilliant fire-ball, which traverses the air at a great speed, sometimes leaving behind it a luminous trail, after which it explodes with a loud sound, and heavy fiery meteoric fragments, diverging in all directions, fall at the surface of the Earth. The name of *Aerolites* or *Meteorolites* is given to these ponderous fragments. As these meteors, before they explode and fall to the ground, have many points of resemblance with the shooting-stars, they are generally supposed to be connected with them, and to have a similar cometary origin. The fact that the aerolites differ widely from each other in constitution, and are all composed of substances found on the Earth, associated with other facts given below, would rather seem to indicate a terrestrial than a celestial origin.

If the aerolites belong to the same class of bodies as the falling stars, differing from them only in size and mass, it is difficult to see why so very few should fall upon the Earth during the great meteoric showers, when thousands of shooting-stars traverse our atmosphere. In Prof. Kirkwood's "Meteoric Astronomy" are given catalogues of all the falls of aerolites and fire-balls which have been observed at the time of the periodic meteoric showers of the 10th of August and the 13th of November, during a period of 221 years for the Perseids, or August showers, and of 318 years for the Leonids, or November showers. During 221 years, 10 falls of aerolites have been witnessed simultaneously with the fall of the Perseids; while during 318 years, only 4 such falls have been recorded as having occurred at the time of the Leonid shower. If there is any close connection between the shooting-stars and the aerolites, we should expect to find a maximum in their fall at the time of the great meteoric displays. So far, no maxima or minima have yet been discovered in the fall of aerolites; they do not seem, like meteoric showers, to be governed by a law of periodicity.

A very remarkable peculiarity of the aerolites is that they seem to have a tendency to fall in certain regions. Such are the southern part of France, the north of Italy, Hindostan, the central states of North America, and Mexico and Brazil. There is a curious contrast existing between the quick cometary motion of the aerolites before their explosion, and the comparatively slow motion of their fragments as they reach the Earth; motion which seems to be no greater than that corresponding to their natural fall impeded by the resistance of the air. In general, their penetration into the soil upon which they fall does not at all correspond to the great velocity with which they move in the atmosphere. The fragmentary structures of the aerolites, their identity of substance with that of our globe, their great resemblance to the volcanic minerals of the Earth, and the fractures and faults which some of them exhibit, do not correspond at all with the idea that they are cometary particles fallen on the Earth. As far as their structure and appearance is concerned, they seem rather to be a volcanic product of the interior of the Earth than parts of disintegrated comets. It must be admitted that their identity with the shooting-stars is far from established, and that they are still involved in mystery.

The so-called meteoric dust gathered at sea and on high mountains may have various origins, and may be partly furnished by volcanic dust carried to great distances in the atmosphere.

Since millions of shooting-stars penetrate our atmosphere every year and remain in it, becoming definitively a part of the Earth, it follows that, no matter how small may be the quantity of matter of which they are composed, they must gradually increase the volume and mass of our globe, although the increase may be exceedingly slow. Supposing every one of the shooting-stars penetrating our atmosphere to contain one cubic millimeter of matter, it has been calculated that it would take nearly 35,000 years to make a deposit one centimeter in thickness all over the surface of our globe. Insignificant as this may appear, it is probable that the quantity of matter of meteoric origin which is added to our globe is much less than has just been supposed.

THE MILKY-WAY OR GALAXY.

PLATE XIII.

DURING clear nights, when the Moon is below the horizon, the starry vault is greatly adorned by an immense belt of soft white light, spanning the heavens from one point of the horizon to the opposite point, and girdling the celestial sphere in its delicate folds. Every one is familiar with this remarkable celestial object, called the *Milky-way* or *Galaxy*.

Seen with the naked eye, the Galaxy appears as an irregular, narrow, nebulous belt, apparently composed of cloud-like luminous masses of different forms and sizes, separated by comparatively dark intervals. These cloud-like masses vary much in luminous intensity, and while some among them are very bright and conspicuous, others are so faint that they are hard to recognize. In general, the brightest parts of the Milky-way are situated along the middle of its belt, while its borders, which are usually very faint, gradually vanish in the sky. Some parts of the Galaxy, however, show very little of the cloudy structure so characteristic of other parts, being almost uniform throughout, except towards the borders, which are always fainter. These parts showing greater uniformity are also the faintest.

Such is the general appearance of the Milky-way on ordinary nights, but on rare occasions, when the atmosphere is particularly pure, it presents one of the grandest sights that can be imagined. At such favorable moments I have seen the Galaxy gleaming with light, and appearing as if composed of star-dust or of precious stones. The strange belt then appeared all mottled over and fleecy, its large cloud-like masses being subdivided into numerous small, irregular cloudlets of great brilliancy, which appeared projected upon a soft luminous background.

The width of the Galaxy is far from being uniform; while in some places it is only 4° or 5°, in others it is 15° and even more. In some places it appears wavy in outline, at others quite straight; then it contracts, to expand a few degrees distant ; while at other places it sends off branches and loops, varying in form, size and direction, some of which are quite prominent, while others are very faint.

Although very irregular in form, the general appearance of the galactic belt is that of a regular curve occupying one of the great circles of the celestial sphere. The Milky-way completely encircles the heavens, but, of course, only one-half is visible at any one moment, since our globe prevents the other half from being seen. If, for a moment, we imagine ourselves left in space, our globe having vanished from under our feet, we should then see the whole Galaxy forming a continuous belt in the heavens, at the centre of which we should apparently be situated.

While only one-half of the galactic belt can be seen at once from any point on the Earth, yet, according to the position of the observer, a larger or smaller portion of the whole can be seen at different times. In high northern or southern latitudes but little more than half can be seen even by continuous observations; but as we approach the equatorial regions, more and more of it becomes visible, until the whole may be seen at different hours and seasons. In the latitudes of the northern states, about two-thirds of the Galaxy is visible, the rest remaining hidden below the horizon ; but from the southern states very nearly the whole can be seen. The half of the Milky-way visible at any one time from any latitude on the Earth never entirely sets below the horizon, although in some places it may be so near the horizon as to be rendered invisible by vapors. In the latitude of Cambridge, when in its lowest position, the summit of its arc is still about 12° or 15° above the northern horizon. The great circle of the celestial sphere, occupied by the galactic belt, is inclined at an angle of about 63° to the celestial equator, and intersects this great circle on one side in the constellation Monoceros in 6h. 47m., and on the opposite side in the constellations Aquila and Ophiuchus in 18h. 47m. of right ascension; so that its northern pole is situated in the constellation Coma Berenices in R. A. 12h. 47m., declination N. 27°, and the southern in the constellation Cetus in R. A. o h. 47m., declination S. 27.°

According to the seasons and to the hours of the night at which it is observed, the galactic arch presents different inclinations in the sky. Owing to its inclination to the equator of the celestial sphere, its opposite parts exhibit opposite inclinations when they pass the meridian of a place. That part of the Galaxy which is represented on Plate XIII., and which intersects the celestial equator in the constellation Aquila, is inclined to the left or towards the east, when it is on the meridian; while the opposite part, situated in Monoceros, is inclined to the right, or towards the west, when it reaches the meridian. The former passes the meridian in the evening in the summer and autumn months; the latter, in the winter and spring months.

By beginning at its northernmost part, represented at the upper part of Plate XIII., situated in "the chair" of the constellation Cassiopeia, and descending southwardly, and continuing in the same direction until the whole circle is completed, the course of the Milky-way through the constellations may be briefly described as follows: From Cassiopeia's chair, the Galaxy, forming two streams, descends south, passing partly through Lacerta on the left, and Cepheus on the right; at this last point it approaches nearest to the polar star. Then it enters Cygnus, where it becomes very complicated and bright, and where several large cloudy masses are seen terminating its left branch, which passes to the right, near the bright star Deneb, the leader of this constellation. Below Deneb, the Galaxy is apparently disconnected and separated from the northern part by a narrow, irregular dark gap. From this rupture, the Milky-way divides into two great streams separated by an irregular dark rift. An immense branch extends to the right, which, after having formed an important luminous mass between the stars γ and β, continues its southward progress through parts of Lyra, Vulpecula, Hercules, Aquila and Ophiuchus, where it gradually terminates a few degrees south of the equator. The main stream on the left, after having formed a bright mass around ε Cygni, passes through Vulpecula and then Aquila, where it crosses the equinoctial just below the star η, after having involved in its nebulosity the bright star Altair, the leader of Aquila. In the southern hemisphere the Galaxy becomes very complicated and forms a succession of very bright, irregular masses, the upper one being in Scutum Sobieskii, while the others are respectively situated in Sagittarius and in Scorpio; the last, just a little above our horizon, being always considerably dimmed by vapors. From Scutum Sobieskii, the Galaxy expands considerably on the right, and sends a branch into Scorpio, in which the fiery red star Antares is somewhat involved.

Continuing its course below our horizon, the Milky-way enters Ara and Norma, and then, passing partly through Circinus, Centaurus and Musca, it reaches the Southern Cross, after having been divided by the large dark pear-shaped spot known to navigators as the "Coal-Sack." In Ara and Crux the Milky-way attains its maximum of brightness, which there surpasses its brightest parts in Cygnus. In Musca, it makes its nearest approach to the south pole of the heavens. It then enters Carina and Vela, where it spreads out like a fan, and terminates in this last constellation, before reaching λ, being once more interrupted by a dark and very irregular gap, on a line with the two star $s\gamma$ and λ. It is noteworthy that this second rupture of continuity of the Galaxy in Vela is very nearly opposite, or at about 180° from the break near Deneb in Cygnus.

Continuing its course on the other side of the break, the Milky-way again spreads out into the shape of a fan, grows narrower in entering Puppis, where it is longitudinally divided by darkish channels. It then passes above our southern horizon, becoming visible to us, passing through part of Canis Major, where its border just grazes the brilliant star Sirius. But from Puppis it gradually diminishes in brightness and complication, becoming faint and uniform. It enters Monoceros and Orion, where it again crosses the equator a little above δ, the northernmost of the three bright stars in the belt of Orion. Continuing its northward course it passes through Gemini, extending as far as Castor and Pollux, and then entering Auriga, where it begins to increase in brightness and in complication of structure. It passes partly through Camelopardus and into Perseus, where an important branch proceeds from its southern border.

This branch beginning near the star θ, advances towards the celebrated variable star Algol, around which it is quite bright and complicated. Continuing its course in the same direction, the branch rapidly loses its brightness, becoming very faint a little below Algol, and passing through ζ Persei, it enters Taurus, leaving the Pleiades on its extreme southern margin; and after having passed through ε, where it branches off, it rapidly curves towards the main stream, which it joins near ζ Tauri, thus forming an immense loop. The ramification projecting near ε Tauri involves in its nebulosity the ruddy star Aldebaran and the scattered group of the Hyades. It then advances towards the three bright stars δ, ε and ζ of the belt of Orion, which, together with the sextuple star θ Orionis, are involved in its faint nebulosity, and joins the main stream on the equinoctial, having thus formed a second loop, whose interior part is comparatively free from nebulosity, and contains the fine stars Betelgeuse and Bellatrix.

That portion of the main galactic stream which is comprised between the star Deneb in Cygnus, and Capella in Auriga, is divided longitudinally by a very irregular, narrow, darkish cleft, comparatively devoid of nebulosity, which, however, is interrupted at some points.   This dark gap sends short branches north and south, the most important of which are situated near ζ Cephei and β Cassiopeiæ.   Another branch runs from γ beyond ε of the constellation last mentioned.   The main stream of the Galaxy after leaving Perseus, enters Cassiopeia, and sending short branches into Andromeda, it completes its immense circle in Cassiopeia's chair, where this description was begun.

When examined through the telescope, the appearance of the Milky-way completely changes, and its nebulous light is resolved into an immense number of stars, too faint to be individually seen with the naked eye.   When Galileo first directed the telescope to the galactic belt, its nebulous, cloud-like masses were at once resolved into stars, even by the feeble magnifying power of his instrument. When, much later, Sir William Herschel undertook his celebrated star-gaugings of the Galaxy, millions of stars blazed out in his powerful telescopes.   The stars composing this great nebulous belt are so numerous that it is impossible to arrive at any definite idea as to their number.   From his soundings Herschel estimated at 116,000 the number of stars which, on one occasion, passed through the field of his telescope in 15 minutes, by the simple effect of the diurnal motion of the heavens ; and on another occasion, a number estimated at 250,000 crossed the field in 41 minutes.   In a space of 5°, comprised between β and γ Cygni, shown on Plate XIII., he found no less than 331,000 stars.   Prof. Struve has estimated at 20,500,000 the number of stars seen in the Milky-way through the twenty-foot telescope employed by Herschel in his star-gaugings.   Great as this number may seem, it is yet far below the truth; as the great modern telescopes, according to Professor Newcomb, would very probably double the number of stars seen through Herschel's largest telescope, and detect from thirty to fifty millions of stars in the Milky-way.

Although the telescope resolves the Galaxy into millions of stars, yet the largest instruments fail to penetrate its immense depths. The forty-foot telescope of Herschel, and even the giant telescope of Lord Rosse, have failed to resolve the Milky-way entirely into stars, the most distant ones appearing in them as nebulosities upon which the nearer stars are seen projected, the galactic stratum being unfathomable by the largest telescopes yet made.

The stars composing the Milky-way are very unevenly distributed, as might easily be supposed from the cloud-like appearance of this belt.   In some regions they are loosely scattered, forming long rows or streams of various figures, while in others they congregate into star groups and clusters having all imaginable forms, some being compressed into very dense globular masses. The intervals left between the clustering masses are poorer in stars, and indeed some of them are even totally devoid of stars or nebulosity. Such are the great and small "coal-sacks" in the southern Galaxy. I have myself detected such a dark space devoid of stars and nebulosity in one of the brightest parts of the Milky-way, in the constellation Sagittarius, in about 17h. 45m. right ascension, and 27° 35′ south declination. It is a small miniature coal-sack or opening in the Galaxy, through which the sight penetrates beyond this great assemblage of stars. Close to this, is another narrow opening near a small, loose cluster.

Although lacking the optical resources which now enable us to recognize the structure of the Milky-way, some of the ancient philosophers had succeeded tolerably well in their speculations regarding its nature. It was the opinion of Democritus, Pythagoras and Manilius, that the Galaxy was nothing else but a vast and confused assemblage of stars, whose faint light was the true cause of its milky appearance.

Before the invention of the telescope, no well-founded theory in regard to the structure of the Milky-way could, of course, be attempted. Although Kepler entertained different ideas in regard to the structure of this great belt from those now generally admitted, yet in them may be found the starting point of the modern conception of the structure of the Galaxy and of the visible universe. In the view of this great mind, the Milky-way, with all its stars, formed a vast system, the centre of which, and of the universe, was occupied by our Sun. Kepler reasoned that the place of the Sun must be near the centre of the galactic belt, from the fact this last object appears very nearly as a great circle of the celestial sphere, and that its luminous intensity is about the same in all its parts.

Half a century later, another attempt to explain the Milky-way was made by Wright, of Durham, who rejected the idea of an accidental and confused distribution of the stars as inconsistent with the appearance of the Galaxy, and regarded them as arranged along a fundamental plane corresponding to that of the Milky-way. These ideas which were subsequently developed and enlarged by Kant, and then by Lambert, constitute what is now known as Kant's theory. According to this theory, the stars composing the Galaxy are conceived as being uniformly arranged between two flat planes of considerable extension, but which are comparatively near together, the Sun occupying a place not very far from the centre of this immense starry stratum. As we view this system crosswise through its thinnest parts, the stars composing it appear scattered and comparatively few in number, but when we view it lengthwise, through its most extended parts, they appear condensed and extremely numerous, thus giving the impression of a luminous belt encircling the heavens. In the conception of Kant, each star was a sun, forming the centre of a planetary system. These systems are not independent, but are kept together by the bonds of universal gravitation. The Galaxy itself is one of these great systems, its principal plane being the equivalent of the zodiac in our planetary system, while a preponderant body, which might be Sirius, is the equivalent of our Sun, and keeps the galactic system together. In the universe there are other galaxies, but as they are too distant to be resolved into stars, they appear as elliptical nebulæ. Such are, in brief, the grand speculations of Kant and Lambert on the Milky-way, and the structure of the universe.

Kant's theory rested more on conjectures than on observed facts, and needed therefore the sanction of direct observations to be established on a firm basis. With this view, Sir William Herschel investigated the subject, by a long and laborious series of observations. His plan, which was that of "star-gauging," consisted in counting all the stars visible in his twenty-foot telescope, comprised in a wide belt cutting the Galaxy at right angles, and extending from one of its sides to the opposite one, thus embracing 180° of the celestial sphere. In this belt he executed 3,400 telescopic star-gaugings of a quarter of a degree each, from which he obtained 683 mean gaugings giving the stellar density of the corresponding regions.

The general result derived from this immense labor was that the stars are fewest in regions the most distant from the galactic belt; while from these regions, which correspond to the pole of the Galaxy, they gradually increase in number in approaching the Milky-way. The star density was found to be extremely variable, and while some of the telescopic gaugings detected either no star at all, or only one or two, other gaugings gave 500 stars and even more. The average number of stars in a field of view of his telescope, obtained for the six zones, each of 15°, into which Herschel divided up the portion of his observing belt, extending from the Galaxy to its pole, is as follows: In the first zone, commencing at 90° from the galactic belt and extending towards it, 4 stars per telescopic field were found; 5 in the second; 8 in the third; 14 in the fourth; 24 in the fifth and 53 in the sixth, which terminated in the

Galaxy itself. Very nearly similar results were afterwards found by Sir John Herschel, for corresponding regions in the southern hemisphere.

From these studies, Herschel concluded that the stellar system is of the general form supposed by the Kantian theory, and that its diameter must be five times as extended in the direction of the galactic plane, as it is in a direction perpendicular to it. To explain the great branch sent out by the Galaxy in Cygnus, he supposed a great cleft dividing the system edgewise, about half way from its circumference to its centre. From suppositions founded on the apparent magnitude and arrangement of stars, he estimated that it would take light about 7,000 years to reach us from the extremities of the Galaxy, and therefore 14,000 years to travel across the system, from one border to the opposite one.

But Herschel's theory concerning the Milky-way rested on the erroneous assumption that the stars are uniformly distributed in space, and also that his telescopes penetrated through the entire depth of the Galaxy. Further study showed him that his telescope of twenty feet, and even his great forty-foot telescope, which was estimated to penetrate to a distance 2,300 times that of stars of the first magnitude, failed to resolve some parts of the Galaxy into stars. Meanwhile, the structure of the Milky-way being better known, the irregular condensation of its stars became apparent, while the mutual relation existing between binary and multiple systems of stars, as also between the stars which form clusters, was recognized, as showing evidence of closer association between certain groups of stars than between the stars in general. Herschel's system, which rested on the assumption of the uniform distribution of the stars in space, and on the supposition that the telescopes used for his gauges penetrated through the greater depths of the Galaxy, being thus found to contradict the facts, was gradually abandoned by its author, who adopted another method of estimating the relative distances of the stars observed in his gaugings.

This method, founded on photometric principles, consisted in judging the penetrating power of his telescope by the brightness of the stars, and not, as formerly, by the number which they brought into view. He then studied by this new method the structure of the Milky-way and the probable distance of the clustering masses of which it is formed, concluding that the portion of the Galaxy traversing the constellation Orion is the nearest to us. This last result seems indicated by the fact that this portion of the Milky-way is the faintest and the most uniform of all the galactic belt.

More recently Otto Struve investigated the same subject, and arrived at very nearly similar conclusions, which may be briefly stated as follows : The galactic system is composed of a countless number of stars, spreading out on all sides along a very extended plane. These stars, which are very unevenly distributed, show a decided tendency to cluster together into individual groups of different sizes and forms, separated by comparatively vacant spaces. This layer where the stars congregate in such vast numbers may be conceived as a very irregular flat disk, sending many branches in various directions, and having a diameter eight or ten times its thickness. The size of this starry disk cannot be determined, since it is unfathomable in some directions, even when examined with the largest telescopes. The Sun, with its attending planets, is involved in this immense congregation of suns, of which it forms but a small particle, occupying a position at some distance from the principal plane of the Galaxy. According to Struve, this distance is approximately equal to 208,000 times the radius of the Earth's orbit. The Milky-way is mainly composed of star-clusters, two-thirds, perhaps, of the whole number visible in the heavens being involved in this great belt. In conclusion, our Sun is only one of the individual stars which constitute the galactic system, and each of these stars itself is a sun similar to our Sun. These individual suns are not independent, but are associated in groups varying in number from a few to several thousands, the Galaxy itself being nothing but an immense aggregation of such clusters, whose whole number of individual suns probably ranges between thirty and fifty millions. In this vast system our globe is so insignificant that it cannot even be regarded as one of its members. According to Dr. Gould, there are reasons to believe that our Sun is a member of a small, flattened, bifid cluster, composed of more than 400 stars, ranging between the first and seventh magnitude, its position in this small system being eccentric, but not very far from the galactic plane.

The study of the Milky-way, of which Plate XIII. is only a part, was undertaken to answer a friendly appeal made by Mr. A. Marth, in the Monthly Notices of the Royal Astronomical Society, in 1872. I take pleasure in offering him my thanks for the suggestion, and for the facility afforded me in this study by his " List of Co-ordinates of Stars within and near the Milky-way," which was published with it.

THE STAR-CLUSTERS.

PLATE XIV.

It is a well-known fact that the stars visible to the naked eye are very unequally distributed in the heavens, and that while they are loosely scattered in some regions, in others they are comparatively numerous, sometimes forming groups in which they appear quite close together.

In our northern sky are found a few such agglomerations of stars, which are familiar objects to all observers of celestial objects. In the constellation Coma Berenices, the stars are small, but quite condensed, and form a loosely scattered, faint group. In Taurus, the Hyades and the Pleiades, visible during our winter nights, are conspicuous and familiar objects which cannot fail to be recognized. In the last group, six stars may be easily detected by ordinary eyes on any clear night, but more can sometimes be seen; on rare occasions, when the sky was especially favorable, I have detected eleven clearly and suspected several others. The six stars ordinarily visible, are in order of decreasing brightness, as follows : Alcyone, Electra, Atlas, Maia, Taygeta and Merope. Glimpses of Celano and Pleione are sometimes obtained.

When the sky is examined with some attention on any clear, moonless night, small, hazy, luminous patches, having a cometary aspect, are visible here and there to the naked eye. In the constellation Cancer is found one of the most conspicuous, called Præsepe, which forms a small triangle with the two stars γ and δ. In Perseus, and involved in the Milky-way, is found another luminous cloud, situated in the sword-handle, and almost in a line with the two stars γ and δ of Cassiopeia's Chair. In the constellation Hercules, another nebulous mass of light, but fainter, is also visible between the stars η and ζ, where it appears as a faint comet, in the depths of space. In Ophiuchus and Monoceros are likewise found hazy, luminous patches. In the southern sky, several such objects are also visible to the naked eye, being found in Sagittarius, in Canis Major and in Puppis; but the most conspicuous are those in Centaurus and Toucan.   That in Centaurus involves the star ω in its pale diffused nebulosity, and that in Toucan is involved in the lesser Magellanic cloud.

When the telescope is directed to these nebulous objects, their hazy, ill-defined aspect disappears, and they are found to consist of individual stars of different magnitudes, which being more or less closely grouped together, apparently form a system of their own. These groups, which are so well adapted to give us an insight into the structure and the vastness of the stellar universe, are called *Star-clusters*.

Star-clusters are found of all degrees of aggregation, and while in some of them, such as in the Pleiades, in Præsepe and in Perseus, the stars are so loosely scattered that an opera glass, and even the naked eye, will resolve them; in others, such as in those situated in Hercules, Aquarius, Toucan and Centaurus, they are so greatly compressed that even in the largest telescopes they appear as a confused mass of blazing dust, in which comparatively few individual stars can be distinctly recognized.   Although only about a dozen Star-clusters can be seen in the sky with the naked eye, yet nearly eleven hundred such objects visible through the telescope, have been catalogued by astronomers.

The stars composing the different clusters visible in the heavens vary greatly in number, and while in some clusters there are only a few, in others they are so numerous and crowded that it would be idle to try to count them, their number amounting to several thousands.   It has been calculated by Herschel that some clusters are so closely condensed, that in an area not more than $\frac{1}{10}$ part of that covered by the Moon, at least 5,000 stars are agglomerated.

When the group in the Pleiades is seen through the telescope it appears more important than it does to the naked eye, and several hundreds of stars are found in it.   In a study of Tempel's nebula, which is involved in the Pleiades, I have mapped out 250 stars, mostly comprised within this nebula, with the telescope of $6\frac{1}{2}$ inches aperture, which I have used for this study.

As a type of a loose, coarse cluster, that in Perseus is one of the finest of its class.   It appears to the naked eye as a single object, but in the telescope it has two centres of condensation, around which cluster a great number of bright stars, forming various curves and festoons of great beauty.   Among its components are found several yellow and red stars, which give a most beautiful contrast of colors in this gorgeous and sparkling region.   In a study which I have made of this twin cluster, I have mapped out 664 stars belonging to it, among which are two yellow and five red stars.

While some clusters, like those just described, are very easily resolvable into stars with the smallest instruments, others yield with the greatest difficulty, even to the largest telescopes, in which their starry nature is barely suspected. Owing to this peculiarity, star-clusters are usually divided into two principal classes. In the first class are comprised all the clusters which have been plainly resolved into stars, and in the second all those which, although not plainly resolvable with the largest instruments now at our disposal, show a decided tendency to resolvability, and convey the impression that an increase of power in telescopes is the only thing needed to resolve them into stars. Of course this classification, which depends on the power of telescopes to decide the nature of these objects, is arbitrary, and a classification based on spectrum analysis is now substituted for it.

The star-clusters are also divided into globular and irregular clusters, according to their general form and appearance. The globular clusters, which are the most numerous, are usually well-defined objects, more or less circular in their general outlines. The rapid increase of brightness towards their centres, where the stars composing them are greatly condensed, readily conveys the impression that the general form of these sparkling masses is globular. The irregular clusters are not so rich in stars as the former. Usually their stars are less condensed towards the centre, and are, for the most part, so loosely and irregularly distributed, that it is impossible to recognize the outlines of these clusters or to decide where they terminate. The globular clusters are usually quite easily resolvable into stars, either partly or wholly, although some among them do not show the least traces of resolvability, even in the largest instruments. This may result from different causes, and may be attributed either to the minuteness of their components or to their great distance from the Earth, many star-clusters being at such immense distances that they are beyond our means of measurement.

As has been shown in the preceding section, the star-clusters are found in great number in the Galaxy; indeed, it is in this region and in its vicinity that the greater portion of them are found. In other regions, with the exception of the Magellanic clouds, where they are found in great number and in every stage of resolution, the clusters are few and scattered.

The star-cluster in the constellation Hercules, designated as No.

4,230 in Sir J. Herschel's catalogue, and which is represented on Plate XIV., is one of the brightest and most condensed in the northern hemisphere, although it is not so extended as several others, its angular diameter being only 7' or 8'. This object, which was discovered by Halley in 1714, is one of the most beautiful of its class in the heavens. According to Herschel, it is composed of thousands of stars between the tenth and fifteenth magnitudes. Undoubtedly the stars composing this group are very numerous, although those which can be distinctly seen as individual stars, and whose position can be determined, are not so many as a superficial look at the object would lead us to suppose. From a long study of this cluster, which I have made with instruments of various apertures, I have not been able to identify more stars than are represented on the plate, although the nebulosity of which this object mainly consists, and especially the region situated towards its centre, appeared at times granular and blazing with countless points of light, too faint and too flickering to be individually recognized. Towards its centre there is quite an extended region, whose luminous intensity is very great, and which irresistibly conveys the impression of the globular structure of this cluster. Besides several outlying appendages, formed by its nebulosity, the larger stars recognized in this cluster are scattered and distributed in such a way that they form various branches, corresponding with those formed by the irresolvable nebulosity. At least six or seven of these branches and wings are recognized, some of which are curved and bent in various ways, thus giving this object a distant resemblance to some crustacean forms. Although I have looked for it with care, I have failed to recognize the spiral structure attributed to this object by several observers. Among the six appendages which I have recognized, some are slightly curved; but their curves are sometimes in opposite directions, and two branches of the upper portion make so short a bend that they resemble a claw rather than a spiral wing. The spectrum of this cluster, like that of many objects of its class, is continuous, with the red end deficient.

A little to the north-east of this object is found the cluster No. 4,294, which, although smaller and less bright than the preceding, is still quite interesting. It appears as a distinctly globular cluster without wings, and much condensed towards its centre. The stars individually recognized in it, although less bright than those of the other cluster, are so very curiously distributed in curved lines that they give a peculiar appearance to this condensed region.

A little to the north of γ Centauri may be found the great

ω Centauri cluster, No. 3,531, already referred to above. This magnificent object, which appears as a blazing globe 20′ in diameter, is, according to Herschel, the richest in the sky, and is resolved into a countless number of stars from the twelfth to the fifteenth magnitude, which are greatly compressed towards the centre. The larger stars are so arranged as to form a sort of net-work, with two dark spaces in the middle.

The great globular cluster No. 52, involved in the lesser Magellanic cloud, in the constellation Toucan, is a beautiful and remarkable object. It is composed of three distinct, concentric layers of stars, varying in brightness and in degree of condensation in each layer. The central mass, which is the largest and most brilliant, is composed of an immense number of stars greatly compressed, whose reddish color gives to this blazing circle a splendid appearance. Around the sparkling centre is a broad circle, composed of less compressed stars, this circle being itself involved in another circular layer, where the stars are fainter and more scattered and gradually fade away.

Many other great globular clusters are found in various parts of the heavens, among which may be mentioned the cluster No. 4,678, in Aquarius. This object is composed of several thousand stars of the fifteenth magnitude, greatly condensed towards the centre, and, as remarked by Sir J. Herschel, since the brightness of this cluster does not exceed that of a star of the sixth magnitude, it follows that in this case several thousand stars of the fifteenth magnitude equal only a star of the sixth magnitude. In the constellation Serpens the globular clusters No. 4,083 and No. 4,118 are both conspicuous objects, also No. 4,687 in Capricornus. In Scutum Sobieskii the cluster No. 4,437 is one of the most remarkable of this region. The stars composing it, which are quite large and easily made out separately, form various figures, in which the square predominates.

Among the loose irregular clusters, some are very remarkable for the curious arrangement of their stars. In the constellation Gemini the cluster No. 1,360, which is visible to the naked eye, is a magnificent object seen through the telescope, in which its sparkling stars form curves and festoons of great elegance. The cluster No. 1,467, of the same constellation, is remarkable for its triangular form. In the constellation Ara the cluster No. 4,233, composed of loosely scattered stars, forming various lines and curves, is enclosed on three sides by nearly straight single lines of stars. In Scorpio the cluster No. 4,224 is still more curious, being composed of a continuous ring of loosely scattered stars, inside of which is a round, loose cluster, which is divided into four parts by a dark cross-shaped gap, in which no stars are visible.

Among the 1,034 objects which are now classified as clusters more or less resolvable, 565 have been absolutely resolved into stars, and 469 have been only partly resolved, but are considered as belonging to this class of objects.   In Sir J. Herschel's catalogue there are 102 clusters which are considered as being globular; among them 30 have been positively resolved into stars.

The agglomeration of thousands of stars into a globular cluster cannot be conceived, of course, to be simply the result of chance. This globular form seems clearly to indicate the existence of some bond of union, some general attractive force acting between the different members of these systems, which keeps them together, and condenses them towards the centre.   Herschel regards the loose, irregular clusters as systems in a less advanced stage of condensation, but gradually concentrating by their mutual attraction into the globular form.   Although the stars of some globular clusters appear very close together, they are not necessarily so, and may be separated by great intervals of space.   It has been shown that the clusters are agglomeration of suns, and that our Sun itself is a member of a cluster composed of several hundreds of suns, although, from our point of observation, these do not seem very close together.   So far as known, the nearest star to us is α Centauri, but its distance from the Earth equals 221,000 times the distance of the Sun from our globe, a distance which cannot be traversed by light in less than three years and five months.   It seems very probable that if the suns composing the globular clusters appear so near together, it is because, in the first place, they are at immense distances from us, and in the second, because they appear nearly in a line with other suns, which are at a still greater distance from us, and on which they accordingly are nearly projected.   If one should imagine himself placed at the centre of the cluster in Hercules, for instance, the stars, which from our Earth seems to be so closely grouped, would then quite likely appear very loosely scattered around him in the sky, and would resemble the fixed stars as seen from our terrestrial station.

Judging by their loose and irregular distribution, the easily resolvable clusters would appear, in general, to be the nearer to us. It is probable that the globular clusters do not possess, to a very great degree, the regular form which they ordinarily present to us.   It seems rather more natural to infer that they are irregular, and composed of many wings and branches, such as are observed in the cluster in Hercules; but as these appendages would necessarily be much poorer in stars than the central portions, they would be likely to become invisible at a great distance, and therefore the object would appear more or less globular; the globular form being simply given by the close grouping of the stars in the central portion. It would seem, then, that in general, the most loosely scattered and irregular clusters are the nearest to us, while the smallest globular clusters and those resolvable with most difficulty are the most distant.

In accordance with the theory that the clusters are composed of stars, the spectrum of these objects is in general continuous; although, in many cases, the red end of the spectrum is either very faint or altogether wanting. Many objects presenting in a very high degree the principal characteristics exhibited by the true star-clusters, namely, a circular or oval mass, whose luminous intensity is greatly condensed toward the centre, have not yielded, however, to the resolving power of the largest telescopes, although their continuous spectrum is in close agreement with their general resemblance to the star-clusters. Although such objects may remain irresolvable forever, yet it is highly probable that they do not materially differ from the resolvable and partly resolvable clusters, except by their enormous distance from us, which probably reaches the extreme boundary of our visible universe.

THE NEBULÆ.

PLATE XV.

Besides the foggy, luminous patches which have just been de-scribed, a few hazy spots of a different kind are also visible to the naked eye on any clear, moonless night. These objects mainly differ from the former in this particular, that when viewed through the largest telescopes in existence they are not resolved into stars,. but still retain the same cloudy appearance which they present to the unassisted eye. On account of the misty and vaporous appear-ance which they exhibit, these objects have been called *Nebulæ*.

Of the 26 nebulous objects visible to the naked eye in the whole heavens, 19 belong to the class of star-clusters, and 7 to the class of nebulæ. Among the most conspicuous nebulæ visible to the unas-sisted eye, are those in the constellations Argo Navis, Andromeda and Orion.

Besides the seven nebulæ visible to the naked eye, a great num-ber of similar objects are visible through the telescope. In Sir John Herschel's catalogue of nebulæ and clusters, are found 4,053 irre-solvable nebulæ, and with every increase of the aperture of tele-scopes, new nebulæ, invisible in smaller instruments, are found. Notwithstanding their irresolvability it is probable, however, that many among them have a stellar structure, which their immense distance prevents us from recognizing, and are not therefore true nebulæ. The giant telescope of Lord Rosse has shown nebulæ so remote that it has been estimated that it takes their light 30 mil-lion years to reach the Earth.

The nebulæ are very far from being uniformly distributed in space. In some regions they are rare, while in others they are nu-merous and crowded together, forming many small, irregular groups, differing in size and in richness of aggregation. The grouping of the nebulæ does not occur at random in any part of the heavens, as might naturally be supposed, but, on the contrary, it is chiefly confined to certain regions. Outside of these regions nebulæ are rare and are separated from each other by immense intervals; so that these isolated objects appear as if they were lost wanderers from the great nebulous systems.

The regions where the nebulæ congregate in great number are very extensive, and in a general view there are two vast systems of nebular agglomeration, occupying almost opposite points of the heavens, whose centres are not very distant from the poles of the Milky-way. In the northern hemisphere, the nebulous system is much richer and more condensed than in the southern hemisphere. The northern nebulæ are principally contained in the constellations Ursa Minor and Major, in Draco, Canes Venatici, Bootes, Leo Major and Minor, Coma Berenices, and Virgo. In this region, which occupies about ⅛ of the whole surface of the heavens, ⅓ of the known nebulæ are assembled. The southern nebulæ are more evenly distributed and less numerous, with the exception of two comparatively small, but very remarkable centres of condensation which, together with many star-clusters, constitute the Magellanic clouds.

These two vast nebular groups are by no means regular in outline, and send various branches toward each other. They are separated by a wide and very irregular belt, comparatively free from nebulæ, which encircles the celestial sphere, and whose medial line approximately coincides with that of the galactic belt. The Milky-way, so rich in star-clusters, is very barren in nebulæ; but it is a very remarkable fact, nevertheless, that almost all the brightest, largest, and most complicated nebulæ of the heavens are situated either within it, or in its immediate vicinity. Such are the great nebulæ in Orion and Andromeda; the nebula of ζ Orionis; the Ring nebula in Lyra; the bifurcate nebula in Cygnus; the Dumb-bell nebula in Vulpecula; the Fan, Horse-shoe, Trifid and Winged nebulæ in Sagittarius; the great nebula around η Argus Navis, and the Crab nebula in Taurus.

Aside from the discovery of some of the largest nebulæ by different observers, and their subsequent arrangement in catalogues by Lacaille and Messier, very little had been done towards the study of these objects before 1779, when Sir W. Herschel began to observe them with the earnestness of purpose which was one of the distinctive points of the character of this great man. He successively published three catalogues in 1786, 1789, and 1802, in which the position of 2,500 nebulous objects was given. This number was more than doubled before 1864, when Sir John Herschel published his catalogue of 5,079 nebulæ and star-clusters. To this long list must be added several hundred similar objects, since discovered by D'Arrest, Stephan, Gould and others. But, as has been shown above, among the so-called nebulæ are many star-clusters which do not properly belong to the same class of objects, it being sometimes impossible in the present state of our knowledge to know whether a nebulous object belongs to one class or to the other.

The nebulæ exhibit a great variety of forms and appearances, and, in accordance with their most typical characters, they are usually divided into several classes, which are: the Nebulous stars, the Circular, or Planetary, the Elliptical, the Annular, the Spiral and Irregular nebulæ.

The so-called nebulous stars consist of a faint nebulosity, usually circular, surrounding a bright and sharp star, which generally occupies its centre. The nebulosity surrounding these stars varies in brightness as well as in extent, and while, in general, its light gradually fades away, it sometimes terminates quite suddenly. Such nebulosities are usually brighter and more condensed towards the central star. The stars thus surrounded do not seem, however, to be distinguished from others by any additional peculiarity. Some nebulæ of this kind are round, with one star in the centre; others are oval and have two stars, one at each of their foci. The nebulous star, ι Orionis, represented at the upper part of Plate XV., above the great nebula, has a bright star at its centre and two smaller ones on the side. The association of double stars with nebulæ is very remarkable, and may in some cases indicate a mutual relation between them.

The so-called planetary nebulæ derive their name from their likeness to the planets, which they resemble in a more or less equable distribution of light and in their round or slightly oval form. While some of them have edges comparatively sharp and well defined, the outlines of others are more hazy and diffused. These nebulæ, which are frequently of a bluish tint, are comparatively rare objects, and most of those known belong to the southern hemisphere. When seen through large telescopes, however, they present a different aspect, and their apparent uniformity changes. The largest of these objects, No. 2,343 of the General Catalogue, is situated in the Great Bear, close to the star β. Its apparent diameter is, according to Sir J. Herschel, 2′, 40″, and "its light is equable, except at the edge, where it is a little hazy." In a study which I made of this object in 1876, with a refractor 6½ inches in aperture, I found it decidedly brighter on the preceding side, where the brightest part is crescent shaped. In Lord Rosse's telescope its disk is transformed into a luminous ring with a fringed border, and two small star-like condensations are found within. Another planetary nebula, near *x* Andromedæ, has also shown an annular structure in Rosse's telescope.

The elliptical nebulæ, as their name implies, are elongated, elliptical objects ; but while some of them are only slightly elongated ovals, others form ellipses whose eccentricity is so great that they appear almost linear. In all these objects the light is more or less condensed towards the centre ; but while in some of them the condensation is gradual and slight, in others it is so great and sudden that the centre of the nebula appears as a large diffused star, somewhat resembling the nucleus of a comet. From the general appearance of these objects, it is not unlikely that some of them are either flattish, nebulous disks, like the planetary nebulæ, or nebulous rings, seen more or less sidewise. The condensation of light at their centres does not appear to be stellar, but nebulous like the rest, and it is a remarkable fact that very few, if any, of these objects are resolvable into stars.

Several elliptical nebulæ are remarkable for having a star at or near each of their foci, or at each of their extremities. Such are the elliptical nebulæ in Draco, Centaurus, and Sagittarius, Nos. 4,419, 3,706 and 4,395 of the General Catalogue, the last of which is in the vicinity of the triple star *μ* Sagitarii. Each of these nebulæ has a star at each of its foci, while No. 1, in Cetus, has a star at each of its extremities.

Among the most remarkable elliptic nebulæ may be mentioned Nos. 1,861 and 2,373 of Sir J. Herschel's catalogue, both situated in the constellation Leo. The first is one of Lord Rosse's spiral nebulæ, and the last, which is a very elongated object, is formed of concentric oval rings, which are especially visible towards its central part. The constellation Draco is particularly remarkable for the number of elliptical nebulæ found within its boundaries. Among them are Nos. 3,939, 4,058, 4,064, 4,087, 4,415, etc., which are quite remarkable objects of their class. No. 4,058, of which I have made a study, is bright, and has a decided lenticular form with a condensation in the centre. Its following edge is better defined than the preceding. In Lord Rosse's telescope this object exhibits a narrow, dark, longitudinal, gap in its interior.

By far the largest and the finest object of this class is the great nebula in Andromeda. Although this object belongs rather to the class of irregular nebulæ, yet it is generally considered as an elliptic nebula, since its complicated structure, being less prominent, was not recognized until 1848, when it was perceived by George P. Bond, Director of the Harvard College Observatory. This, the first nebula discovered, was found in 1612 by Simon Marius. It is situated in the constellation Andromeda, in the vicinity of the star ν, and almost in a line with the stars μ and β of the same constellation. It is visible to the naked eye, and appears as a faint comet-like object. It is represented at the upper left hand corner of Plate XIII., on the border of the Milky-way, as it appears to the naked eye.

The nebula in Andromeda is one of the brightest in the heavens, and is closely attended by two smaller nebulæ. Perhaps it would be rather more correct to say that it has three centres of condensation, as the two small nebulæ referred to are entirely involved in the same faint and extensive nebulosity. Its general form is that of an irregular oval, upwards of one degree in breadth and two and a half degrees in length. Its brightest and most prominent part, which alone was seen by the earlier observers, consists in a very elongated lenticular mass, which gradually condenses towards its centre into a blazing, star-like nucleus, surrounded by a brilliant nebulous mass. At a little distance to the south of this central condensation is found one of the lesser centres of condensation noted above, which is globular in appearance, with a bright, star-like nucleus like the former. The other centre of condensation is found to the north-west of the centre of the principal mass, and is quite elongated, with a centre of condensation towards its southern extremity, but it is not so bright as the others. Close to the western edge of the bright lenticular mass first described, and making a very slight angle with its longer axis, are found two narrow and nearly rectilinear dark rifts, running almost parallel to each other, and both terminating in a slender point in the south. These dark rifts, which are almost totally devoid of nebulous matter, are quite rare in nebulæ, and afford a good opportunity to watch the changes which this part of the nebulæ may undergo.

This nebula has never been positively resolved into stars, although Prof. Geo. Bond and others have strongly suspected its resolvability. In a study which I have made of it, with the same instrument employed by Bond, and also with the great Washington telescope, I detected a decided mottled appearance in several places, which might be attributable to a beginning of resolvability ; but I do not consider this a conclusive indication that the nebula is resolvable. The continuous spectrum given by this nebula, showing that it is not in the gaseous state which its appearance seems to indicate, warrants the conclusion, however, that it will ultimately be found to be resolvable. This object, being situated on the edge of the Galaxy and involved in its diffused light, has a great number of small stars belonging to this belt projected upon it. During my observations I have mapped out 1,323 of these stars, none of which seems to be in physical connection with the nebula.

Among the circular and elliptical nebulæ a few exhibit a very remarkable structure, being apparently perforated, and forming either round, slightly oval, or elongated rings of great beauty. These Annular nebulæ are among the rarest objects in the heavens. In Scorpio, two such nebulæ are found involved in the Milky-way, and also one in Cygnus. One of those in Scorpio has two stars involved within its ring, at the extremities of its smallest interior diameter. A very elongated nebula in the vicinity of the fine triple star γ Andromedæ is also annular, and has two stars symmetrically placed at the extremities of its greatest interior axis. Another elongated annular nebula is also found north of η Pegasi.

The grandest and most remarkable of the annular nebulæ is found in the constellation Lyra, about midway between the two stars β and γ. It is slightly elliptical in form, and according to Prof. E. S. Holden, its major axis is 77″.3 and the minor 58″. From a study and several drawings which I have made of this object, with instruments of various apertures, I have found it decidedly brighter towards its outer border, at the extremities of its minor axis, than at the ends of the major axis. On very favorable occasions, some of its brightest parts have appeared decidedly, but very faintly mottled, and I have recognized three small centres of condensation. Its interior, in which Professor Holden has detected a very faint star, is quite strongly nebulous. In Lord Rosse's telescope, this nebula is completely surrounded by wisps and appendages of all sorts of forms, which I have failed to trace, however, both with the refractor of the Harvard College Observatory and with that of the Naval Observatory at Washington ; Rosse, Secchi and Chacornac, have seen this nebula glittering as if it were a "heap of star dust," although its spectrum indicates that it is gaseous.

The nebula No. 1,541, in Camelopardus, of which I have also made a study and a drawing, is closely allied to the class of annular nebulæ. This object, which is quite bright, has a remarkable appearance. It consists principally of somewhat more than half of an oval ring, surrounding a bright, nebulous mass which condenses around a star; this mass being separated from the imperfect ring by a dark interval. Upon the bright portion of the ring, and on opposite points, are found two bright stars, between which lies the star occupying the central mass. The central mass extends at some distance outside of the ring on its open side. Several stars are involved in this object.

The Spiral nebulæ are very curious and complicated objects, but they are visible only in the largest telescopes. Prominent above all is the double spiral nebula No. 3,572, in Canes Venatici, which is not far from η Ursa Majoris. In Lord Rosse's telescope, this object presents a wonderful spiral disposition, looking somewhat like one of the fire-works called pin-wheels, and forming long, curved wisps, diverging from two bright centres. The spectrum of this object, however, is not that of a gas. In the constellation Virgo, Rosse has detected another such nebula. In Cepheus, Triangulum, and Ursa Major, are found other spiral nebulæ of smaller size. Lord Rosse has recognized 40 spiral nebulæ and suspected a similar structure in 30 others.

The class of the Irregular nebulæ, which will be now considered, differs greatly in character from the others, and includes the largest, the brightest and the most extraordinary nebulæ in the heavens. The nebulæ of this class differ from those belonging to the other classes by a want of symmetry in their form and in the distribution of their light, as well as by their capricious shapes, and their very complicated structure. Another and perhaps the principal difference between them and the objects above described, consists in the remarkable fact already stated, that they are not, except in rare cases, to be found in the regions where the other nebulæ abound. On the contrary, they are found in or very near the Milky-way, precisely where the other nebulæ are the most rare. This fact, recognized by Sir J. Herschel, led him to consider them as "outlying, very distant, and as it were detached fragments of the great stratum of the Galaxy." It seems very probable that the reason why these objects differ so greatly from the other nebulæ in size, brightness and complication of structure, is simply because they are much nearer to us than are most of the others. They are perhaps nebulous members of our Galaxy. The same remark which has been made of star-clusters may be applied to nebulæ. The nearer they are to us, the larger, the brighter and the more complicated they will appear, while the farther they are removed, the more simple and regular and round they will appear, only their brightest and deepest parts being then visible.

The Crab Nebula of Lord Rosse, near ζ Tauri, No. 1,157, is one of the interesting objects of this class. It has curious appendages streaming off from an oval, luminous 'mass, which give it a distant resemblance to the animal from which it derives its name. The Bifid nebula in Cygnus, Nos. 4,400 and 4,616, is another object of this class. It consists of a long, narrow, crooked streak, forking out at several places, and passing through *x* Cygni. Observers, having failed to recognize the connection existing between its different centres of brightness, have made distinct nebulæ of this extended object.

The Dumb-bell nebula in Vulpecula, No. 4,532, is a bright and curious object, with a general resemblance to the instrument from which it derives its name. Lord Rosse's telescope has shown many stars in it, projected on a nebulous background, and Prof. Bond seems to have thought that it showed traces of resolvability, although in the study which I made of this nebula with the same instrument used by the latter observer, I failed to perceive any such traces. Dr. Huggins finds its spectrum gaseous.

The star-cluster, No. 4,400, in Scutum Sobieskii, which is described by Sir J. Herschel as a loose cluster of at least 100 stars, I have found to be involved in an extensive, although not very bright, nebula, which would seem to have escaped his scrutiny. In a study and drawing of this nebula made in 1876, its general form is that of an open fan, with the exception that the handle is wanting, with deeply indented branches on the preceding side, where the brightest stars of the cluster are grouped. From its peculiar form, this object might appropriately be called the Fan nebula.

The Omega or Horse-shoe nebula, in Sagittarius, No. 4,403, of which I have made a study and two drawings, one with a refractor 6¼ inches in aperture, and the other conjointly with Prof. Holden, with the great telescope of the Naval Observatory, is a bright and very complicated object. Its general appearance in small instruments, with low power, is that of a long, narrow pisciform mass of light, from which proceeds on the preceding side, the great double loop from which it derives its name. But in the great Washington refractor its structure becomes very complicated, forming various bright nebulous masses and wisps of great extension. Prof. Holden, who has made a careful, comparative study of the published drawings of this object, thinks there are reasons to believe that its western branch has moved relatively to the stars found within its loop. The spectrum of this nebula is gaseous.

The Trifid nebula, No. 4,355, in the same constellation, is also a very remarkable object, although it is not so bright as the last. This nebula, which I have studied with the refractor of the Cam--

bridge Observatory, consists of four principal masses of light, separated by a wide and irregular gap branching out in several places. These masses, which are brighter along the dark gap, gradually fade away externally. A group of stars, two of which are quite bright, is found near the centre of the nebula, on the inner edge of the following mass, and close to the principal branch of the dark channel. A little to the north, and apparently forming a part of this nebula, is a globular-looking nebula, having a pale yellow star at its centre. Prof. Holden's studies on this nebula show that the triple star, which was centrally situated in the dark gap from 1784 to 1833, was found involved in the border of the nebulous mass following it, from 1839 to 1877 ; the change, he thinks, is attributable either to the proper motion of the group of stars or to that of the nebula itself.

In the same vicinity is found the splendid and very extensive nebula No. 4,361, in which is involved a loose, but very brilliant star-cluster. This nebula and cluster, which I have studied and drawn with a 6⅓ inch telescope, is very complicated in structure, and divided by a dark irregular gap into three principal masses of light, condensing at one point around a star, and at others forming long, bright, gently-curved branches, which give to this object a strong resemblance to the wings of a bird when extended upwards in the action of flying. From this peculiarity this object might appropriately be called the Winged nebula. Its spectrum is that of a gas.

The variable star η Argus is completely surrounded by the great nebula of the same name, No. 2,197, first delineated by Sir J. Herschel, during his residence at the Cape of Good Hope, in 1838. This object, which covers more than ⁴⁄₄ of a square degree, is divided into three unequal masses, separated by dark oval spots, comparatively free from nebulosity, and is suspected to have undergone changes since Herschel's time.

In the same field with the double star, ζ Orionis, the most easterly of the three bright stars in the belt of Orion, is found another irregular nebula of the Trifid type. From the drawings which I have made of this object, it appears to be composed of three principal unequal masses, separated by a wide, irregular, dark channel, two of the masses being quite complicated in structure, and forming curved, nebulous streams of considerable length and breadth. This nebula, like the next to be described, seems to be connected with the Galaxy by the great galactic loop described in another section.

By far the most conspicuous irregular nebula visible from our

northern States, is the great nebula in Orion, No. 1,179, represented on Plate XV. This object, visible to the naked eye, is the
brightest and the most wonderful nebula in the heavens. It is situated a little to the south of the three bright stars in the belt of
Orion, and may be readily detected surrounding the star θ, situated
between and in a line with two faint stars, the three being in a
straight line which points directly towards ε, the middle star of the
three in Orion's belt. The area occupied by this nebula is about
equal to that occupied by the Moon.

In its brightest parts the nebula in Orion appears as a luminous
cloud of a pentagonal form, from which issue many luminous appendages of various shapes and lengths. This principal mass is
divided into secondary masses, separated by darkish, irregular intervals: These secondary masses in their turn appear mottled and
fleecy. Towards the lower part of the pentagonal mass is found a
roundish dark space, comparatively devoid of nebulosity, in which
are involved four bright stars forming a trapezium, and several
fainter ones. The four bright stars of the trapezium constitute the
quadruple star θ Orionis, from which the nebula has received its
name. The cloud-like pentagonal form is brightest on the north-
west of the trapezium, and is surrounded on three sides by long,
soft, curved wisps, fading insensibly into the outer nebulous mass in
which they are involved. On the east a broad, wavy wing spreads
out, and sends an important branch southward. South-east of the
trapezium are found several curious dark spaces, comparatively devoid of nebulosity, especially those on the east, which give to this
nebula a singular character. Close to the north-eastern part of
the nebula, or rather in contact with it, is found a small, curiously-
shaped nebula, condensing around a bright star into a blazing nucleus. From this centre it continues northward in a narrow diffused
stream, which spreads out in passing over the stars c^1 and c^2; and
after having sent short branches northward, it curves back to the
south and joins the main nebula on the west of its starting point,
having thus formed a great loop which is not shown on the Plate.
The nebula also forms a loop towards the south, which is partly
shown on Plate XV., a small branch of which, passing through ι
Orionis, the nebulous star shown at the top of the Plate, and extending southward, is not here represented.

On ordinary nights the nebula in Orion is a splendid object, and
inspires the observer with amazement; but this is as nothing compared with the grand and magnificent sight which it presents during the very rare moments when our atmosphere is perfectly clear

and steady. I have seen this nebula but once under these favorable circumstances, and I was surprised by the grandeur of the scene. Then could be detected features to be seen at no other time, and its fleecy, floculent, cloud-like masses glittered with such intensity that it seemed as if thousands of stars were going to blaze out the next moment. Although I observed the nebula under such favorable conditions, and with the fifteen-inch refractor of the Cambridge Observatory, yet I was disappointed in my expectations, and distinguished no new stars or points of light, and nothing more than a very bright mass, finely divided into minute blazing cloudlets. Although I failed to resolve this nebula into stars, yet Lord Rosse, Bond and Secchi thought they had caught glimpses of star dust. Its spectrum, however, proves to be mainly that of incandescent gases, probably hydrogen and nitrogen. In the curved wisps found in this nebula, Lord Rosse and others saw indications of a spiral structure.

Several bright stars are found scattered over this nebula, and besides those forming the trapezium, there are three in a row, a little to the south-east of that group, which are quite bright and remarkable. Among the stars involved in this nebula, few show signs of having a physical connection with it, although it seems probable that the group of the trapezium is so connected. Some of these stars are variable. The small stars represented on this Plate, as on others of the series, are somewhat exaggerated in size, as was unavoidable with any process of reproduction which could be adopted.

In 1811, W. Herschel was led to suspect that some changes had occurred in this nebula, but changes in such complicated and delicate objects are not easily ascertained, since, for the most part, we have for comparison with our later observations only coarse drawings made by hands unskilled in delineation.

Although comparatively rare, double and multiple nebulæ may be found in the sky. When this occurs, their constituents most commonly belong to the class of spherical nebulæ. Sometimes the components are separated and distinct, at other times one of them is projected upon the other, either really or by the effect of perspective. Sometimes one is round and the other elongated. It is probable that while some of these nebulæ are physically associated and form a system, others appear to be so only because they happen to be almost in a line with the observer. A double nebula in Draco, Nos. 4,127 and 4,128, which I have drawn, is a fair type of those which are separated. The first is a globular nebula, and the last an oval one, with a star at its centre. The double nebula, Nos. 858 and 859, in Taurus, which I have also studied, is a type of the cases in which one nebula is partly projected on another. In this instance both the nebulæ are globular.

The nebulæ in general show very little color in their light, which is ordinarily whitish and pale. Some, however, present a decided bluish or greenish tint. The great nebula in Orion has a greenish cast, and we have seen that some planetary nebulæ are bluish.

It has been a question whether nebulæ are changing. It has already been stated that Prof. Holden believes there is ground to suspect that the Trifid and Horse-shoe nebulæ have undergone some changes. A nebula near ε Tauri has been lost and found again several times. Two other nebulæ in the same constellation have presented curious variations. One, near a star of the tenth magnitude, exhibited variations of brightness like those of the star itself, and for a time disappeared. The other, near ζ Tauri, increased in brightness for three months, after which it disappeared. In 1859 Tempel discovered a nebula in the Pleiades, which has shown some fluctuations. In 1875 I made a long study of this object, and drew it carefully a dozen times, but I was not able to see any changes in it within the two or three months during which my observations were continued. But on Nov. 24, 1876, it was found of a different color, being purplish and very faint. On Dec. 23, 1880, it was found just as bright and visible as when I drew it in 1875, and on Oct. 20, 1881, it appeared faint and purplish again, as in 1876. On this last night, and on those which followed it, it was impossible for me to trace the nebulosity as far as in 1875. I consider this as due to a variation in the light of this object, which in 1875 was bright enough to be well seen while the Moon after her First Quarter was within ten or fifteen degrees from the Pleiades.

From the observations of M. Laugier, it appears that some nebulæ have a proper motion, comparable to that of stars. From the displacement of the lines of their spectra by their motion in the line of sight, Dr. Huggins found that no nebula observed by him has a proper motion surpassing 25 miles per second. The Ring nebula in Lyra appears, to move from us at the rate of 3 miles per second, and that in Orion recedes about 17 miles per second.

The important question arises, are all the irresolvable nebulæ in the heavens to be considered as so many star-clusters, differing only from them by the minuteness of their components, or their immense distance from us; or are they cosmical clouds, composed of luminous vapors, similar to the matter composing the heads and tails of comets? Originally, W. Herschel, with many astronomers, thought that all these objects were stellar aggregations, too distant to be resolved into stars; but he subsequently modified his opinion, and accepted the idea that some of them are of a gaseous nature.

No direct proof that the nebulæ are gaseous could be obtained, however, before the spectroscope was known. The attempt to analyze the light of the nebulæ with this instrument was made in 1864, by Dr. Huggins, who directed his spectroscope to the planetary nebula, No. 4,373, in Draco. Its spectrum was found to consist of three bright, distinct lines, the brightest of which corresponded with the strongest nitrogen line, and the feeblest with the hydrogen C line. Besides these lines, it gave also a very faint, continuous spectrum, apparently due to a central point of condensation. By this observation, the gaseous nature of a nebula was for the first time demonstrated.   Dr. Huggins thus analyzed 70 nebulæ, of which one-third gave a gaseous spectrum, consisting òf several bright lines, the brightest of which invariably corresponded with the lines of nitrogen.   The others gave a continuous spectrum, with the red end usually deficient.   These results indicate that if some of the so-called nebulæ are due to an aggregation of stars, either too minute or too remote in space to be individually resolved, others are in a gaseous state.   Yet the faint, continuous spectrum, given by some nebulæ, in addition to their gaseous spectra, seems to show that these nebulæ have some stars or matter in a different state, either involved in them or projected on their surface.

The idea of diffused matter distributed here and there in space, and gradually condensing into stars, is by no means new.   As early as 1572, Tycho Brahé proposed such an hypothesis, to explain the sudden apparition of a new star in Cassiopeia, which he considered as formed by the recent agglomeration of the " celestial matter " diffused in space.   Kepler adopted the same idea to explain the new star which appeared in Ophiuchus, in 1604. Halley, Lacaille, Mairan and others, entertained the same opinion.   The hypothesis of a self-luminous, nebulous matter diffused in space, and forming here and there immense masses, has been proposed from the origin of the telescope, and was adopted by Sir William Herschel, who in his grand speculations on the universe considered the nebulæ as immense masses of phosphorescent vapors, gradually condensing around one or several centres into stars or clusters of stars.   The evidence afforded by the spectroscope seems to be in favor of such an hypothesis, and shows us that gaseous agglomerations exist in space.

According to our modern conception, the visible universe is but an infinitely small portion of the infinite universe perceived by our mind. The great blazing centre around which our little, non-luminous globe pursues its endless journey, is only an humble member of a cluster comprising four hundred equally powerful suns, as they are believed to be, although they appear to us as little twinkling stars. The nearest of these stars is 221,000 times as far from the Sun as the Sun is from the Earth, and yet this entire cluster is only one among the several hundred Star-clusters composing the great galactic nebula in which we are involved, comprising thirty or fifty millions of such suns. Among the 4,000 irresolvable nebulæ in the sky, perhaps over one-half are supposed to be galaxies, like our own galaxy, composed of star-clusters, and millions of stars. Besides these remote galaxies, vast agglomerations of yet uncondensed, nebulous matter exist in space, and form the nebulæ proper, in which the genesis of suns is slowly elaborated. Although the visible universe is limited by the penetrating power of our instruments, yet we see in imagination the infinite universe stretching farther and farther; but we know not whether this invisible universe is totally devoid of matter, or whether it also is filled with millions and millions of suns and galaxies.

APPENDIX.

KEY TO THE PLATES.

[The numerals in brackets refer to pages of the MANUAL. The letters *a, b, c,* designate respectively the upper, middle and lower portions of the page.]

PLATE I.—GROUP OF SUN-SPOTS AND VEILED SPOTS.

Observed June 17, 1875, at 7h. 30m. A. M.

The background shows the sun's visible surface, or *photosphere* [2b], as seen with a telescope of high power at the most favorable moments, composed of innumerable light markings, or granules [3c], separated by a network of darker gray. The granules, each some hundreds of miles in width [4a], are thought to be the flame-like [5a] summits of the radial filaments or columns of gas and vapor [5c] which compose the photospheric shell [10a, 17a]. The two principal sun-spots [8a] of the group [15b] here represented show the characteristic dark *umbra* in the centre [9b], overhung by the thatch-like *penumbra* [10b], composed of whitish gray filaments. The penumbral filaments are not supposed to differ in their nature from those constituting the ordinary photosphere, save that they are seen here elongated and violently disturbed by the force of gaseous currents [10b]. Both spots are traversed partly or wholly by bright overlying *faculæ* [6a], or so-called *luminous bridges* [10c], depressed portions of which, in the left-hand spot, form the *gray and rosy veils* [9c] commonly attendant upon this class of spots [13c]. In each of these spots, also, the inner ends of projecting penumbral filaments have fallen so far within the umbra [11a] as to appear much darker than the rest. At the right of the upper portion of the left-hand spot, is a mass of white facular clouds [14b], honey-combed by dark spaces, through which are seen traces of the undeveloped third spot of the triple group first observed [17b]. If seen upon the sun's limb, this would have presented the appearance of a *lateral spot* [13b]. Above the right-hand spot is a small black "dot," or incipient spot, without distinct penumbra [9b]. The irregular dark rift below the two large spots and connecting them is a spot of the *crevasse* type [14a], with very slight umbra, a still better example of which is seen in a westward [vi. c] prolongation of the penumbra of the left-hand spot. In the upper left-hand corner of the Plate are seen several small *faculæ* [6a], appearing as irregular whitish streaks amongst the granules [7c]. In the pear-shaped darkening of the solar surface below and at their left, is seen a *veiled spot* [16c], two of which attended this group [17b].

Approximate scale, 2500 *miles*—1 *inch.*

PLATE II.—SOLAR PROTUBERANCES.

Observed May 5, 1873, at 9h. 40m. A. M.

A view of an upheaval of the *chromosphere* [18a], or third outlying envelope of the sun [3a], as observed with the tele-spectroscope, or telescope with spectroscope attached.

The *method of the observation* requires a word of explanation. Save on the rare occasions of a total solar eclipse, no direct telescopic view of the solar prominences or flames is possible, owing to the fact that the intense white light from the sun's main disk entirely obscures [3a] the feeble pink light of the chromosphere [26a]. A few years ago Messrs. Janssen and Lockyer [18b] found that a spectroscope of high dispersive power so weakens the spectrum of ordinary sun-light as to show the spectrum of bright lines given by the chromosphere [21a], on any clear day. The telescope is adjusted so that a portion of the sun's limb, usually near a group of active sun-spots [21a], shall be presented before the opened slit of the spectroscope. The light of the chromosphere thus admitted along with some diffused sun-light from the earth's atmosphere, produces a spectrum of intensely bright lines, widely separated, on the fainter background of the strongly dispersed spectrum of sun-light. The most prominent of these bright lines are those known as the C line (*scarlet*), F line (*blue*), which with several others are due to the hydrogen present in the chromosphere, the D_3 line (*orange*) ascribed to a little known substance called "helium" [5a], and occasionally the sodium lines D_1, D_2, (*yellow*). By adjusting the slit upon the scarlet C line, the appearances represented in Plate II. were observed as through an atmosphere of scarlet light: in the D or F lines identical appearances may be seen, but somewhat less clearly defined, as through yellow or blue light respectively. Hence the solar flames, as here observed with the spectroscope in the hydrogen C line, are seen through a portion only (the scarlet rays) of the light coming from but one substance (hydrogen) of the companion incandescent substances present in the chromosphere. The color of the collective chromospheric light is seen directly with the telescope during an eclipse (See Plate III.) to be a delicate rosy pink [26a.]

Description of the Plate.—The black background represents the general darkness of the eye-piece to the spectroscope. The broad red stripe stretching from top to bottom of the Plate is a portion of the red band of the spectrum, magnified about 100 times as compared with the actual spectroscopic view. The upper and lower edges of the cross-section of dusky red correspond with the edges of the slit, opened widely enough to admit a view of the chromospheric crest and of the whole height of the protuberances at once. With a narrower opening of the slit this background would have been nearly black, its reddish cast increasing with the amount of opening and consequent admission of diffused sun-light. Rising above the lower edge of the opening is seen a small outer segment of the chromosphere, which, as a portion of the sun's eastern limb, should be imagined as moving directly towards the beholder. The seams and rifts by which its surface is broken, as well as the distorted forms of the huge protuberances show the chromosphere to be in violent agitation. Some of the most characteristic shapes [19c] of the *eruptive protuberances* [20a] are presented, as also *cloud-like* forms overtopping the rest. In the immediate foreground the bases of two towering columns appear deeply depressed below the general horizon of the segment observed, showing an extraordinary velocity of motion of the whole uplifted mass toward the observer [21c]. The highest of these protuberances was 126,000 miles in height at the moment of observation [22a]. The triple protuberance at the left with two drooping wings [21b] and a tall swaying spire tipped with a very bright flame, shows by its more brilliant color the higher temperature (and possibly compression) to which its gases have been subjected [18c]. The irregular black bands behind this protuberance indicate the presence there of less condensed and cooler clouds of the same gases [20c]. The dimmer jets of flame rising from the chromosphere are either vanishing protuberances [20c], or, as in the case of the smallest jet shown at the extreme right of the horizon, are the tops of protuberances just coming into view.

Approximate scale, 6000 miles—1 inch.

PLATE III.—TOTAL ECLIPSE OF THE SUN.

Observed July 29, 1878, at Creston, Wyoming Territory.

A telescopic view of the sun's *corona* or extreme outer atmosphere [3b] and of the *solar flames* or *prominences* [25c] during a *total eclipse* [23c]. At the moment of observation the dark disk of the moon, while still hiding the sun's main body, had passed far enough eastward to allow the rosy pink chromospheric prominences to be seen on its western border [20c]. On all sides of the sun's hidden disk, the *corona* [25b] shows its pale greenish light [26a] extending in halo-like rays and streamers, and two very remarkable wings [26b] stretch eastward and westward very nearly in the plane of the ecliptic and in the direction of the positions of Mercury and Venus respectively at the time of observation. The full extent of these wings could not be shown in the Plate without reducing its scale materially, since the westerly wing extended no less than twelve times the sun's diameter [27b], and the easterly wing nearly as far, or over ten million miles. A circlet of bright light immediately bordering the moon's disk is the so-called *inner corona*, next to which the wings and streamers are brightest, thence shading off imperceptibly into the twilight sky of the eclipse [25b]. Other noteworthy peculiarities of the corona, as observed during this eclipse [26b], are the varying angles at which the radiating streamers are seen to project, the comparatively dark intervals between them, and the curved, wisp-like projections seen upon the wings. An especially noticeable gap appears where the most westerly of the upward streamers abruptly cuts off the view of the long wing. The largest and brightest of the curving streamers on the westerly wing coincides with the highest flame-like protuberance [26b]. To some observers of this eclipse the upward and downward streamers seemed pointed at their outer extremities and less regular in form.

Approximate scale, 135,000 miles—1 inch.

PLATE IV.—AURORA BOREALIS.

As observed March 1, 1872, at 9h. 25m. P. M.

The view presents the rare spectacle of an aurora spanning the sky from east to west in concentric arches [28c]. The Polar Star is nearly central in the back-ground, the constellation of the Great Bear on the right and Cassiopeia's chair on the left. The large star at some distance above the horizon on the right is Arcturus. The almost black inner segment [28b] of the aurora resting upon the horizon, has its summit in the magnetic meridian [32a], which was in this case a little west of north, its arc being indented by the bases of the ascending streamers [28c]. Both streamers and arches were, when observed, tremulous with upward pulsations [29b] and there was also a wave-like movement of the streamers from west to east [29a]. The prevailing color of this aurora is a pale whitish green [28c] and the complementary red appears especially at the west end of the auroral arch. The summits of the streamers are from four hundred to five hundred miles above the earth [31a] and the aurora is therefore a phenomenon of the terrestrial atmosphere [32b] rather than of astronomical observation proper.

PLATE V.—THE ZODIACAL LIGHT.

Observed February 20, 1876.

An observation of the cone of light whose axis lies along the Zodiac [36b], whence it derives its name. It is drawn as seen in the west [41a], with its base in the constellation Pisces, and its apex near the familiar group of the Pleiades in the constellation Taurus. The first bright star above the horizon in the base of the cone is the planet *Venus* and at some distance above is the reddish disk of *Mars*, the two being in rare companionship as evening stars. Above the constellation Pisces, two bright stars of Aries lie just outside the cone at the right. The nearest bright star above these at the right is *Beta*, the leading star of the constellation Triangula. Further at the right the three prominent stars nearly in a line are, in ascending order, *Delta, Beta and Gamma* of the constellation Andromeda. Above these at the left, the brightest star of a quadrangular group of four is the remarkable variable star *Algol (Beta)* of the constellation Perseus, which changes from the second to the fourth magnitude in a period of less than three days. At the left and a little above the Pleiades is the ruddy star *Aldebaran*, one of the Hyades and chief star in the constellation Taurus. These are the principal stars visible in this portion of the sky at the time of the observation. Their relative positions are represented as seen in the sky and not by the common method of star-atlases, which allows for the change from a spherical to a plane surface. Their magnitude in the order of brightness is indicated only approximately [41a].

PLATE VI.—MARE HUMORUM.

From a study made in 1875.

A view of one of the lunar plains [47c], or so-called *seas (Maria)*, with an encircling mountainous wall [45a] consisting of volcano-like craters [45c, 46c] in various stages of subsidence and dislocation [48a]. The sun-light coming from the west casts strong shadows from all the elevations eastward, and is just rising on the *terminator* [44c], where the rugged structure of the Moon's surface is best seen. The lighter portions are the more elevated mountainous tracts and crater summits [45a]. The detailed description of this Plate given in the body of the MANUAL [51-2] is repeated here for convenience of reference: The Mare Humorum, or sea of moisture, as it is called, is one of the smaller gray lunar plains. Its diameter, which is very nearly the same in all directions, is about 270 miles, the total area of this plain being about 50,000 square miles. It is one of the most distinct plains of the Moon, and is easily seen with the naked eye on the left-hand side of the disk. The floor of the plain is, like that of the other gray plains, traversed by several systems of very extended but low hills and ridges, while small craters are disseminated upon its surface. The color of this formation is of a dusky greenish gray along the border, while in the interior it is of a lighter shade, and is of brownish olivaceous tint. This plain, which is surrounded by high clefts and rifts, well illustrates the phenomena of dislocation and subsidence. The double-ringed crater Vitello, whose walls rise from 4,000 to 5,000 feet in height, is seen in the upper left-hand corner of the gray plain. Close to Vitello at the east is the large broken ring-plain Lee, and farther east, and a little below, is a similarly broken crater called Doppelmayer. Both of these open craters have mountainous masses and peaks on their floor, which is on a level with that of the Mare Humorum. A little below, and to the left of these objects, is dimly seen a deeply imbedded oval crater, whose walls barely rise above the level of the plain. On the right-hand side of the great plain is a long *fault*, with a system of fracture running along its border. On this right-hand side may be seen a part of the line of the terminator, which separates the light from the darkness. Towards the lower right-hand corner is the great ring-plain Gassendi, 55 miles in diameter, with its system of fractures and its central mountains, which rise from 3,000 to 4,000 feet above its floor. This crater slopes towards the plain, showing the subsidence to which it has been submitted. While the northern portion of the wall of this crater rises to 10,000 feet, that on the plain is only 500 feet high, and is even wholly demolished at one place where the floor of the crater is in direct communication with the plain. In the lower part of the sea, and a little to the west of the middle line, is found the crater Agatharchides, which shows below its north wall the marks of rills impressed by a flood of lava, which once issued from the side of the crater. On the left-hand side of the plain is seen the half-demolished crater Hippalus resembling a large bay, which has its interior strewn with peaks and mountains. On this same side can be seen one of the most important systems of clefts and fractures visible on the Moon, these clefts varying in length from 150 to 200 miles.

Approximate scale, 15 miles—1 inch.

Plate VII.—PARTIAL ECLIPSE OF THE MOON.

Observed October 24, 1874.

A view of the Moon partially obscured by the Earth's shadow [53a], whose outline gives ocular proof of the earth's rotundity of form. The shadowed part of the Moon's surface is rendered visible by the diffused sun-light refracted upon it from the earth's atmosphere [55a]. Its reddish brown color is due to the absorption, by vapors present near the earth's surface [55a], of a considerable part of this dim light. On both the obscured and illuminated tracts the configurations of the Moon's surface are seen as with the naked eye [56b]. The craters [45c] appear as distinct patches of lighter color, and the noticeably darker areas are the depressed plains or *Maria* [47c]. The large crater *Tycho*, at the lower part of the disk, is the most prominent of these objects, with its extensive system of *radiating streaks* [49a]. The largest crater above is *Copernicus*, at the left of which is *Kepler* and still above are *Aristarchus* and *Herodotus* appearing as if blended in one. Above and at the left of the great crater *Tycho*, the first dark tract is the *Mare Humorum* of Plate VI., seen in its natural position [vi.c], with the crater *Gassendi* at its northern (upper) extremity and *Vitello* on its southern (lower) border [51b]. The advancing border of the shadow appears, as always, noticeably darker than the remainder, an effect probably of contrast. The illuminated segment of the Moon's disk has its usual appearance, the lighter portions being the more elevated mountainous surfaces, and the dark spaces the floors of extensive plains.

Approximate scale, 140 miles—1 inch.

Plate VIII.—THE PLANET MARS.

Observed September 3, 1877, at 11h. 55m. P. M.

A view of the southern hemisphere of Mars [64a], when in the most favorable position for observation [61b], and when exceptionally free from the clouds, which very frequently hide its surface configurations [63b]. Since, of all the planets, Mars is most like the earth [71c], Plate VIII. may give a fair idea of the appearance of our globe to a supposed observer on Mars. The dark gray and black markings [63c], are regarded as tracts of water [65b], or of some liquid with similar powers of absorbing light; and, for the same reason, the lighter portions, of a prevailing reddish tint [70c], are supposed to be bodies of land [65b], while the bright white portions are variously due to clouds [68b], to polar snow or ice [65b, 67b], and the bright rim of white along the limb, to the depth of the atmosphere through which the limb is seen

[70c]. The chief permanent features of the planet's surface have been named in honor of various astronomers.

The large dark tract on the left is *De La Rue Ocean*, the isolated oval spot near the centre is *Terby Sea*, and on the right is the western end of *Maraldi Sea*, with strongly indented border. Directly north of (below) De La Rue Ocean, is *Maedler Continent;* above it stretches *Jacob Land;* and surrounding Terby Sea is *Secchi Continent*. Extending into the centre of De La Rue Ocean is a curious double peninsula, called, in consequence of the dimness of former observations, *Hall Island* [69a]. The sharply defined, white-crested northern borders of De La Rue Ocean and Maraldi Sea may indicate the existence there of lofty coast ranges, more or less constantly covered with opaque clouds [63b] strongly reflecting light [65b]. The white spot in the centre of Maedler Continent, of a temporary nature, has a similar explanation [69c]. The intervals of olivaceous gray on Secchi Continent and elsewhere may perhaps be ascribed [65c] to the flooding and drying up of marshes and lowlands, as these markings have been observed to vary somewhat in connection with the change of seasons on Mars [71c]. The greenish tints observed along the planet's limb, alike on the darker and lighter surfaces, are probably due to an optical effect, the green being complementary to the prevailing red of the disk. The brilliant oval white spot near the southern (upper) pole of the planet is a so-called polar spot [65-67], in all probability consisting of a material similar to snow or ice [67b] and here observed in the midst of a dark open sea [67c].

Approximate scale, 300 miles—1 inch.

PLATE IX.—THE PLANET JUPITER.

Observed November 1, 1880, at 9h. 30m. P. M.

This planet is perpetually wrapped in dense clouds [75b] which hide its inner globe from view. The drawing shows Jupiter's outer clouded surface with its usual series of alternate light and dark belts [74b], the disk as a whole appearing brighter in the centre than near the limb. The darker gray and black markings [74c] indicate in general the lower cloud-levels; that is, partial breaks or rifts in the cloudy envelope, whose prevailing depth apparently exceeds four thousand miles [79c-80c]. While the deepest depression in the cloudy envelope is within the limits of the Great Red Spot [77a], the vision may not even here penetrate very deeply. Two of Jupiter's four moons [77c] present bright disks [78c] near the planet's western limb, and cast their shadows [79a] far eastward on the disk, that of the " second satellite " falling upon the Red Spot [82a]. On the Red Spot are seen in addition two small black spots [77a], no explanation of which can yet be offered. The broad white ring of clouds bordering the Red Spot [77b] appeared in constant motion. The central, or equatorial belt [74c], shows brilliant cloudy masses of both the *cumulus* and *stratus* types, and the underlying gray and black cloudy surfaces are pervaded with the pinkish color characteristic of this belt. The dark circular spots on the wide white belt next north showed in their mode of formation [76c] striking resemblances to sun-spots [82a]. They afterward coalesced into a continuous pink belt. The diffusion of pinkish color over the three northernmost dark bands, as here observed, is unusual [75a]. About either pole is seen the uniform gray segment [75a] or polar cap. The equatorial diameter is noticeably longer [73c] than the polar diameter, a consequence of the planet's extraordinary swiftness of rotation. To the same cause may also be due chiefly the distribution of the cloudy belts parallel to the planet's equator [74b], though the analogy of the terrestrial trade-winds fails to explain all the observed phenomena.

Approximate scale, 5,500 miles—1 inch.

Plate X.—THE PLANET SATURN.

Observed November 30, 1874, at 5h. 50m. P. M.

Saturn is unique amongst the planets in that its globe is encircled by a series of concentric rings [96c], which lie in the plane of its equator, and consist, according to present theories, of vast throngs of minute bodies revolving about the planet, like so many satellites, in closely parallel orbits [97c]. The globe of Saturn, like that of Jupiter, is surrounded by cloudy belts parallel to its equator [85c]. The broad equatorial belt, of a delicate pinkish tint, is both brighter and more mottled [85c] than the narrower yellowish white belts, which alternate with darker belts of ashy gray [86a] on both the north and south sides, but are seen here only on the northern side. The disk has an oval shape, owing to the extreme polar compression of the globe [85b].

The outer, middle and inner rings, with their various subdivisions [86c], are clearly shown in Plate X., and are best seen on the so-called *ansæ*, or handles, projecting on either side. The gray *outer ring* is separated by the dusky *pencil line* [86c] into two divisions, both of which appear slightly mottled on the ansæ, as if with clouds [87a]. The *middle ring* has three subdivisions which are clearly distinguishable, although separated by no dark interval, viz., a brilliant white outer zone, distinctly mottled, as seen on the extremities of the ansæ, and two interior zones of gradually diminishing brightness [87a]. The *gauze* or *dusky ring* is seen at its full width on the ansæ, but on the background of the strongly illuminated globe only its outer and presumably denser border [87c] is visible. The shadow of the globe on the rings [88b] is seen on the lower portion of the eastern ansa. The shadow on the dusky ring [88c] is with difficulty perceptible; the shadow on the middle ring is slightly concave toward the planet, which concavity is abruptly increased on the outer zone of this ring [89a]; while the shadow on the outer ring slants away from the globe. These appearances are fully accounted for by supposing a general increase of level from the inner edge of the dusky ring to the outer margin of the middle ring, and a uniform lower level on the outer ring. Other observers have regarded the deflection of the shadow as an effect of irradiation [89-90]. The inner margin of the double outer ring presents on both ansæ a number of slight indentations, which, if not actual irregularities in the contour of this ring, may be explained as shadows caused by elevations on the outer border of the middle ring, or possibly by overhanging clouds.

Approximate scale, 6,500 miles—1 inch.

Plate XI.—THE GREAT COMET OF 1881.

Observed on the night of June 25-26, at 1h. 30m. A. M.

A view of the comet 1881, III., drawn as if seen with the naked eye, the minute details, however, being reproduced as seen with the telescope [vi.c]. The star-like *nucleus* [103b] is attended by four conical wings [104a] which cause it to appear diamond-shaped. The *coma* [105b] appears double, the brilliant inner coma, immediately enveloping the nucleus, being surrounded by a fainter exterior coma [106a], which has a noticeable depression corresponding to that of the inner edge of the principal coma. The tail is divided lengthwise by a dark rift [106b] and is brightest on its convex or forward side [106c]. An inner portion of the tail, brighter than the rest, is more strongly curved, as if by solar repulsion [105c, 113]. Stars are seen through the brighter parts of the tail, as they may be seen even through the coma and nucleus, with little diminution of their light [111b].

Plate XII.—THE NOVEMBER METEORS.

As observed on the night of November 13-14, 1868.

A partially ideal view of the November Meteors [116c], combining forms observed [vii.a] at different times during the night of Nov. 13th, 1868. It is not, however, a fanciful view [118c], since a much larger number of meteors were observed falling at once during the shower of November, 1833, and at other times [116b]. The locality of the observation is shown by the Polar Star seen near the centre of the Plate, and Cassiopeia's Chair at the left. The general direction of the paths of the meteors is from the north-east, the *radiant point* [120a] of the shower having been in the constellation Leo [121a], beyond and above Ursa Major. While the orbits of the meteors are, in general, curved regularly and slightly, [117a], several are shown with very eccentric paths [117b], among them one which changed its course at a sharp angle. In the upper left-hand corner appear two vanishing trails of the "ring-form," and several others still further transformed into faint luminous patches of cloud [118b]. Red, yellow, green, blue and purple tints were observed in the meteors and their trails [118b], as represented in the Plate.

Plate XIII.—PART OF THE MILKY WAY.

From a study made during the years 1874, 1875 and 1876.

The course of the portion of the Galaxy [130] represented in Plate XIII. is as follows: From Cassiopeia's chair, three bright stars of which appear at the upper edge of the Plate, the Galaxy, forming two streams, descends south, passing partly through Lacerta on the left, and Cepheus on the right; at this last point it approaches nearest to the Polar Star, which is itself outside of the field of view. Then it enters Cygnus, where it becomes very complicated and bright, and where several large cloudy masses are seen terminating its left branch, which passes to the right, near the bright star *Deneb*, the leader of this constellation. Below *Deneb*, the Galaxy is apparently disconnected and separated from the northern part by a narrow, irregular dark gap. From this rupture, the Milky-way divides into two great streams, separated by an irregular dark rift. An immense branch extends to the right, which, after having formed an important luminous mass between the stars *Gamma* and *Beta*, continues its southward progress through parts of Lyra, Vulpecula, Hercules, Aquila and Ophiuchus, where it gradually terminates a few degrees south of the equator. The main stream on the left, after having formed a bright mass around *Epsilon Cygni*, passes through Vulpecula and then Aquila, where it crosses the equinoctial just below the star *Eta*, after having involved in its nebulosity the bright star *Altair*, the leader of Aquila. In the southern hemisphere the Galaxy becomes very complicated and forms a succession of very bright, irregular masses, the upper one being in Scutum Sobieskii, while the others are respectively situated in Sagittarius and in Scorpio; the last, just a little above our horizon, being always considerably dimmed by vapors. From Scutum Sobieskii, the Galaxy expands considerably on the right, and sends a branch into Scorpio, in which the fiery red star *Antares* is somewhat involved. In the upper left-hand corner of the Plate, at some distance from the Milky-way, is seen dimly the Nebula in Andromeda, which becomes so magnificent an object to telescopic view [147c].

Plate XIV.—STAR-CLUSTER IN HERCULES.

From a study made in June, 1877.

In the constellation Hercules [137c], a small nebulous mass is faintly visible to the eye [138b], a telescopic view of which is presented in Plate XIV. It is one of the most beautiful of the easily resolvable [139a] globular clusters [139b]. The brilliancy of the centre gives the cluster a distinctly globular appearance, while the several wings [140b] curving in various directions, have suggested to some observers an irregularly spiral structure [140c]. The large stars of the cluster are arranged in several groups which correspond, in a general way, with the faintly luminous wings.

PLATE XV.—THE GREAT NEBULA IN ORION.

From a study made in the years 1875-76.

This nebula, which is one of the most brilliant and wonderful of telescopic objects, readily visible to the naked eye as a patch of nebulous light immediately surrounding the middle star of the three which form the sword of Orion, and a little south of the three well-known stars forming the belt [153a]. The small stars in this, as in other Plates of the series, are somewhat exaggerated in size, as was unavoidable with any mode of reproduction that could be employed [41a]. The bright pentagonal centre of the nebula [152b] is traversed by less luminous rifts, the several subdivisions thus outlined being irregularly mottled as if by bright fleecy clouds [154a]. Toward the lower part of this bright pentagonal centre is a comparatively dark space containing four bright stars which form a trapezium and together constitute the quadruple star *Theta Orionis*, which, to the naked eye, appears as the single star in the centre of the sword. On three sides of the central mass extend long bright wisps, whose curves fail, however, to reveal the spiral structure often attributed to this nebula [154b]. On the east a broad wing, with wave-shaped inner border, stretches southward [153b]. East of the trapezium are two especially noticeable dark spaces. Close to the main nebula on the north-east, a small faint nebula surrounds a bright star, and a branch from another faint stream of nebulous matter forming a loop to the southward, encloses the nebulous star (*Iota Orionis*) shown at the top of the Plate.

www.ingramcontent.com/pod-product-compliance
Lightning Source LLC
Chambersburg PA
CBHW031113020726
47495CB00007B/2179